PISCES RISING

PETER CAVE was born in London in 1940 and now lives in Torquay, Devon. He is the author of twenty-seven novels written under various pseudonyms. His interests include hang-gliding, skiing, tennis, swimming, snorkelling, playing pool and travel. Some years ago he spent nearly a year living in France as an itinerant folk singer and busker. Since then he has travelled extensively in Europe, North Africa, the Canary Islands, Canada and the United States. His current major ambition in life is to survive into the twenty-first century and still be able to see planet earth with some sort of future.

MARGARET WREDDEN is currently working as a teacher in Devon. She began this career in the East End of London, later moving into the world of the theatre for some years. She had the extreme good fortune to work for Brian Way of Theatre Centre as a wardrobe mistress and costume designer, after which she worked for a summer season with Bernard Delfont. She then took off for six months and travelled through India, Afghanistan, Iran and Europe. Her interests include sailing, skiing and all stages of textile production, from weaving and spinning to dressmaking.

PISCES RISING

For marine biologist Heinz Grossman the giant underwater complex being built by Merton Ellis gave him the opportunity to realize a dream. He was able to prove that man could descend to the ocean floor; he could study and try to understand thousands of new life-forms. But like many visionaries, Grossman was too much of an optimist. Where he saw hope and future harmony, others saw only profits to be ruthlessly exploited.

This latest threat to marine life snaps the already tenuous co-operation between the dry lands and the liquid world. The liquid world revolts, it fights back in a co-ordinated attack inconceivable to man, and as Grossman's dream dies, the world's nightmare begins.

PETER CAVE and MARGARET WREDDEN

Pisces Rising

FONTANA/Collins

First published in Great Britain in 1978 by
Sidgwick & Jackson Limited
First issued in Fontana Books 1979

© Peter Cave and Maggie Wredden

Made and printed in Great Britain by
William Collins Sons & Co Ltd, Glasgow

TO THE FUTURE – WITH HOPE!
. . . And a debt of gratitude to
Herman Hesse, Colin Wilson and Bob Dylan

The Great Legend of the Liquid World

'In the beginning, in the time of the first time, the earth was dry land, with little water upon it. Of its creatures, none was more powerful than Man, to whom was entrusted the great and terrible secrets of earth, fire and heaven.

'Earth was man's domain, and locked in its dust and rocks were the secrets of change, which could bring forth metals and precious things. With his knowledge of these secrets, man rode upon the earth and beneath it in his machines. In ships which rode on fire he conquered the heavens, soared through the star-holes in the black canopy of space to the other worlds beyond. Man had the power of the gods, but not the wisdom or the compassion. Greed was within him, a festering disease. His heart was not pure, and he carried the seeds of his own destruction.

'Time passed. The great dry-creature man prospered and grew until his tribes were many and covered the flat-lands. He grew rich with the gifts of earth and heaven, but still his greed was not satisfied. Tribes made war amongst themselves, fighting for possessions which were not theirs to possess. They plundered the earth anew, drawing out new metals to forge into weapons. They learned to kill, and death came upon the earth like a terrible plague.

'In the dying days of the first time, man drew the ultimate secret of the Great Fire from the bowels of the earth, turning it into his final and most terrible weapon. He released the dreadful energy locked in the very core of earth itself, and, too late, he realised that the Great Fire knew no pity. Earth shook, the flat-lands split asunder, and molten death spewed up from the depths below. Mountains opened like angry mouths, spitting the great fire across the land and all its creatures. The earth became a ball of fire, and all life ceased.

'The Great-God-Of-All-Things looked upon the inferno and was torn with sorrow. Huge tears fell from his eyes, dropping from heaven on to the burning land and putting out the flames. The tears cascaded down the mountainsides in mighty rivers, until the great fire was dead.

'There was a new earth – a place of vast areas of water

broken only by small islands of dry land. All was sterile, for the water was pure, as befitted the tears of a god.

'But the Great-God-Of-All-Things created life anew. Reaching down from heaven, he stirred the waters with his finger until a thousand new life-forms populated the barren planet. Of these, one family was his favourite – the tuna, the largest of which was the bluefin tuna, or horse mackerel. The Great-God-Of-All-Things selected a leader, and breathed the wisdom of the gods into its mouth. This was Nah-Ep, the Wise One, supreme ruler of the liquid world. All who lived within it would respect him, and as a symbol of that power he bore a trident – the sign of the trinity that supports the life-chain of the liquid world. These are the plankton, which drift with the currents; the benthos, which crawl upon the ocean floor; and the nekton, which swim free throughout all waters, choosing their own destiny.

'In his new wisdom and godliness, Nah-Ep rose to the surface, to the place of light water. There he looked upon the dry lands where no life existed, and great sorrow came upon him. Seeing this the Great-God-Of-All-Things was moved to bring new life there also.

'Thus man lived again, but he paid the penalty for his past sins. No longer wise and powerful, he was condemned to be a small and puny creature, living wild in the steaming rain-forests of the dry lands.

'The new earth was in ten parts, three being dry land and seven being the liquid world.

'And the time of the second time began, set to run for a thousand million years.

'Whilst the liquid world flourished, and life within it was ever abundant, there came strange and terrible changes upon the dry land. Vast areas of rain-forest dried and became desert, falling barren. There came a time of great cold, when the waters of the seas rose even to the towering mountains and froze in huge silver sheets.

'In time, a new god arose in the heavens to challenge the powers of Nah-Ep and the Great-God-Of-All-Things. This was Tiki, the sun-god, who was well disposed towards the creature man. Under Tiki's warm beneficence, the ice melted, the earth was freed from its cold grip, and man grew to regain some of his former glory. He once again built ships and dared to move upon the waters, spreading himself anew.

'But life upon the dry land was harsh and uncompromising.

Sometimes the sun burned too fiercely, drying and burning the delicate skins of the man-creature. Sometimes angry storms raged, and water fell from the heavens to extinguish the fires man built to warm himself in times of cold. Their dwelling places were destroyed, the crops they grew to feed themselves were flattened and flooded.

'Learning this, Nah-Ep felt compassion for the pitiful dry-creature, for his numbers were few and the creatures of the liquid world were many. Nah-Ep pledged that the life-chain of the sea should encompass man and bestow on him the gift of god. For ever afterwards, fish would swim into the nets and traps of man, sacrificing themselves in order to sustain man in his bleak existence upon the dry land.

'In time, man came to know something of Nah-Ep, and of his liquid domain. In their strange language they called him Nah-Ep-Tuna. A time of great harmony followed, for both fish and man knew their place and kept to it, for only death bridged the void between the two worlds. The delicate balance of life between earth and water was understood and honoured, pleasing the gods.

'But the creature man grew strong again, and his greed was still within him. A powerful tribe of the man-creatures re-discovered some of the old powers and plotted with certain members of the liquid world to steal the great secrets of the sea.

'Nah-Ep arose in a mighty anger, for man had broken his trust. In his wrath he cleaved the very floor of the ocean, creating the black and terrible Abyss, where no dry-creature could survive. There, Nah-Ep buried the great secrets for all time, so that no man should ever know them. His anger still unappeased, Nah-Ep chose two of the men-creatures, a male and a female, and led them to the mouth of the Abyss. There they learned the greatest and most terrible secret of change – transmutation of living things. Nah-Ep trapped them for ever in the liquid world, so that they could never return to the dry land and reveal what they had learned. Their bodies were altered; the two legs they used to walk upon the dry land were taken from them. For ever afterwards, the new creatures which Nah-Ep had created would live in the sea but suffer a bond of longing for the dry-creature man. Nah-Ep named these new creatures dolphins.

'The fish that had joined in the dry-creatures' plot also knew Nah-Ep's vengeance, and they, too, suffered the terrible fate of change. They became monstrous, horribly deformed parodies of their former selves and were banished to the dark and fearful Abyss, there to live out their wretched existence for all eternity.

'Yet Nah-Ep's anger was still not fully appeased. In his rage, he released all the awesome powers of the liquid world so that man should for ever know and fear them. The seas boiled and frothed, the Great Fire erupted again from the core of the earth beneath the waters, and a vast continent of dry land was consumed and destroyed, with all the creatures that lived upon it.

'For ever after, even until the time of the third time, when man once again conquered the heavens, all men spoke in awe of the land which had been swallowed by the mighty sea. They called it Atlantis.'

Chapter One

Heinz Grossman ran the complicated list of figures through the computer for the twentieth time, reading the print-out carefully. It checked yet again, leaving absolutely no possibility of error! A surge of elation rippled through him.

Still clutching the torn-off print-out, Grossman crossed the computer room floor and headed out through the hermetically-sealed doors towards the biology laboratories. Passing through, he caught a glimpse of his face reflected in the gleaming stainless steel. He broke his step, stopping to look more closely at that face. In it he saw no trace of vanity, but a deep, unselfish look of pride. It was the look of a man who had proved himself, who had stood against scepticism and overt opposition and had come through with his optimism unscathed. His face no longer looked its full forty-one years. The light blonde hair, receding from a high brow, did not seem quite so thin; the lines etched below the piercing blue eyes from years of squinting into a microscope, not so pronounced.

With a spring in his step Grossman cleared the doors, which closed behind him electronically. He strolled through the laboratory, savouring his feelings of achievement and personal pleasure. He felt good – both as a marine biologist, and as a man. His theories and dreams had at last been proved. Man *could* descend to the ocean floor and live, without cumbersome and expensive hardware. For the first time in its history, mankind could investigate the whole of his planet earth, and not just a small fraction of it. He could explore the oceans of the world and discover their mysteries. He could study and try to understand thousands of strange new life-forms.

Grossman glanced at his watch. It was almost two-thirty. Merton Ellis would arrive exactly on time. He always did. Grossman walked out of the lab and down the corridor to the main reception area to greet him.

'Ah, Grossman.' Ellis was briskly efficient, a brief nod sufficing for formal greeting. The biologist was his employee, not his friend. 'I trust we are making good progress?'

Grossman found it difficult to conceal the triumph he felt.

'Everything is going well, Mr Ellis.'

'Good, good.' Ellis began to move towards the main elevator shaft. 'Are we ready to test?'

'Perfectly,' Grossman assured him, jumping a step ahead to reach the elevator doors before him and press the button. The steel doors slid back soundlessly. Ellis stepped in, with Grossman close behind him.

Grossman pressed his lips against a small metal grille built into the side of the cage. 'Sub-level fifteen,' he murmured quietly. For security reasons, the elevator was designed to work only upon the specific voice-prints of Grossman, Ellis and a handful of trusted security personnel.

Ellis felt his stomach lurch briefly as the elevator cage began to drop. The descent took nearly two whole minutes, finally slowing to a gentle stop. The doors slid back, opening directly on to the main laboratory.

For once, Grossman led the way. Here, he was the boss. This was his domain, a private world of strange secrets to which he alone held the key. The two men walked across the lab, past rows of water-filled tanks containing a weird assortment of animal life. Rats, guinea-pigs, small squirrel monkeys and even a large German shepherd dog moved sluggishly, obviously alive even though completely immersed in water. Each animal wore a small flat pack on its back, from which an assortment of plastic pipes ran to their throats and main blood pressure points.

Ellis had seen this before. Hardly bothering to observe the unnatural phenomena, he followed Grossman to the far end of the lab, where a thick steel door blocked further passage. Grossman punched out a code sequence on a digital panel. After a few seconds, the door began to slide back, allowing access to another, slightly smaller, laboratory. Ellis followed the scientist into it, completely unprepared for what he then saw.

The three water-filled tanks lined up against the far wall of the inner laboratory were much larger than those in the main lab. Their inhabitants looked even more bizarre in their liquid environment.

Three naked men!

Ellis stared at them with cold fascination. Although the sight aroused his sense of wonder, the men themselves meant little more to him than the other experimental animals.

Grossman saw them through different eyes.

'There you are, Mr Ellis. Pioneers of a new frontier.'

Ellis smacked his lips. 'You surprise me, Grossman. I had no idea you'd progressed this far. I thought we were going to try some tests with the dog today.'

Grossman's eyes flashed excitedly. 'I conducted those tests five days ago, with perfect results. It was time to move on to the next stage. All three divers volunteered to bring the schedule forward by two weeks, just for your benefit. You have brave men there, Mr Ellis.'

Ellis let out a small snort of doubt. 'Brave?' he queried. 'Who else ever got paid a hundred thousand dollars a month for a guaranteed minimum period of three years?'

Grossman dared to disagree. 'You can't buy courage, Mr Ellis.'

Ellis stared him in the eye, mocking scornfully. 'You can buy *anything*, Grossman . . . provided you know the price,' he said coldly. He turned away from the tanks, waving his hand around the laboratory in a sweeping gesture. 'I bought all this, everything you needed to make your wild ideas work. I bought *you*, Grossman . . . never forget that.'

A momentary chill wiped away all of Grossman's excitement. The old doubts about Ellis crowded in on him again, filling him with fear. Had the man fooled him all along? Had he allowed his professional zeal to cloud his better judgement, sell out his dream to a totally unprincipled financier?

Ellis seemed to sense that he had gone too far. He did not want to disillusion and antagonise the scientist, not yet. That would come soon enough, when Grossman realised that all his work and the patents of his invention belonged to the Ellis Corporation, and that the benefaction of humanity was the last thing in its president's cunning mind. For the moment, Ellis still wanted Grossman's enthusiasm and co-operation. There was quite a long way to go before the man was dispensable.

Ellis forced a smile. 'You're right, of course, Grossman. Sometimes I find it difficult to remember the basic humanities, to switch off the cynicism which pervades the world of high finance. I survive in a cut-throat environment, Grossman; exposure to it can taint a man. make him hide behind a hard protective shell. Being a millionaire unfortunately brings with it the attendant problems of remaining so . . . and deciding how best to use that wealth and power for the greatest good.

As he spoke, Ellis observed Grossman's face from the corner

of his eye. The scientist appeared to be pacified, for the time being. To reinforce the bluff, Ellis moved towards the three men in the tanks, affecting a greater interest. He observed them for several moments before something unnatural struck him. With a look of alarm on his face, he turned back towards Grossman.

'These three men aren't breathing. Is there something wrong? Are they dead?'

Grossman failed to notice that the man's voice betrayed no compassion, only disappointment. 'No, they're not breathing, but I can assure you they are far from dead.'

'Anaesthetised?'

Grossman nodded. 'Heavily. The pressurisation process would be intolerably painful without it. They show no signs of normal breathing simply because their lungs have been deliberately collapsed,' he explained. 'The gill-unit they wear on their backs is drawing natural oxygen from the water in exactly the same way that a fish's gills do. It is being pumped directly into their blood supply. The lungs have become totally superfluous.'

'You say they're already pressurised, yet they appear to be quite normal,' Ellis said. 'I expected them to be all bloated up.'

Grossman shook his head patiently. 'No, Mr Ellis. The pressure being forced into their bloodstreams and body tissues exactly matches the water pressure in the tanks. That, by the way, is 1,000 pounds to the square inch, roughly equivalent to a depth of 2,000 feet. When the tanks are lowered to that depth, and the inner and outer pressures align exactly, the tanks will open automatically. From then on, the gill-units will adjust the divers' pressure automatically, so that they can move freely at almost any depth.'

Ellis shook his head, not quite understanding the technical aspects of the process but astute enough to realise that it was a real breakthrough. 'I sure have to hand it to you, Doc.'

Grossman smiled wistfully, remembering the early days of ridicule. 'I couldn't possibly have done any of it without your help, Mr Ellis,' he said, quite sincerely. 'Most of my fellow biologists thought I was crazy for believing that a man could venture into the ocean depths virtually unprotected. Our thinking was back to front for years, but I always had that sneaking suspicion that a different answer was looking us in the face all the time. All it took, really, was some lateral thinking. Every law of science seemed to indicate that man could only descend into deep water protected against the incredible pressures by an outer, rigid shell. First the diving-suit, then the bathyscape. When biologists first discovered soft-bodied life forms existing in the extreme depths, it appeared to make nonsense of logic. To me, the answer was immediately clear: not to protect against pressure from the outside, but to compensate for it from within. Now I know that I was right.'

Ellis nodded enthusiastically. 'You sure are.'

Grossman suddenly felt a little embarrassed at singing his own praises. In a brisk, businesslike voice, he snapped: 'Well, I expect you would like to get on with it, Mr Ellis.'

'Right.' Ellis nodded emphatically. 'The sooner the better.'

Grossman checked the pressurised tanks one more time. The men inside were beginning to stir as the effects of the numbing anaesthetic gradually wore off. In a few minutes, they would be fully conscious and alert. He moved to the wall, speaking into an intercom unit. 'Charles, have the tanks conveyed down to the main airlock, will you? I want to be ready for a test dive in about thirty minutes from now.' Without waiting for an acknowledgement, Grossman snapped off the intercom and returned to Ellis's side. 'If you would like to follow me, Mr Ellis.' Then, on an afterthought: 'Of course, you haven't actually been inside the tunnel before, have you?'

Ellis shook his head. 'I've been too busy,' he lied adroitly. It seemed a much better excuse than admitting the truth; that he had been terrified, and still was. Only the fact that the tunnel had been functioning perfectly for several months slightly allayed his fears. He followed Grossman back through the main laboratory to the elevator shaft. Entering the cage, the two men dropped down a further five levels.

The tunnel would eventually be the nucleus and focal point of the giant Atlantis Hotel complex. At present, only a cluster of half-finished shore buildings tucked neatly into the cliffs of Cape Romano showed the faintest promise of what was to come. When it was finished, the Florida complex would be unique – a fabulous, futuristic showpiece which was designed to impress, dazzle . . . and conceal. A battery of elevators would take thousands of visitors down through solid rock to a point some 500 feet below sea level. There, surrounded by bars, discotheques and restaurants, would be the entrance to the tunnel, the most extravagant and exciting spectacle in the world. A long, multi-windowed tunnel which would run out from the land directly into the sea, dropping gently down along the ocean bed for some four miles out towards the Thousand Isles and the Gulf of Mexico beyond. Safely inside its pressurised and airconditioned luxury, the visitors would be able to look out of the thick glass windows on to a strange and alien world. On top of the weird beauty of the visual spectacle, their senses would be assaulted by the tingling accompaniment of nervous fear – a unique and powerful experience. The fact that the tunnel looked out towards the mysterious Bermuda Triangle only added to the allure, for despite cold scientific explanations of its supposed mysteries, the legends of the area never abated.

Just as this combination of facts would make the Atlantis Hotel a guaranteed commercial success, so would they suit Ellis's ulterior motives. The hotel was just a cover. While its multiple facilities kept visitors happy spending their dollars, the Ellis Corporation's other business would be going on unnoticed. Any activities going on in the area of the Bermuda Triangle were unlikely to come under close scrutiny, for sailors the world over still avoided it if possible, and any odd happenings went straight into the fabric of myth.

The seabed itself would become the new headquarters of the massive Ellis Corporation, and the plunder could begin.

'We're going to be space-age pirates, Clive, plundering the riches of the sea,' Ellis had said to Clive Podmore, a director of one of the sixteen interconnected holding companies which made up the Ellis empire. 'It's all down there – gold, uranium, manganese, oil. Just waiting to be extracted and sold to the highest bidder. And deuterium, the power and wealth of the next century. One ounce of that stuff contains the potential energy of 300 gallons of gasoline, and the sea is lousy with it.'

That was Merton Ellis's dream. Exploiting the ocean and seabed, using the complex as a base, and Grossman's gill-units to create a new breed of worker. Unknown to the biologist, he was being used to bring on a new and accelerated destruction of the sea he loved and respected.

Ellis had been smart, of course. Grossman might have suspected a purely altruistic motive. So the Atlantis Hotel fulfilled yet another role – an admitted commercial motivation with which Grossman was willing to compromise. He was willing to give his skills to the project because Ellis's money made his own dream possible. The fact that Ellis would turn his research into profits for himself was partly offset by the knowledge that thousands of visitors would be able to view some of the wonders of the sea, and hopefully come to respect it and its creatures as he did.

Heinz Grossman had been a find in a million, Ellis congratulated himself. The scientist's unique combination of character traits was perfect for the purpose. His brilliant scientific mind was not hidebound by narrow, restricted thinking. In a highly specialised field, he was able to see visions and think at a tangent. He was an idealist, and as such more naïve than a man with the cynicism of realism. He believed in Ellis's story because he wanted to believe, and because he had his own dreams.

Grossman stopped by a solid metal bulkhead. Built into it was the hatchway which would lead into the 600 feet of tunnel already completed.

Thoughts of future riches faded from Ellis's mind as Grossman opened the hatch and stepped through. Glancing from side to side apprehensively, Ellis followed him along the uncarpeted steel and concrete floor, acutely aware that he was now literally surrounded by death.

Grossman stopped by one of the huge windows. 'Look,' he breathed, pointing out into the water. A large shoal of angel fish was swimming by, the bright light from the tunnel making them look like a living, shimmering rainbow.

Ellis followed the scientist's pointing finger, nodding with satisfaction. The tunnel was going to be one hell of a tourist attraction, that was for sure.

'Beautiful sight, isn't it?' Grossman went on enthusiastically. 'Windows on to a new world . . . a glimpse into man's future.'

'Damn well ought to be,' Ellis grumbled. 'Each one of those windows cost $3,000 apiece.'

Grossman spread his hands in a gesture of apology. 'Nothing comes cheap down here, Mr Ellis, especially not human life. To be completely safe, those windows had to be eighteen inches thick, with special titanium elements fused into the glass for extra strength. Producing windows that thick which are also optically true is no easy matter.'

'But they *are* safe?'

Grossman smiled. 'Oh yes. I assure you that those windows would safely withstand a pressure over five times what it is out there right now.' He gestured to one of the heavy steel bulkheads buried at frequent intervals in the walls of the tunnel. 'In any case, if one of the windows gave in for any reason, the water would immediately trigger off the electronic sensors on the floor, and those bulkheads would seal off the affected area in seconds, making the rest of the tunnel water-tight at once.'

'I guess I'll have to take your word for it,' Ellis muttered, staring out into the dark green water moodily.

Grossman continued on down the tunnel until he came to the end, marked off with a massive double-walled bulkhead. He stepped across to the nearest window. 'We should have a fairly good view of the divers from here, Mr Ellis.' He glanced down at his watch. 'They should be going out of the lower airlock in a few minutes.'

Ellis joined him, peering out into the murky depths. A faint stirring of movement attracted his attention and he strained to identify it. From the general gloom a darker shape materialised, heading at some considerable speed towards the side of the tunnel.

Ellis jumped back instinctively as something large, sleek and grey-black loomed up, suddenly blocking all vision out of the window, and then was gone again, slipping sideways out of sight.

'What the hell was that?' Ellis asked, glancing at Grossman.

Grossman pressed his face against the glass, peering out. 'Hammerhead,' he announced in a quiet, casual voice. 'In fact, there are three or four of them out there. It must be the tunnel lights attracting them.'

'Hammerheads?' Ellis croaked. 'You mean hammerhead sharks?'

Grossman noted the man's fear with a slight satisfaction. He smiled gently, nodding. 'Yes, hammerhead sharks, Mr Ellis. They're quite common in these waters.'

'Jesus!' Ellis shivered uncomfortably. 'Guess I know now how a pickled herring feels. We must look like food in a jar to them.' A second thought struck him. 'What about the divers? Will they be safe out there, with those damned things swimming around?'

Grossman nodded thoughtfully. 'Oh, I should think so,' he murmured, still apparently casual. 'Contrary to popular belief, sharks rarely attack man unless provoked, and almost never in deep water. When sharks do attack, it is usually inshore, when they're feeding. They see a swimmer's legs dangling below the surface of the water and mistake them for a pair of white, juicy fish. In deep water, seeing the creature man as a whole, they usually reckon he's just a little too large to take on, and give him a wide berth. They'll cruise around, of course, purely out of curiosity.'

Ellis looked far from convinced. Grossman smiled inwardly, quietly enjoying himself. 'Of course, it can be a bit different with a great white,' he went on. 'They're that much bigger, you see . . . have a much larger set of teeth and jaws specially adapted for shredding and tearing.'

Ellis had a pained look on his face. He was feeling slightly sick.

'Anyway, the divers have been well coated with shark repellant, just as an added precaution,' Grossman assured him, finishing off his brief joke. 'And they know what they're doing. They'll be on the lookout for trouble. They know only too well that sharks are amongst the minor dangers of the sea.'

'Minor?' Ellis found it difficult to conceive of a worse fate than being torn to pieces by jagged teeth.

'Oh yes.' Grossman nodded absently. 'There are certain species of jellyfish . . . I've heard grown men screaming out, begging death to come just a few seconds quicker, just to end the agony . . .' He broke off abruptly as a sudden, booming crash echoed the full length of the tunnel.

Ellis jumped nervously. 'What in God's name was that?'

Grossman didn't have time to answer him. From the dark waters outside, the huge grey shape of a hammerhead loomed up again. Its thick snout crashed against the window as it swam at full speed head-on into the glass. As the wicked-looking creature glanced off, a second shark made a run at the same window, catching it only a glancing blow as it veered off just a fraction of a second too soon. Dull vibrations rocked the tunnel. Seconds later, a third hammerhead smashed its snout against the side of the tunnel, just below the level of the window. Ellis saw the wicked set of its teeth as it curved upwards and swam away to turn in a circle and head in for another assault.

'My God, the bloody things are attacking us!'

Grossman's face registered puzzlement, but he remained calm. 'Not us, Mr Ellis. If they are indeed attacking anything at all, it's the tunnel itself.'

'What the hell are you talking about?' Ellis was sweating as another impact shook the walls of the tunnel.

'The tunnel has no right to be here, in their eyes,' Grossman explained 'This is their world, after all. Something strange and alien which suddenly appears in it must necessarily be regarded as an interloper, probably an enemy. Look at it this way, how would you feel if you suddenly found a Martian spaceship hovering outside your office window?'

As he spoke, Grossman delved into the pocket of his white coat, bringing out a small black plastic box. 'Anyway, this should get rid of them.' He pressed the box flat against the metal side of the tunnel and thumbed a small red button. A shrill electronic bleeping filled the air.

Almost at once the circling sharks shied away from the sides of the tunnel and swam off at speed. Grossman grunted with satisfaction and transferred the box to his pocket. 'That should take care of them for a while,' he muttered.

Ellis stared in amazement. 'What was that?'

'High frequency sound,' Grossman explained. 'Sound waves travel much better under water, you see. The metal walls of the tunnel transmitted the sonic wave out into the water, amplifying it like a simple resonator. Sharks can't stand loud noises, especially high-pitched ones. They're very sensitive to sound and vibration.'

'Oh,' Ellis said quietly. Now that his immediate fears had subsided, he felt a trifle foolish.

Grossman pressed his face against the window once again. A broad smile spread over his face. 'Ah, here they come,' he announced happily.

Ellis rushed to his side, peering out of the same window into the green murk. The sight which greeted him was like something out of a dream. The three naked divers were cruising effortlessly up towards the tunnel from the depths, their bodies seemingly weightless. It reminded Ellis of astronauts in free-fall under zero-gravity conditions. There was none of the usual awkwardness or clumsy movements of scuba divers. These underwater swimmers seemed as much in their natural element as any one of the thousands of small, brightly-coloured fish which danced around them.

'Everything must be functioning perfectly,' Grossman breathed, his tone betraying a degree of relief. 'If they can come up from 1,000 feet to this level with no ill effects, they can go virtually anywhere.'

The leading diver neared the window, checking his slow and graceful ascent with gentle fluttering movements of his hands. He hovered outside, treading water before pressing his face to the glass and grinning broadly. He raised a hand, the thumb extended upwards in a clear signal that everything was just fine.

Grossman smiled back, returning the gesture. Then he jabbed a finger, first towards his mouth and then to his ear.

The diver nodded understandingly, pointing downwards to the second diver who was swimming up towards him. He held a small black box, identical to the one which Grossman had used to chase away the sharks. The lead diver took it from him, his fingers hovering over two faintly glowing luminescent panels.

Grossman took out his own pocket computer, staring at it intently as the diver's fingers moved over the buttons. Ellis, peering over the scientist's shoulder, saw the panel of his calculator light up. White letters clicked into place upon it, spelling out a message: 'Down . . . again . . . now . . . query.'

Grossman touched the buttons of his own set. On the diver's calculator the answer lit up: 'Yes.'

The diver responded with a further question. 'What . . . depth . . . time . . . query.'

Grossman tapped out his answer. '2000 feet . . . 15 mins . . . good . . . luck.' The diver acknowledged the instruction and turned away from the window, jacknifing effortlessly in the water to face down towards the depths once again. With no more than a faint paddling motion, he and his two companions began to descend. Ellis and Grossman watched until the three divers disappeared into the dark waters below.

Ellis nodded towards Grossman's calculator. 'Quite a little box of tricks,' he murmured, impressed.

The biologist shrugged modestly. 'It's only a slightly modified pocket calculator,' he said. 'It's the only form of communication we have open to us, unfortunately.' Seeing the man's obvious puzzlement, he explained further. 'Normal communication is impossible, so we use these, and talk in basic computer language, binary code. The calculator translates the code into a visual print-out, enabling us to communicate clearly and quickly with each other. Think of it as a highly up-to-date form of Morse code transmitter and receiver if you like.'

He broke off to study the print-out panel as the lead diver transmitted the first of his regular progress reports. '400 feet . . . OK . . . yellow . . . gone.'

Ellis tapped the biologist on the shoulder. 'What does that mean, yellow gone?'

Grossman smiled patiently. 'As you go deeper into water, the colours of the spectrum gradually disappear,' he explained. 'The depth of the water filters light out in progressive stages. At only fifty feet, the colour red can no longer be distinguished clearly. Deeper still, and orange and green begin to disappear. At 350 to 400 feet, all yellow light ceases to penetrate the water and you can only see shades of green and blue. When you pass the violet end of the spectrum, it's as black as pitch.'

'Then how will they see at 2,000 feet?' Ellis demanded.

'Simple, they have electron torches with them,' Ellis explained. As he spoke, another message flashed up on his communicator. 'Indigo . . . going . . . switching . . . on . . . lights . . . all . . . OK.' Grossman showed the message to Ellis. 'You see?'

Ellis nodded absently. It meant little or nothing to him. He was not really interested in the inner workings of things, provided that they did work. However, feigning interest in all aspects of his work seemed to keep Grossman happy and Ellis was a great believer in keeping the workers happy — especially if it cost nothing. It kept them from asking too many awkward questions.

'Good God!' Grossman's voice showed that his scientific mind had been severely rattled for once.

'What is it?' Ellis looked quickly over the scientist's shoulder at the bizarre message which had flashed up on the communicator. 'We . . . have . . . visitors.'

Grossman tapped out a hasty question. 'Explain.' He waited patiently for several seconds, but no answer came.

McAllister, the lead diver, felt his communicator slip from his fingers. He made a desperate grab at it, knowing that it was irretrievably lost even as he moved. His fingers clawed empty water. The beam of his powerful torch picked out the shape of the small black box just once as it plunged towards the ocean floor. Then it was gone.

He looked up again at the nerve-shattering sight which had caused him to lose his grip on the communicator. The huge, ghostly shapes had suddenly appeared out of the total blackness. Silently, magically, they had materialised into the beams

22

of the electron torches like so many lumps of grey-white ectoplasm. McAllister and his two companions seemed to be enclosed in a ritual circle, a circle too geometrically true to be dismissed as pure chance. Something deep in McAllister's brain told him that he was facing an intelligence – creatures with a precise and definite sense of purpose.

It was weird, horribly unreal. McAllister glanced sideways at each of his fellow divers in turn as they clustered around him defensively. In the glow of their torches, McAllister could read the fear in their eyes. A jarring thought struck him. He should be feeling terror himself, real, gut-chilling fear. Yet he wasn't. The incredibly powerful emotion he was experiencing was something else, subtly different, something tantalisingly just outside his range of human experience.

He returned his attention to the hovering creatures. They had begun to close in now, tightening the perfect circle. There could no longer be any doubt that they were acting in a definite, rational way, and somehow linked together in their purpose. Even as logic insisted that such a thing was impossible, McAllister knew it to be so. In a way which he couldn't hope to explain, he could actually feel the creatures around him thinking. It was like a dull pain in his temples as if some ancient memory was struggling towards the light, too important to lie buried any longer.

The creatures moved even closer, sinking down through the water towards the three divers. Still McAllister could not feel the sense of fear which he knew he ought to feel. There was a sense of menace, certainly, but it was muted, cloaked in something else which was definitely not malicious. The pain in his head became more acute.

McAllister was vaguely aware that his two companions had began to thrash wildly in the water beside him, kicking out with frantic strokes of their flippered feet to escape from the closing circle. For just a moment, their total, uncompromising terror was communicated to him, but his overriding concern was the new, the very real, danger they were placing themselves in.

Panic was the greatest enemy of the deep-sea diver, greater than sharks, faulty equipment, jagged rocks. Panic, the irrational fear which sent adrenalin coursing through the system, playing havoc with the delicate blood-oxygen supply and the normal processes of the brain. Under its deadly influence, a diver forgot all the basic rules of survival. It sent him scurrying blindly towards the supposed safety of the surface, forgetting that the changing pressures would work upon the already disrupted body chemistry to bring terrible agony, and sometimes death.

There was nothing McAllister could do to stop his companions as they kicked away from him and began to fight towards the surface. He could only hope that the Grossman gill-unit would cope with the abrupt changes in pressure they would experience.

Alone now, McAllister found a strange new calm, centred firmly in his survival instinct. He must not make the same mistake as his companions. In the presence of the unknown, only rational consideration would serve him, and sudden movement was definitely out.

Not that he could have moved suddenly even if he had wanted to. As the pain in his head increased, McAllister sensed a gradual numbness coming over his body. He trod water slowly and automatically, keeping his position in the water. It took a distinct effort to turn his head enough to look once more at the bizarre scene around him.

There were eight of the creatures in all. They had closed the circle completely now, so that the tips of their huge wings actually touched. Eight gigantic manta rays, each one at least twenty feet in span. They hovered in the water, their massive triangular wings pulsating gently in a regular wave-like motion which travelled around the entire circle in a continuous ripple.

McAllister found his gaze drawn by the circle of bulbous, protruding eyes. They were cold and expressionless, yet oddly penetrating. McAllister felt, without the slightest trace of a doubt, that the rays were observing him with intense interest. Watching . . . waiting . . . thinking.

Again, that inexplicable conviction that the creatures were actually thinking objectively. The pain in McAllister's temples shifted slightly, centralising itself high in his forehead, between the eyes. A strange thought flashed, unbidden, into his mind. The third eye, the pineal gland . . . something lost, or discarded, a long, long time ago.

McAllister struggled desperately against the pain, trying to remember. There was a clue somewhere, if only he could dredge it up from the dark recesses of his brain. It was so tantalisingly close, yet it refused to surface. MsAllister felt a strong and terrible sadness, as though an important promise had been expected, waited for, and then broken.

Time seemed to slow down and stop for an indefinite period. The pain was like a hot knife now, twisting slowly inside his skull. If he could have screamed, McAllister would certainly have done so.

Suddenly, it was gone, switched off immediately. As if upon a silent signal, the manta rays moved. In a quick, perfectly co-ordinated motion, the circle broke up. With all the grace and precision of an acrobatic manoeuvre, each giant ray performed a back-flip and glided away from its companions. McAllister caught a brief glimpse of their long, spear-like tails in the torchlight, and then they disappeared into the inky blackness as quickly, silently and mysteriously as they had come.

McAllister's limbs came to life again as free thought returned. Automatically, he began to paddle firmly, making his way slowly towards the security of the airlock and the laboratory beyond it. He rose about fifty feet, then paused for a while to allow the gill-unit to compensate. Gently treading water, he thought back to his recent experience, turning it all over in his mind. One vague, misty idea prickled in the back of his brain, niggling at him. The manta ray had been trying to convey something to him, something which did not quite translate into words. It was not hate, that was too strong, too human an emotion. It wasn't even quite resentment, although McAllister couldn't help but feel there had been a certain element of that between him and the fish. The feeling he had picked up, and was struggling to identify, fell somewhere between the two, on a unique level of understanding which was not within a man's compass.

Staring back down into the black depths, McAllister knew that he would always carry the image of those flat, grey, alien creatures hovering silently around him.

He shivered, briefly, then kicked out and once again began swimming towards the airlock.

Chapter Two

Pyramus the manta ray hovered in the black depths, looking back towards the Secret Place and the three retreating invaders. Faintly, he saw the bright, dancing light of the strange creatures as they rose up through the murky waters towards the surface. The creatures puzzled and worried him, for they were like no denizens of the liquid world he had ever seen before, and their presence so close to the Secret Place was most disturbing. Pyramus was one of the guardians, entrusted by no lesser a being than Cacha the Elder himself to patrol the sacred entrance, keeping all creatures at a respectable distance.

He remained motionless, trying to think clearly. Try as he might, he could make little sense of the weird creatures or their behaviour. They had swum away towards the place of light water, so it seemed logical to assume that there was their natural habitat. Yet they had borne glowing, phosphorescent appendages, like the creatures of the dark Abyss. The two facts did not fit together.

Stranger still, Pyramus nursed a strong suspicion that he had not managed to communicate with them. It was quite unthinkable that any creature of the liquid world should not understand basic thought-speech. Even the proud and independent dolphins, who often openly displayed their contempt by loudly chattering amongst themselves, would never fail to understand and respond to the one true language of the liquid world.

Delicate vibrations in the water around his gill-slits made Pyramus turn, his huge wings beating slowly. Rasta, his second-in-command, was approaching him. The two manta rays hovered in the water, facing each other.

Pyramus felt the faint prickle in his brain which announced Rasta's intention to communicate with him confidentially. Automatically, Pyramus cut off all outward thought at once, so that the other manta rays could not share in the private conversation.

'What did you think of those strange creatures?' Rasta asked, sounding even more puzzled than Pyramus himself.

Pyramus's thought returned: 'They baffled me, Rasta. They were like no life-form I have ever seen before.'

'Nor I,' Rasta agreed. 'Where can they have come from?'

'The dry world, perhaps?' Pyramus communicated, doubting the thought even as he expressed it. 'They appeared to have two legs, just like the dry-creature itself.'

Rasta's thoughts were vague, full of doubt and puzzlement. 'There was a likeness, certainly. Yet they blew out no air bubbles. Besides, they wore no diving helmets and we know that no dry-creature, even the Great One itself, can descend to these depths without the protection of a submarine.'

'True, Rasta, true,' Pyramus admitted. 'Yet just the same, I am troubled. I communicated to them the great command of the forbidden places here in the place of dark water, but they did not seem to understand me. Either that, or they planned to violate the command anyway, and trespass into the Secret Place, despite my warning. I even invoked the name of the great Nah-Ep himself, but still they showed no humility or fear.' Pyramus lashed his tall in the water, creating swirling eddies around him. His wings fluttered briefly, preparatory to swift movement. 'I feel I must report this strange occurrence to the great Cacha himself. This is a matter for an Elder to consider.'

Pyramus opened his mind, letting his thoughts spread out to embrace all the other mantas in the area. 'Rasta will take command in my absence. You must all return to the Secret Place and guard it well.'

'At once, Pyramus.' Rasta replied, swimming away quickly to round up the other guardians and escort them back to duty.

Pyramus hovered in the water for a few more seconds after they had gone. Then, making a final decision, he beat his huge wings powerfully against the water, sluicing round in a curving, diving arc and heading down to the deep sounding-place beyond the coral city.

Pyramus was spared the full journey. He had swum only a few miles when he came upon Cacha the Elder. The huge whale was not alone, and certainly not in the most dignified situation for an important and sombre discussion.

Cacha was engaged in yet another of his seemingly interminable conflicts with Kraka the giant squid. Whenever the chance presented itself, the two giants of the ocean locked together in bloody battle, living out the vestiges of an ancient and terrible blood feud.

Pyramus stopped well clear of the battle arena, only too well aware of the dangers of approaching too closely to the fight. More than one member of his species had been stunned or badly hurt by a wild blow from Cacha's mighty tail, or scarred for life by a raking lash from Kraka's tentacles and their deadly hooked suckers. Pyramus hovered in the water, fascinated and repelled at the same time by the titanic clash being enacted before his eyes. He found it difficult to understand how Kraka could dare to challenge one of the Great Elders. Even more puzzling was Cacha's apparent willingness to demean himself by such brawling.

He shuddered as Kraka's longest tentacle raked out and wrapped itself around the sperm whale's broad, oily-black back, fastening into position with hundreds of limpet-like, claw-rimmed suckers. Bellowing with rage, Cacha tore himself free from the unwelcome embrace, but the squid's razor-like weapons ripped huge, disc-shaped pieces of flesh from his body. Cacha lashed out with his powerful tail, stirring his huge bulk into sudden forward movement. Circling round with surprising agility for his size, he crashed into the soft body of the giant squid, his massive blunt snout thrusting the creature against a knife-like outcrop of jagged coral. But the big whale turned away too slowly to make the most of his temporary advantage, and Kraka managed to strike a quick blow with his savage, parrot-like beak as the whale turned, gouging a deep furrow of flesh in his tail.

Pyramus forgot his disapproval as the fight progressed. It was not really his place to question a feud which had been going on for thousands upon thousands of generations – reputedly since the time of the first time itself. It was a battle older than the Great Council, and deeper than rational thought. Everyone in the liquid world had long forgotten the original reason for the feud, but it carried on unabated. The two ocean monsters battled endlessly in an instinctive but vain attempt to demonstrate some vague concept of superiority. When they were not fighting, the two species fed upon each other's young in a murderous attempt to gain superiority by sheer numbers. It did not bear thinking about, Pyramus reflected. Still, it was exciting.

From the corner of one protruding eye, Pyramus noticed a pair of nurse sharks glide into view, no doubt attracted by the strong scent of freshly spilled blood and sensing easy prey. Recognising the participants, and feeling foolish, they turned and slipped away again as discreetly as they could.

Cacha also noticed their movement in the water. Distracted from the fight for just a moment, he turned to follow the departing sharks and his eyes fell upon the waiting Pyramus.

A shock thought of pure embarrassment hit Pyramus. He felt the Elder's acute regret. It was not seemly to be caught scrapping, especially by one of the guardians.

The massive whale backed away from his enemy's flailing tentacles, transmitting a terse, somewhat angry thought. 'What do you want, Pyramus?'

The manta ray shielded his thought-speech from Kraka. 'I must converse with you upon an urgent matter, Great Cacha.'

Kraka, crafty as ever, took full advantage of his opponent's diverted attention. Expelling all the water from his huge sac in one mighty gush, he jetted down through the water under Cacha's belly, spreading his tentacles out to their full 100-foot length and encircling the whale's body in a sticky embrace. It was one of Kraka's favourite tricks, a hold which worked well on young and smaller whales. With his limpet-like hold, he could often keep a young sperm whale from rising to the surface for precious air. A sperm whale can remain submerged for an hour and a half, but Kraka could drown one easily if he cared to wait it out.

Cacha was too big and powerful to fall prey to the move. He squirmed to be free of the squid's clam-like grip. The cruel hooked suckers tore at him again, this time tearing great lumps of soft flesh out of his underbelly. Pyramus, still linked in thought-contact with the Elder, flinched at the shared sensation of pain.

Cacha noticed the manta's discomfort and sent out an apologetic thought. 'Forgive me, Pyramus. Just let me get rid of this great blundering bag of arms and I will give you my full attention.' Cacha snapped off his thoughts abruptly as Kraka's vicious beak began to slash across his belly. He turned his attention back to the fight with renewed vigour, eager to bring it to an end. Threshing his massive tail in the water, Cacha threw all his strength into one last burst of speed and power. He had one little trick of his own to pull out of the bag.

Despite the giant squid's prodigious weight, Cacha's strength sent him surging forwards through the water. The luckless Kraka, clamped tightly to the whale's belly in a back-to-front position, realised the vulnerability of his position too late.

29

The gushing water buffeted against the back of his gill-slits, forcing its way in. To a fish, such a thing is the same as a dry-creature drowning. Kraka had no choice but to unfasten himself quickly from the speeding whale before he blacked out.

Cacha was ready for him. As the giant squid floated free, he curved round in the water, lashing out sideways with his powerful tail in a chopping movement. The smashing blow took Kraka full in the mantle, just below the funnel, knocking him several yards through the water. As the squid retracted his tentacles instinctively, Cacha followed up the move with a high-speed charge, butting the squid with his huge, blunt snout. Backing off a little, Cacha dropped his lower jaw, exposing his fine set of teeth.

It was more than enough for the squid. Quickly losing all taste for further fight, he discharged his ink sac in a thick, clouding spurt. With his tentacles trailing behind him, Kraka jetted away at full speed, soon disappearing into the darkness.

Cacha turned slowly in the water to face Pyramus, regaining his composure. He concentrated his thoughts. 'Yes, trusted guardian. What news?'

Pyramus began to recount his story of the three strange creatures, omitting nothing. Cacha listened attentively until he had finished, then floated, almost motionless, as he considered the facts. Pyramus tried to probe the Great Elder's thoughts, but Cacha had erected a strong mental shield. Nevertheless, Pyramus was surprised and a little dismayed to discover that although he could not read the whale's thoughts clearly, fear emanated from him in quite powerful waves. It was obvious that the Elder took the whole matter very seriously indeed.

Finally, Cacha lifted his shield, letting only his direct thoughts flow out. 'You were right to come to me, Pyramus. You have done your duty as a guardian well, with wisdom.'

'Thank you, Great Cacha.' Pyramus was genuinely pleased, as well as being rather relieved. He had feared that he might have been wasting the Elder's time, bothering him with a trivial matter. He hovered in the water uncertainly, not quite sure whether to go or stay. Curiosity filled him, urging him to try and discuss the matter with Cacha, attempt to prise open the Great Elder's mind. Respect, and a strong sense of duty, fought against these temptations. It was not really his place to attempt familiarity with someone of Cacha's position.

Cacha read the manta ray's thoughts clearly, feeling a slight sympathy for the creature's concern. However, he could tell Pyramus nothing at this point, for the matter appeared far too important to be reduced to the level of gossip. He chose his thoughts carefully, anxious not to hurt the guardian's feelings. 'You must return to duty at once, Pyramus, and be especially vigilant in case these creatures return. Discuss this matter with no one.' He softened the harshness of the command with a final thought. 'I place great faith and trust in you, Pyramus. I know you will not let me down.'

'Of course, Great Cacha,' Pyramus responded, swelling with pride. 'I will do exactly as you command. No one shall hear of this matter from me.'

Cacha let out a brief, unshielded thought of ironic humour. 'Every creature in the liquid world shall hear of it soon enough. I think the great Nah-Ep himself will deem it important enough to summon a meeting of the Great Council.'

Pyramus was stunned. The Great Council! Nah-Ep himself! It was unheard of in his lifetime, and only rumoured amongst the very ancient ones in the places of dark water. Indeed, memories of a Great Council meeting were so remote that some fish dared to suggest that it, and Nah-Ep himself, were not real at all, merely myths and legends.

The guardian's shock registered clearly with Cacha, who projected a grave thought back to him. 'Yes, Pyramus, now you realise the full importance of the news you have brought me.' Cacha moved in the water, pointing his massive blunt head up towards the surface. 'I must go now, Pyramus, for my air supply is all but exhausted. I will need a strong, refreshed body to undertake the descent into the Secret Place and the Chamber of Echoes.'

With a few sluggish flips of his tail, Casha propelled his bulky body upwards towards the place of light water. Pyramus followed him at a respectful distance for a few hundred feet, until he reached light green water. Here, nearer the surface, he could make better speed, and it suddenly seemed of prime importance to return to duty as soon as possible.

Cacha swam towards the surface slowly, not wishing to overtire himself. The journey down to the Chamber of Echoes was a long and perilous one, and the fight with Kraka had taken a lot out of him. Cacha needed a little time to recover his full strength, and also time to reflect.

It was a supremely important decision he had made, to summon the Great Council. Cacha could only hope that it was the right one. Nah-Ep would not take kindly to being roused from the Secret Place for nothing.

The more he thought about it, the more his doubts evaporated, and his fears grew. There seemed little question that the three strange invaders had been dry-creatures. From the detailed description furnished by Pyramus, there seemed no other possible explanation.

It had only been a matter of time anyway, Cacha pondered gloomily. Sooner or later the dry-creature man had been bound to apply his powerful brain to the problem of conquering and exploiting the liquid world. Nothing stopped him for long. The legends told of the great greed, the strange driving force which pushed the dry-creature onward, for ever destroying anything which stood in his path.

Already the liquid world had suffered terribly. The dry-creature's poisons filled the oceans, his great ships ploughed the places of light water, bringing destruction to thousands. Now he had found his way into the places of dark water, and Cacha had no doubt that the dry-creature would bring his greed and destruction down with him.

Cacha dismissed the last lingering doubts with a heavy heart. No, he had not been wrong in deciding to summon the Great Council. If ever there had been a reason to do so, this was it.

He broke the surface, floating lazily in the light water and enjoying the tingling, somewhat erotic effect of the sun caressing his black, oily back, drying out the few droplets of water which had collected around his blowhole. Taking air was a process which could not be hurried. It would take nearly a quarter of an hour for his body to recharge itself. In that time Cacha was almost helpless, his keen sense of sound and vibration greatly diminished. His weak eyes, never very keen, were virtually useless in the bright glare of daylight.

Something light and shimmering broke against his flesh, tickling the softer parts of his underbelly. A large shoal of krill were swimming past him. He opened his mouth gratefully, gulping down thousands of the tiny, shrimp-like creatures to sustain him on his long journey. Oblivious of anything but the endless life-chain of the sea in which they played their part, the krill swam unconcernedly into the whale's gaping jaw, to change their form and become the substance from which life itself sprang.

At last Cacha was refreshed and ready for his journey. His black tail rose and fell, slapping the surface of the water and creating a large, powerful vortex into which his body sank. Almost vertically, he sank down towards the coral city.

With a grace and agility which belied his huge bulk, Cacha slipped down through the green waters at the very edge of the Continental Shelf. The low, sloping rock formations of the light waters were cleaved here and there with deep, jagged canyons, black holes yawning up from the inky depths of the Abyss far below. Flattening his body into a steep, angled dive, he cruised over the weed-festooned rocks, searching out a passageway to the depths large enough to accommodate his body.

He hardly noticed the vivid splendour of the coral city and its millionfold inhabitants as he progressed downwards. Normally, Cacha took great pleasure in observing the riot of colour and texture which now passed him by. Whole forests of glowing green and red seaweed swayed gently in the turbulence of his wake. Delicate sea fans and brilliantly coloured sponges brushed against his belly. In front of him, the lurid Moorish idols and the rainbow colours of the parrotfish danced in a beautiful, technicoloured ballet, but Cacha's mind was on more serious things.

The water darkened gradually, the soft pinks and yellows of the coral outcrops giving way to the lower end of the spectrum. A colony of golfball sponges glowed blood-red in the dim light, the colours of the prancing, preening fish changed to blues, searing violets, and glistening black scales, broken by bands of almost luminescent silver. From its lair deep in a rocky crevice, the polka-dotted head of a spotted eel snaked out, jaws open wide to snap up a luckless butterfly fish which had been swept its way by Cacha's passage.

Cacha's weak eyes strained ahead, past the complex, living city all around him. A few hundred feet further on, all movement ceased. The thin growths of seaweed hung lifelessly in the dark green water, with no undersea currents to waft them from side to side. No shoals of coloured fish moved in this area, for Cacha had come to one of the gigantic tunnels which led down to the Abyss, and the icy waters of the depths rose to chill the surrounding area and chase away the denizens of the warm Gulf currents.

Cacha had no fear of the cold water. Unlike his fishy fellow beings with whom he shared the sea, he had the great advantage of having the warm-blooded body of a mammal, and unique insulating properties inherent in his blubber-filled flesh. As he neared the rim of the yawning crater, his body adjusted automatically to adapt to the changing temperatures around him. Rich, highly-oxygenated blood flowed to fill the spaces between the layers of fatty tissue, raising his internal heat to compensate for the cold outside.

Cacha hovered above the pit for several seconds, gazing down into its depths with a certain awe. For a few hundred feet there would be a little residual light to guide him. After that he would be in total and utter blackness, blind except for his remarkable sonic radar. In the Abyss he would feel his way by sending out sound waves, judging size, shape and distance by the echoes which returned to him. It was a poor defence against some of the horrible dangers which lurked in the gloomy depths.

Carefully, Cacha floated out into the very centre of the pit before starting his descent, for the greatest danger would be near the sides of the vertical shaft. The tunnel plunged down for several thousand feet; the sides were irregular, and lined with jagged, knife-edged outcrops of rocks. Cacha had no wish to slice open his delicate flesh against them.

Other more unpleasant dangers would also be lurking in the blackest places between the rocks. Here, on the very threshold of the Abyss, were the banished creatures – the monstrous life-forms whose deformed and grotesque bodies were mercifully hidden by the darkness. Some were no more than hideous, gaping mouths, for ever open to snap up whatever titbits came their way. Behind these floating teeth, their stunted, pathetic little bodies were no more than an afterthought. Cacha had seen some of the ghastly creatures before, whilst others were merely rumours – stories of hobgoblins and vampires which served to warn young and impressionable fish to stay away from the Secret Place. One particularly repugnant monster was real enough, however, and Cacha had no wish to become its wretched victim. This blind, vicious creature would latch itself on to the body of any fish who was foolish enough to venture into its domain. Needle-like teeth and limpet-like suckers enabled the monster to attach itself to its prey, eating into the body of its host and living embedded there as a parasite, devouring the flesh and blood of its living home. Cacha would be an ideal victim, for these disgusting creatures particularly relished a large and healthy host who could carry them away from their dark and dismal prison. Cacha's high position was no protection, for the banished creatures of the Abyss respected nothing from the places of light water, and held especial hatred for any of the Elders.

Cacha pushed his fears aside, for he could not afford to waste time. His air was limited, and there was a long way to go. He curved his body, pointing his blunt head down into the chasm. With slow but strong pulses of his powerful tail, he began to propel himself towards the Secret Place.

A few feet below him, Cacha picked out one of the first of the many unpleasant sights which heralded the approach to the Abyss. Across his path a white, misty haze hung motionless in the water. In the dullish red light, the millions of fine, fibrous tentacles and filaments of the giant polyp colony seemed to shimmer like a tracery of exposed veins in torn flesh, pulsing with blood. Behind the tightly interwoven web of stinging tentacles, a thousand fiery-red eyes peered out hopefully. Cacha pushed through the colony regardless. This particular horror of the deep was no threat to a creature of his size. It relied on tiny, almost microscopic creatures for its food supply. Brushed aside in Cacha's wake, the colony of polyps retracted their tentacles, rolling into a huge tight ball which drifted off towards the side of the tunnel to spread its web in more hopeful waters.

A large female angler fish floated by, its squat, ugly body bristling with strange branched appendages. It bared its huge curved teeth momentarily at Cacha, then decided that discretion was the better part of valour. With a flurry of movement from its withered tail, it scuttled away. Cacha shuddered as he saw the tiny, stunted body of the male hanging from its underbelly. That too lived the life of a parasite, eating its way into the larger body of the female and becoming a useless passenger for ever afterwards. For the most part, the denizens of this hellish place accepted such revolting habits as an unfortunate but inescapable fact of their wretched existence.

The main shaft of the tunnel widened as Cacha descended, opening out into a vast underwater grotto. A rich, luxuriant growth of purple weed festooned the sides and floor of the cavern, providing a home for thousands of tiny luminous fish. In the indigo darkness, their flashing discharges of energy created a shimmering carpet of tiny fairy lights, revealing glimpses of startlingly bright orange and scarlet bodies. Larger fish floated above the weed, with huge bulbous eyes constantly reviewing the scene below them. Like the smaller fish upon which they preyed, their bodies glowed with an eerie, luminescent sheen.

Cacha skimmed above them, his sound waves pulsing out ahead of him to locate the next tunnel entrance. There were three to choose from at the far end of the grotto. As he neared them, Cacha could see that they all glowed with a dull reddish tint, looking for all the world like three huge open mouths, open and ready to swallow him up. Here, the rocks themselves seemed to be alive, for they throbbed with the colours of fire. Darting in and out of the alternating patches of light and darkness, Cacha saw more of the obscene angler fish, now bigger and even more deformed. Some of them were no more than shapeless masses of branches, each one ending in a glowing bulbous tip dripping with a thick mucous.

Unexpectedly a ten-foot specimen launched itself out of the gloom towards Cacha's eyes. He recoiled instinctively from the gaping mouth, lined with three rows of curved and barbed teeth. His massive lower jaw dropped open, exposing his own set of teeth. Unaware of the danger, the giant angler pressed forward with his attack, confident in his knowledge that most of the whales had only horny cartilage lining their mouths.

It was a fatal mistake. The angler died soundlessly and suddenly as Cacha's powerful jaws crushed its distended body. Tossing the dead creature aside in disgust, Cacha watched its body drift slowly down towards the tunnel floor. A group of its own species gathered around the corpse at once, ripping it apart with snapping bites of their vicious teeth. Cacha swam on quickly, eager to leave the unpleasant sight behind him. Like many of the other unsavoury ways of the Abyss, he found cannibalism repugnant.

The tunnel narrowed. Cacha's huge bulk was almost touching the sides. Reflecting upon the unexpected attack of the angler, he felt a little uneasy. He tensed himself, letting out a deep, bellowing grunt which echoed and reverberated along the tunnel walls. Cacha was proud of his unique ability to make the loudest noise of all marine creatures. It was virtually guaranteed to drive away any other would-be attackers. He redoubled his efforts to reach the end of the final tunnel. He would have little time to spare for the return journey, and on the way back he would be weaker and less able to make good speed.

The tunnel ended at last, opening out into the real Abyss. Immediately, Cacha moved from the dull light of the fire rocks into a blackness which was absolute. It even seemed to have a thick texture of darkness to it, like the oil which man poured into the sea from his huge ships.

Cacha sent out waves of sound at random, searching out a passageway in the black void. The echoes which came back were faint and indistinct, so vast was the underworld of the Abyss. For a moment Cacha felt almost panicky, he was so utterly lost.

Then faith returned, warming and cheering him. He was an Elder, with access to the Secret Place. He was so near to Nah-Ep's domain now that the great sea-god would send help to guide him.

It came. From out of the blackness a cluster of glowing violet globes appeared, hovering around his weak eyes. Slowly, they pressed forward in the water, leading him towards the Chamber of Echoes.

Cacha followed his strange guides gratefully, thankful that his great task was nearly completed. The pulsing violet globes dropped downwards, taking him to the absolute depths of the Abyss, the heart and centre of the liquid world.

Deep in the ocean, on the very bed of the inner earth, lay the vast domed vault of the Chamber of Echoes. In the pale light cast from the glowing orbs, Cacha looked around in wonder. In the Chamber even an Elder felt utterly insignificant.

Settling himself, Cacha began the solemn ritual which would summon Nah-Ep and relay his message to all creatures of the liquid world. In the forbidden language of the Ancients, Cacha began to chant the incantation.

The strange clicking sounds which emanated from Cacha's head flowed into the surrounding water, pulsing outwards in widening concentric ripples until they reached the walls of the Chamber. There, intricately inlaid slabs of metallic rock amplified the signals, bouncing them off in thunderous, rolling echoes which would permeate the length and depth of the entire liquid world.

The violet globes glowed brighter and brighter as Cacha incanted the ritual, finally becoming haloes of pure white brilliance. As Cacha emitted the last syllable of the ancient message, the very walls of the Chamber seemed to come alive, vibrating with power.

A throbbing sound filled the water, growing louder and louder until Cacha felt that he could not bear the pain of it. Then, with a final shrieking burst of intensity, it broke through the walls of the Chamber of Echoes to find its way into the open sea. Silence and blackness descended quickly again. Cacha remained motionless for several minutes, stunned with awe.

Then, moving painfully, he began the slow and perilous return to the place of light water. His job was done. Nah-Ep was roused, and all the mighty powers of the liquid world were abroad.

Chapter Three

Grossman paced the floor of the main lab irritably, glancing at his watch every fifteen or twenty seconds without really reading the time. His obvious nervousness affected Ellis, bringing home to him the disquieting knowledge that things were not as they should be; the all-important test dive had not gone as planned.

'What the hell happened down there?'

'I don't know,' Grossman snapped, equally tersely. Yet again he glanced at his watch abstractedly, then crossed the lab to the intercom unit. 'Charles, is anything happening down there yet?'

From the airlock below, Charles Flaxman's voice grated over the speaker, unusually clipped. 'The tanks are on their way up now. You're not going to like it, Heinz.'

'Get up here fast,' Grossman said, snapping off the intercom. He resumed his nervous pacing, ignoring Ellis.

Minutes later, Flaxman entered the laboratory and supervised the conveyance of the pressure tanks on to their respective podiums. He checked the gauges, made a couple of minor adjustments to the settings, then walked across to Grossman. His face was pulled into a taut, grim frown. 'It's nasty,' he muttered, simply.

Grossman regarded the three tanks and their occupants with horrified fascination. Only McAllister floated passively in the water. Both his companions were in a constant state of agitation, their torsos and extremities convulsing and twitching spasmodically, churning the water into swirling, distorting patterns which made them look less than human. Their eyes rolled from side to side wildly, seeing nothing.

Ellis looked, briefly, then turned away in disgust. The sight was vaguely obscene.

'Bloody fools,' Grossman spat out suddenly, anger against the divers surging up as a reaction to his own sense of guilt. 'What the hell got into them? Every basic rule they had drummed into them just forgotten, ignored.'

'What are you talking about?' Ellis didn't understand.

Grossman stared at the jerking figures in the tanks, his anger subsiding as pity took over. 'The poor devils must be going through hell,' he muttered, through gritted teeth. 'The agony must be unbelievable.'

'They're in pain?' Ellis had not fully grasped this fact.

'The sort of pain which drives a man insane,' Flaxman put in. 'God only knows what made them panic like that. They came up far too fast, it was suicidal.'

'You mean they have the bends?' Ellis had heard the term, although he didn't fully understand what it involved. He rounded on Grossman accusingly. 'You told me this gill-unit of yours was self-compensating.'

'It is,' Grossman snapped. 'But adapting to pressure changes takes a certain amount of time under any circumstances. God dammit, they knew that well enough. It's like a first commandment to any diver, a thought as natural as self-preservation itself. Something down there spooked them so much that they couldn't even think straight.'

'Will they be all right?' Ellis spoke with the concern of a man with vested interests.

Grossman shrugged helplessly. 'They have a fair chance of survival,' he admitted. 'But if they do live, they'll never dive again, that's for sure. They may never be able to live normal lives again; the muscular and cardiac damage could be immense.' He broke off, slamming his clenched fist into the opposite palm. 'What made them do it, for God's sake?'

He turned to Flaxman. 'Did you see anything?'

The man shook his head sadly. 'Nothing. I wasn't expecting them back for at least twenty minutes. Brandon and Caffrey hit the airlock like there was a race on.'

'Is there any way we can communicate with them, ask them what happened?' Ellis asked.

Grossman shook his head. 'No, and that's my damned fault. A stupid oversight. I didn't take into account the possibility of losing the communicator. I should have fitted the tanks with their own pressure locks so that we could have introduced replacements.'

As he spoke, a sudden thought occurred to him. Grossman crossed the laboratory to the valves controlling the pressure in the tanks. He adjusted two of them slightly and moved to his workbench, picking up a small gas cylinder. Carrying it over to the tanks, he linked it into the supply pipes and made a last delicate adjustment.

'Sorry. I should have thought of that,' Flaxman murmured.

'What? What have you done?' Ellis wanted to know.

Grossman finished the job before answering. 'I've just introduced a little anaesthetic into the water. It will ease their pain somewhat. It's all I can do for them, unfortunately.'

'You only treated two of the tanks,' Ellis pointed out.

Grossman nodded. 'McAllister is all right, thank God. He kept his cool and came up comparatively slowly. It was obviously enough to let the gill-unit adjust.' He turned to study the man in question. 'Even so, he's not quite normal. He's far too quiescent for my liking.'

'Nitrogen narcosis?' Flaxman suggested.

'Could be. Then again, it could be shock. If they saw anything down there terrifying enough to send Brandon and Caffrey into a blind panic, McAllister could be having a late reaction. It can happen.'

'The sharks . . . how about those sharks,' Ellis blurted out.

Grossman smiled with exaggerated patience. 'I've seen McAllister tickle a shark's belly. They don't frighten him at all. As a matter of fact, McAllister has always shown an affinity with marine life that I've quite envied. No, it would have to be something pretty unusual to faze him.'

Grossman seemed to come to a sudden decision. He turned away from the pressure tanks abruptly, snapping an order to Flaxman over his shoulder. 'Look after them, Charles. I'm going down into the tunnel.'

'Sure,' Flaxman said. 'Want me to put the tanks on visual, so you can keep an eye on them?'

'Good idea.' As Grossman headed towards the door, Flaxman

adjusted the security scanners so that they focused on the three tanks. The picture would be relayed over the closed-circuit T.V. system throughout the complex.

Grossman paused at the door, turning back to Ellis. 'Want to come down, Mr Ellis?'

'What do you expect to see?' Ellis asked, a trifle uncertainly.

Grossman shrugged. 'I don't know. All I do know is that they saw something, and the tunnel is the only place I'm likely to get any clues as to what it was. Well?'

Ellis paused for a few seconds more. Finally, his fear of the tunnel was overcome by curiosity, fuelled by greed. Everything was suddenly at stake, the entire future of utopian riches threatened. Ellis wanted to know what unforeseen factor posed that threat. With a slight nod he followed Grossman to the elevator.

Grossman strode briskly along the tunnel until he came to the end bulkhead. Stepping to the wall, he opened a small service hatch, pulling out a large wrench and a box of assorted tools. Wielding the heavy wrench with the clumsy touch of a man used only to more delicate tools, he began to loosen the first of the massive hexagonal bolts on the steel bulkhead.

'What are you doing?' Ellis shouted in fright. Beyond the double bulkhead, the tunnel was only partially completed. 'You'll kill us both, for Chrissakes.'

Grossman did not stop his work. Grunting from the exertion of tackling the rock-tight bolts, he spoke over his shoulder. 'There's another 150 feet of the tunnel which is watertight. It's just the safety mechanisms which haven't been connected up yet. The tunnel goes deeper beyond this bulkhead, and there's a slight curve. If we're going to see anything at all, we stand our best chance from there.'

The last bolt came free. Grossman tugged at the heavy bulkhead, swinging it open. Beyond, the dark unlit section of the tunnel dropped gradually downwards.

Warily, Ellis followed the scientist into it, stepping slowly down the curving slope towards the end of the tunnel. As his eyes accustomed themselves to the gloom, he was aware of the pale, greenish light which filtered in through the windows from the sea outside. It lent an eerie, unworldly sheen to the bare concrete and steel walls.

Grossman pressed his face against the glass of the final

41

window, raising himself on to the tips of his toes to look downwards as much as possible.

'See anything?' Ellis asked.

Grossman shook his head uncertainly, dropping on to the soles of his feet again. He cocked his head slightly to one side, a puzzled expression on his face. After a few seconds, he pressed his ear against the window. 'I think I can hear something, though.'

'Hear something? What?'

'Quiet.' Grossman turned on Ellis with unusual savagery. He placed his ear against the window again. 'My God,' he breathed softly, after a couple of moments.

Ellis moved to another window, copying Grossman. As he placed his ear against the cold glass, he heard it too.

It was like no sound Ellis had ever heard before. A dull yet insistent throbbing, rising and falling in a vague melody and increasing in volume every second.

Alarmed by the unknown, Ellis jumped away from the window. 'What the hell is it?'

Grossman moved also. 'I don't know,' he admitted. 'But from the way it's growing, I don't think we'd better stay here.' He moved quickly, tugging at Ellis's sleeve and breaking into a loping run back towards the lighted part of the tunnel. Jumping through the bulkhead, he swung it closed and began to swing the wheel-lock round.

Ellis stood rooted to the spot. He no longer had to go anywhere near the windows to hear the weird sound now. It was pulsing into the interior of the tunnel with ever-increasing intensity. Now that it was louder, it reminded Ellis of a distant thunderstorm, coming rapidly closer.

Grossman finished closing the bulkhead and ran back to the nearest window, staring out in confusion. There was no visual sign that anything was wrong; the water seemed calm enough. Yet the grumbling, rolling sounds were rapidly building up into a crescendo. At their peak they seemed to change slightly, blurring into an overlapping, continuous pulsing noise which seemed to seep into the very fabric of the tunnel setting up a regular vibration.

Ellis looked pale and shaken. 'It's an earthquake,' he shouted suddenly. 'That's what it is, a bloody underwater eruption.'

The same thought occurred to Grossman more or less simultaneously. He ran along the tunnel to consult a panel of instruments built into the walls. He ran back to Ellis, who was shaking with fear. 'It's not a quake,' Grossman shouted, above the growing din. 'I've just checked the seismograph, there are no tremors out there at all. It's purely sonic in origin, just sound waves, that's all.'

If Ellis heard him, he took no comfort from the information. He had retreated to the inner wall of the tunnel, where he leaned back and tried to control the trembling in his legs. The whole tunnel was throbbing now. The metal girders bracing the structure had picked up the pulsing rhythm and were beginning to sing musically, with rising and falling harmonic notes which echoed out into the soundbox of the hollow interior.

Grossman returned to the window, staring out without comprehension. He could think of nothing to explain the phenomena. In this vacuum a snatch of fantasy intruded. A brief mythical quotation rose to his lips. Grossman mouthed it quietly, under his breath: 'Walk in awe, mortal man . . . lest the Kraken wakes.'

The vibrations in the tunnel began to fade. The volume of sound was dropping now, at a faster rate than it had grown. In a matter of seconds it had dwindled to a low murmur, and then was gone. The silence which followed had its own ominous quality.

Grossman continued to stare out into the dark green water. Suddenly, a flash of movement caught his eye. He strained his eyes through the murk towards it. Abruptly the waters surrounding the tunnel were green no more, they were alive with all the colours of the spectrum, flashing between patches of darkness like sheets of multi-coloured lightning, as thousands of brightly-hued fish swept past the windows.

Fascinated, Grossman gazed open-mouthed at the entrancing sight. The light of the tunnel flickered back from a million silver, green and blue scales, creating an almost stroboscopic, hypnotising effect. It lasted for several minutes and then that strange phenomenon, too, disappeared as quickly as it had begun.

Ellis, who had missed it all, came quietly up behind Grossman, trying to peer over his shoulder. 'What can you see out there?'

'Nothing,' Grossman answered him in a strange voice. 'Absolutely nothing. It's incredible!'

'Nothing? Incredible?' Ellis echoed dumbly, failing to understand.

Grossman stepped back from the window, urging Ellis forward to take his place. 'Look out there. What do you see? Nothing at all, not a single fish.'

Ellis checked this fact for himself, finally shrugging. 'Yeah, right. No fish, so what?'

Grossman shook his head in disbelief. 'Don't you understand, Mr Ellis? A few minutes ago, the waters out there were teeming with fish, millions upon millions of them. The water all around us should be alive with different life-forms, yet there is absolutely nothing moving out there, not as far as the eye can see. It's as if this entire area has suddenly become totally and utterly lifeless, sterile.'

Ellis remained unimpressed. 'Guess that bloody racket must have scared them off.'

Grossman allowed himself a faint smile. 'You don't know much about fish, Mr Ellis. Curiosity is an emotion they possess in abundance. Fear is not.'

He turned and began walking back along the tunnel. 'Let's get back. I want to see if the computer can give us any data on that disturbance.'

They walked towards the elevator. Grossman suddenly stopped dead in his stride as a wall-mounted T.V. monitor caught his eye and presented him with yet another weird sight. In the pressure tanks, the divers' behaviour had changed noticeably. Brandon and Caffrey were quieter now, their agonised convulsions reduced to minor twitches. The anaesthetic had done its work. But it was McAllister who fascinated Grossman. He had sunk to the very bottom of his tank, against the natural buoyancy of his body, and he was deliberately keeping himself there by quite powerful beatings of his hands.

Chapter Four

As always, the coral city was a colourful, bustling metropolis, teeming with the myriad, interconnected life-forms which sustained it.

Raspus the cleaner wrasse, the dominant male of his small family unit, was busier than most, his blue, black and gold body constantly on the move, checking his territorial borders, keeping invaders and poachers at bay and trying to attend to his own business at the same time. He enjoyed his busy life. There was something exciting about swimming into the very mouths of fish which would normally devour him, protected absolutely by the code of truce which prevailed within the defined area of the cleaning station. This truce was necessary to both wrasse and customer, for while the larger fish hovered sluggishly in the water, Raspus and his fellow creatures scoured every inch of their bodies, seeking out and devouring the hundreds of microscopic parasites which infested them. It was a perfect relationship; the wrasse were adapted to this unique food supply, and their customers were well rid of the unwanted organisms which would otherwise irritate and possibly destroy them if left unchecked.

Once, Raspus had been a female, leading a much more sedentary life. This was yet another strange feature of his species – the ability to change sex at will when the eco-balance of the family unit demanded it.

He busied himself with his largest, and certainly most important customer of the day – Gamma, the giant bass, a member of the Inner Council. Such an exalted patron deserved particularly fussy attention. Raspus edged carefully into Gamma's delicate gill-slits, his fine teeth nibbling at pieces of debris lodged between the sensitive membranes.

The big body of the giant bass shuddered suddenly, unexpectedly. Raspus darted out backwards, alarmed at such uncharacteristic motion. Under all normal circumstances, a fish being cleaned remained perfectly still and tranquil.

Now, Gamma was far from tranquil. The small wrasse felt thought-waves of unprecedented intensity all around him. Suddenly, something like a psychic shock-wave spread throughout the area. All activity ground to a halt almost simultaneously. The coral city became transfixed, paralysed.

The first of the sonic ripples from the Chamber of Echoes shivered through the water to reach the petrified community. It was no more than a delicate prelude to the throbbing concerto which was to come, but it was enough to start things moving. Raspus looked up with a sense of wonder as the mass exodus from the place of light water began. Like a rain of coloured confetti, the first of millions of tiny fish began to swim downwards towards the coral city, abandoning their usual habitat nearer the surface. Butterfly fish, parrotfish, clownfish, rock beauties and blueheads sank to the sea-bed, turning it into a moving, shimmering carpet designed and coloured by some mad surrealist painter. Without fully understanding why, the denizens of the liquid world were blindly obeying a command, a vague folk memory, which had never actually been invoked during their own brief lifetimes.

Only Gamma, one of the oldest of his species, had the faintest glimmer of what was happening. The Inner Council met quite frequently, to discuss and review the constant, yet ever-changing balance of the liquid world. Part of the ritual processes involved was rehearsing the major mechanics of a Great Council summons, even though it had never seemed necessary to activate them before. This knowledge alone enabled Gamma to recognise the meaning of the growing vibrations in the water around him. They were the first passages from an ancient ritual in the old language, the full text of which was known only to the Council of Elders and Nah-Ep himself. As the rippling waves built up, Gamma knew that they could only emanate from the Chamber of Echoes. Whilst the smaller, younger fish around him panicked, Gamma remained calm, concentrating his mental powers.

Above the confusion and prickling barrage of loose thoughts, the giant bass shielded his mind, directing a single, concen-trated thought at Raspus. He received the concentrated thought clearly. Gamma would guide him to the Great Council Chamber. Leaving the pandemonium of the coral city behind them, the two fish slipped quietly away into the dark green waters, plunging down into the tranquillity of the nether-world between the dark waters and the Abyss. The intense power of Cacha's sonic echoes assumed an almost tactile quality as they descended. The very water seemed heavier, offering pulsating waves of resistance, like strong tidal cur-rents. Raspus found that he had to swim hard to keep up with the giant bass, who cleaved the water ahead of him with muscular flips of his large, powerful tail. A certain heavi-ness descended upon the small wrasse as they progressed towards their destination. At first, he thought that it was merely fatigue from the struggle to keep pace with his guide, but as the sounds in the water intensified, he realised that an impending sense of destiny, tempered with a little fear, was throwing a thick mental blanket over his mind. Raspus re-doubled his efforts to keep close on Gamma's tail as the waters darkened around them.

In contrast to the vivid colours of the coral city, the Great Chamber was a dull, sombre place, carved out of the dark rocks by the passage of tides and time. The dark browns and greens of the surrounding seascape seemed perfectly in keeping with the solemnity and reverence of the ancient place, as though the great and wise elders who had met there since the Time of the First Time had each left something of themselves in the ambience of the place.

Slowly now, Gamma and Raspus swam into the vast underwater amphitheatre, skirting around the outer perimeter in search of an uncrowded place. There seemed little hope of finding one. Already, many thousands of creatures had found their way to the Secret Place. At least one representative of each of the countless species was present. An unspoken truce prevailed within the Great Chamber. Hunter and prey, host and parasite – all natural enemies forgot their differences here, hovering side by side in the water, conscious of the mighty powers which dwarfed their petty struggles.

Gamma and Raspus found themselves a relatively clear patch of water and stopped, staring down into the massive sandy bowl on the ocean bed. All around them the waters seethed with loose, unshielded thought-images of fear, wonder, and wild speculation. What sudden catastrophe threatened the ordered life of the liquid world? Would the mighty Nah-Ep himself appear before them? What strange and terrible changes threatened their futures? So many wild and powerful thoughts seared at the mind, causing actual physical pain. Gamma summoned his greatest mental powers, erecting a strong shield and extending it to embrace Raspus out of pity for the small fish. Raspus was on one of the lowest levels of purely instinctive intelligence. His mental capacities were limited to simple communication and could not possibly stretch to maintaining an adequate defence against so many other, stronger minds.

Two of the three Great Elders had taken their places in the centre of the Great Chamber, awaiting only Cacha's return from the Chamber of Echoes. Poda the Octopus, the Elder of the places of dark water, squatted on the sea floor, her tentacles retracted around her soft body. She had brought a new compassion and sensitivity to the harsh world on the very brink of the Abyss, for the octopuses were on a level of intelligence only slightly inferior to the whales and dolphins, and Poda tempered this intelligence with understanding.

Quench the crayfish, Elder of the places of broken water, was a deceptive figure. His size was dwarfed by the massive bodies of the aquatic mammals, yet he ruled the shallow waters where the tides broke upon the dry lands with an iron grip out of all proportion to his stature. He was feared and respected by all members of the Inner Council, for he had many times brought swift and terrible retribution to those in his domain who had brought pain or death to the dry-creature in the places where the liquid world and dry land met and mingled. Of all the Elders, Quench had the greatest knowledge and understanding of the dry-creature, for it was in his world that the two species came closest together, and at times when the tides retreated, many crustaceans and molluscs shared the constant torment of the dry-creature, burning under his sun, shrivelling on the dry, unforgiving sands and shingles.

Finally Cacha arrived, his mighty bulk moving sluggishly through the water, every fibre of his body wearied by the long and perilous descent to the Abyss. With his arrival, the Great Council was complete. Gamma lowered his shield, marvelling at the way in which a sudden and complete peace had descended upon the vast Chamber. Such was the concentrated power of the Great Council, they could stun every living creature within range by thought-power alone.

A long and terrible silence prevailed, as every living creature present in the Great Chamber sensed the imminent presence of a being a thousand, a million times greater than themselves. It was a time of the utmost wonder, the deepest possible recognition of total humility, supreme unimportance of the individual but the ultimate importance of the whole.

After a while, the circular walls of the Chamber began to glow softly with a deep indigo hue. It changed slowly through the spectrum, purple giving way to blue, blue becoming ultramarine, light dawning in the form of a fine mist dissipating into the murky water to create a faintly luminous dome which formed a canopy over the Chamber and bathed the sandy bowl in soft illumination.

The creatures of the liquid world were as one now, bonded together in the awesome knowledge that they were in the actual presence of their god, the Great Nah-Ep, the Wise One, supreme ruler of the liquid world.

It was a presence that could not truly be seen, yet it could be felt so intensely that it was a picture absorbed into the brain of every creature present. Patterns of light, shivering shapes and forms, traceries of brief, transient outlines blurred and re-formed themselves in the quivering water. In a strange image which could be known and yet not seen, Nah-Ep suddenly existed among them.

Within the shifting, uncertain disturbance in the water lay the image of every fish, mammal and creature which ever had, or ever would, swim in the open seas, crawl upon the ocean floor or drift in the limbo of moving waters. Each representative of the liquid world recognised something of his own species, if only for a fleeting instant. Fin, tentacle, tooth and shell overlapped in the flickering, changing image of a totally omnipotent, all-embracing being.

Nah-Ep permeated every atom of the surrounding water, knowing no limits or barriers, every assembled creature, both individually and collectively. He was at once both the nucleus and the furthermost boundary of life itself, and of the endless life-chain which bound them all.

Nah-Ep settled his being into the minds of the three chosen Elders, bestowing his great gifts upon them. Together, their three minds working as one, the Elders began to recount the Great Legend, which told of the three times upon planet earth, the great creation of the dry world, the liquid world and the Abyss, and of Nah-Ep the sea-god, entrusted keeper of the Secret Place.

With the telling of the Great Legend, a greatly strengthened sense of awe and reverence fell upon the Great Chamber. Every creature present seemed to sense, instinctively, that a sudden and radical change in their existence was imminent. A critical point had been reached and a new danger threatened them. The ancient powers of the sea must again be invoked to maintain the delicate balance of life upon the earth.

Relayed through the minds of the three Elders, Nah-Ep's thoughts came to the assembled creatures, and there was a momentary flash of pity, an apology for what was to come. Before the dawning of a new understanding, before the liquid world could again hope to confront the creature man, there had to be an end to innocence; a dark and terrible secret had to be made known.

The secret was death. The image was one of total evil, on a scale unparalleled or dreamed of in the liquid world.

There was no death in the liquid world, for living never ceased, it merely changed form. In the perfectly balanced life-chain of the seas, there was only new-life, when one creature became the foodstuff, the sustaining life-force of another, and by doing so merely became a different link in the chain, sacrificing only a temporary identity. There was no killing other than that necessary to sustain life. It was the way of the liquid world, and any other way was utterly alien to its creatures.

Now, they had to face the horror that it might well have to become a reality of their survival, for the creature man had violated the greatest of the sacred truths. He had invaded the forbidden territory of the Secret Place. Man, the creature who spread death around himself like a black plague, had found a way into the freedom of the liquid world, perhaps even to the forbidden Abyss. There was a terrifying possibility that he would bring his greed and death with him, to pollute the seas anew. It was a threat which had to be faced, and dealt with.

Nah-Ep's powerful thought-waves subsided, but it was only a temporary respite to enable the assembled delegates to assimilate what they had learned. There was a buzz of frenzied speculation as they debated what Nah-Ep's ruling would be.

When it finally came, it was simple, and direct. Man had transgressed, and would be punished. The liquid world would take back the concession it had once granted him. Man was to be cut from the life-chain, as its single weak, and therefore dangerous, link. The gift of food from the seas would no longer be his.

Abruptly, the Great Council meeting was ended. There would have to be other meetings of course, to keep the situation under review, plan future courses of action. For the moment, however, it was sufficient that fish should avoid all contact with the creature man. The liquid world was on a state of alert, adopting passive resistance for the time being. Pelargic creatures would join their demersal brothers in deeper waters, avoiding man's fishing nets. The creatures of broken water would keep their distance from the tidal dry lands, and the aquatic mammals were to exercise especial care in keeping out of man's sight.

The waters gradually darkened again as Nah-Ep's presence faded from the Great Chamber. Almost at once a mental furore broke out as wild and loose thought-images prickled through the water. Deprived of Nah-Ep's powers, the three Elders could no longer maintain their blanketing shield. It was useless to even try. Cacha stirred himself into life with lazy flips of his huge tail. It was inevitable that a period of bedlam would follow the sombre tone of the meeting, and there could well be turbulent times ahead. Cacha knew that his powers of responsibility would be taxed and tested to their utmost. To give of his best, he would need the tranquillity of reflection, the wisdom that only deep meditation could bring.

Chapter
Five

Heinz Grossman gazed out into the still, lifeless water outside the tunnel. It was over a week now since the strange disruption, and still he had not seen a single fish. It was as if all life in the sea had been exterminated in an instant, as if with the flicking of a switch. He nodded his head in a vague gesture at something far beyond the dark waters pressing around the tunnel. 'Some people believe that the real Atlantis was out there, somewhere,' he said to the man who stood quietly beside him.

McAllister's lips moved slightly, curving into a gentle smile. 'Oh it is,' he muttered, the softness of his tone belying the strange assurance of his words. He fell silent again, not wishing to pursue the matter any further.

Grossman regarded the man quizzically, still unable to understand him or open up anything approaching normal channels of human communication with him. The diver had been out of the decompression unit for three whole days now, and his entire conversation had been limited to similar brief, often cryptic statements. He showed no physical ill effects, but he was oddly withdrawn, retreating into a guarded silence whenever he was questioned directly about his experience. A layman might have taken it as a sign of amnesia, but Grossman had enough basic grounding in human psychology to realise that McAllister was deliberately withholding information. He had released only one fact : that a number of manta rays had spooked his two fellow divers. When Grossman pressed him to expand, McAllister became defensive, then aggressive, suggesting that there was a bug in Grossman's gill-unit which caused divers to hallucinate, to succumb to that strange phenomenon that had been tagged 'the raptures of the deep'. What Grossman could not possibly know was that McAllister was himself unsure of what he had seen, what he had imagined. Until he could sort it all out in his own head, he was keeping quiet.

Grossman sensed the man's obvious mental turmoil and did not press him too far. McAllister was his only chance of finding out what had happened down there in the dark waters below the tunnel. Caffrey was dead, and Brandon was fighting for his life in a naval hospital at Key West. It seemed sensible to temper his curiosity with a little patience. McAllister would talk, eventually, when he felt sure that he had some thing to say. In the meantime, the diver submitted quite willingly to a battery of physiological and psychological tests which would at least show up any flaws in the actual functioning of the gill-unit or the effects of altered body chemistry upon the human brain.

Grossman's pocket bleeper shrilled out a brief call message. He turned and walked towards the nearest monitor screen, where Flaxman's face greeted him. 'Got the results of that last series of tests through, Heinz. Something quite interesting has just shown up. Don't quite know what to make of it though.'

Grossman thumbed the transmitter button on the monitor. 'O.K. Charles, I'm on my way up.' He turned back to McAllister. 'We'd better get back to the lab. It's time for you to take some more rest.'

'Sure.' McAllister nodded compliantly. He fell into step beside Grossman and the two men walked leisurely back to the laboratory.

Flaxman was waiting for them, studying a computer print-out of the latest set of readings. He looked up as Grossman approached him. 'No illuminating answers, I'm afraid.'

'What have we got?'

Flaxman gave a wry smile. 'Some more questions. Interesting ones, though.'

Grossman reached out to take the paper from his colleague's hands, then hesitated on an afterthought. He turned round towards McAllister, who promptly turned his back, walked across the laboratory and lay down on a day bed. He rolled up his left sleeve and clenched his fist a couple of times.

Grossman stared in surprise. Not a word had been said about administering an injection, yet McAllister had quietly gone ahead and prepared himself. It was almost as if he had anticipated Grossman's movements.

It was a ridiculous thought. Grossman thrust it out of his mind. He had mentioned that McAllister was due for another rest period. It was quite natural and logical for the man to assume he would be given a sedative. Grossman crossed the lab, prepared a hypodermic and shot a moderate dose of Valium into McAllister's arm. He waited twenty-five seconds, his finger curled around the man's pulse. Satisfied that McAllister had sunk into a deep, drugged sleep, he placed his arms across his chest and covered him with a thin blanket.

He strolled back to Flaxman. 'So, what's new?'

His colleague handed him a long roll of grid paper. 'This is the latest electro-encephalograph. McAllister wasn't sedated when we questioned him that time.'

Flaxman handed him another roll. 'Now compare it with this graph, the result of verbal questioning under sodium pentothal. A rather interesting link showed up.'

Grossman rolled the papers out on a workbench, studying the patterns of trace lines carefully. One thing became immediately apparent: each time McAllister had been asked a direct question about his dive the brainwave pattern showed up as a massive peak on both the graphs. Grossman tapped his finger on one of them. 'These, you mean?'

Flaxman nodded. 'They're quite incredible. They swamp out every other channel of neural activity. I've never seen anything quite like it before, except under abnormal experimental conditions.'

'Abnormal?' Grossman raised one eyebrow quizzically.

'The only time I've seen peaks remotely like these is with a subject under the influence of hallucinogens, or in deep narco-hypnosis. Oh, and once when I helped study a subject in a yogic trance.'

'Conclusion?'

Flaxman shook his head. 'None, really.' He bent over Grossman and ran his finger along the most regular of the trace lines. 'This is the alpha rhythm trace. As you see, it's perfectly normal, exactly as it should be. It indicates a perfectly relaxed state of wakefulness. It's those peaks which bother me. In a drugged state, McAllister shouldn't have the mental strength to register a block like that.'

'They are definitely blocks?' Grossman queried.

'Well, they seem to be. They're on both graphs and they fit in exactly with the pattern of questioning. Somehow, and for some reason, McAllister appears to be maintaining an incredibly strong mental shield.' Flaxman broke off for a second to let this sink in. 'Which brings me to the other thing,' he murmured. 'And as one scientist to another, you'll have to treat it as strictly off the record.'

'Agreed.' Grossman was fascinated.

Flaxman gave him a slightly apologetic smile as a prelude to what he was about to say. 'As you know, we sent to the U.S. Navy for McAllister's service record. It arrived this morning. Did you know he spent nearly eight months at the California Psychic Research Foundation?'

Grossman shook his head. 'He never mentioned it to me.'

'Nor to me, but it's a matter of record. While he was there, he displayed quite amazing parapsychic powers under carefully controlled laboratory conditions. He showed limited telekinetic ability. Observers noticed appreciable movement of a ping-pong ball inside a partially evacuated glass bowl. He was able to swing a suspended magnetic needle ten to twenty degrees off course almost at will . . . and this, I might add, was done inside a Faraday cage.'

Grossman whistled through his teeth. 'You're saying that McAllister can move physical objects with the power of his mind?' he muttered incredulously.

Flaxman gave his sheepish grin again. 'I'm saying that that was the conclusion the boffins at the research centre came to,' he corrected gently. 'And that's not all. His score for predicting the fall of random dice correctly was an amazing thirty-seven per cent; that's way above the laws of chance. Tested with a pack of Zener cards, he managed to get consistent scores of eighteen to twenty correct symbols out of the twenty-five cards. The normal score is around five. All in all, it would appear that our friend McAllister is a person with very special powers of E.S.P.'

Grossman regarded his assistant closely for several seconds. 'You have a theory, don't you?' he prompted at last.

Flaxman shook his head in a gesture of bewilderment. 'You know me, Heinz. I'm a scientist, and I can only deal in known facts which I can observe with my own eyes or test with proven chemical or biological formulae. I don't like to venture theories or wild guesses, let alone dabble in paranormal mumbo-jumbo.' He broke off, his words hanging on a knife-edge.

'But?' Grossman put in, understanding his colleague's embarrassment.

'But, if I were forced to venture an opinion upon this flimsy evidence,' Flaxman went on, pointing to the E.E.G.s, 'I might be very tempted to suggest that McAllister's mind is operating on a wavelength we cannot identify or try to understand. When he is asked a specific question about what he saw out there, it's just as if a jamming signal cuts into his brain, preventing him from answering. Almost like a post-hypnotic suggestion, if you like, but in this case I would say self-induced.'

Grossman was becoming more and more bewildered. 'It doesn't make sense.'

Flaxman laughed, without humour. 'No, not a lot, I agree. But it'll have to do for the moment, I'm afraid.'

'Is there the slightest scrap of scientific evidence to support such a theory?' Grossman was clutching at straws.

'There are certain parallels in contemporary brainwashing techniques,' Flaxman said. 'It's generally accepted that the C.I.A., and most probably the Soviets as well, use a forced conditioning process to induce a similar reaction in their top agents. Basically, it's a conditioning which ensures that they will "cut off" if they are tortured, or subjected to drugs or sensory deprivation technique. It's crude at the moment, but some progress is being made.'

'I wish the same could be said for us,' Grossman sighed. He gritted his teeth in frustration, and glanced across to the unconscious McAllister. A feeling almost akin to anger shook him. He felt tempted to cross the lab and physically assault the man, try to shake the secrets from his sleeping mind.

Flaxman seemed to interpret his thoughts. 'I know how you must feel, Heinz, but there really isn't much we can do except wait, and persevere. I've no doubt we can get past McAllister's block eventually. It's a question of finding the right key.'

'No,' Grossman spat out suddenly. 'The key is down there, under our feet.' He jabbed his forefinger at the floor of the lab. 'Dammit, Charles, I've got to go and take a look for myself. I'm going down there.'

Flaxman's eyes closed to a squint. 'I hope you're not going to ask me to pressure you up,' he said coldly, 'because I'll flatly refuse, Heinz, I tell you that right now. In the light of what happened to Caffrey and Brandon, we need months of animal tests with those units before we sacrifice any more human guinea-pigs.'

Grossman was touched by his colleague's concern. He smiled gently. 'No, I wouldn't ask you that,' he murmured. 'I'll go down as far as I can with conventional scuba gear. Hell, I could do with a swim.'

'You'll take a camera, of course,' Flaxman put in.

Grossman was silent for a few moments, thinking. 'I'll do better than that,' he said finally. 'I'm going to get hold of some deep-water sonar and T.V. equipment, and go over the entire area around the tunnel with a fine tooth comb.'

Flaxman looked openly dubious. 'You're talking about thousands of dollars' worth of equipment, Heinz. I can't see Ellis sanctioning that sort of expenditure on what he would see as non-productive research.'

'Screw Ellis,' Grossman said carelessly. 'Why try to buy at the corner store when you can raid the supermarket.'

'I'm not with you.' Flaxman looked puzzled.

'The good old U.S. Navy,' Grossman said, with a laugh. 'I think I've got enough pull to borrow everything I need for a few days.'

Chapter Six

Actually being in the water brought home the full impact of the strange phenomenon to Grossman. Peering out through glass and seeing no fish within a strictly limited field of vision was one thing, but swimming freely over large areas utterly devoid of life was quite another. Once or twice Grossman had caught a flash of movement in the strangely still environment and pursued it hopefully. In each case, the object had turned out to be a piece of plastic or paper waste drifting in the faint currents.

These minor visual reminders of man-made pollution had triggered off a promising theory. On his second dive Grossman had painstakingly collected water samples over an area of about five square miles, from differing depths. Back in the laboratory, the theory crumbled. Grossman expected a sudden rise in poisonous pollutants; he found nothing. Certainly there were traces of man's toxic wastes, but the levels were no higher than they had been for years, and laboratory specimens swam in them quite happily, with no obvious ill effects.

After a third deep dive which involved him in nearly three-quarters of an hour of decompression time, Grossman was convinced that no human eye was going to find an answer.

It was time to rely on more scientific equipment. Grossman rose the last twenty-five feet to the surface and began swimming towards the eighteen-foot launch he had borrowed from the local coastguards.

Flaxman helped to pull him aboard and strip the twin air-tanks and harness from his back. Grossman removed the mouthpiece and drew in short, sharp breaths for a few minutes before allowing himself to breathe normally.

'See anything this time?' Flaxman queried.

Grossman shook his head. 'Not a bloody thing,' he said. 'Even the sea-urchins seem to have dropped off the rocks.'

Flaxman sighed, shaking his head. 'I'll get the equipment ready.' He crossed the deck and began to unpack the contents of several crates.

Half an hour later they had erected a small but efficient gantry and were preparing to lower the first video camera over the side. It was followed by an infra-red scanner, four highly sensitive underwater microphones and the U.S. Navy's most sophisticated and up-to-date sonar equipment. Grossman let it all down to a depth of about ten feet and checked it out with the on-board instruments. Everything was functioning perfectly.

He nodded to Flaxman, who began to pay out the steel-reinforced support cables from a massive drum. As the equipment dropped towards the ocean floor, Grossman kept his eyes glued to the instruments. Not one of them gave out so much as a bleep or a flicker. After fifteen minutes, when Flaxman had paid out all the available cable, there was nothing else to do except begin the slow and laborious process of winching all the equipment up again and moving the launch to a new location.

The frustrating performance was repeated half a dozen times

as the day wore on. By four o'clock, Grossman was almost ready to give up.

'One more try?' Flaxman called out, as he cut the engine of the launch.

Grossman was leaning over the side, peering moodily down into the dark, secretive waters. 'Yes, why not?' he said, without enthusiasm. He stood up and went to help Flaxman go through the whole charade yet again.

Deep in the water Kraka the giant squid felt the throbbing motion of a disturbance in the place of light water, and identified it at once. It was a small boat which carried dry-creatures across the surface of the water.

The throbbing ceased, and Kraka knew from experience and observation that without it, there was no movement. That meant that the dry-creatures were hovering directly above him.

Nah-Ep's warning came to mind. Obeying the directive, Kraka curved in the water, jetting vertically down through the depths to put as much distance between himself and the men as possible. It was only as he descended towards the ocean floor that he realised that he was close to the Great Chamber.

The thought troubled him. This was the second time recently that the dry-creature had neared one of the secret places, and the first had already caused an upheaval in the liquid world. Nervous, but without fear, Kraka came to a stop, watching and waiting.

'I think we've got something at last.' Grossman's excited cry caused Flaxman to look up quickly, taking his hand off the slow-release mechanism controlling the armoured cable. The drum sped up as the heavy equipment dragged several hundred feet of cable after it.

'Damn.' Flaxman cursed under his breath, slowing the revolving drum gently to prevent damage to the sensitive equipment. When he was satisfied that it was safe, he slipped on the locking catch and went to join Grossman at the instruments.

The loudspeaker was belting out a cacophony of sound. The delicate microphones had picked up the rushing passage of water as they were dragged behind the heavier sonar equipment. That, and the vibrations from the cable as Flaxman had brought the sudden descent to a halt, were playing havoc with the sound readings.

Grossman glanced up in annoyance, knowing something was wrong. 'What the hell happened? I was picking something up then.'

'Sorry. The slow-release catch slipped. It'll be all right in a few moments.'

The sound gradually faded to a murmur. Grossman turned his attention to the controls which would turn the remote T.V. camera round in a 360-degree sweep. 'Right, now let's take a look at what we've got down there.'

Kraka saw the bright lights plunging down towards him and reacted instinctively. Attack was the best form of defence. He shot up through the water to intercept the strange illuminated creature diving upon him. His massive tentacles closed around it in a vice-like grip, tugging it savagely. With his whole mass wrapped around the creature, Kraka used his jet propulsion to drag it away and down to the ocean floor, where he could use the jagged rocks as a purchase for his tentacles, and something to smash the creature's body against.

As he dragged it down, Kraka saw that the creature was not just a single entity. It had various appendages attached to it, connected to the main body by a series of thin tentacles. Still maintaining his crushing grip upon the body of the creature, Kraka began to slash out with his savage beak at the connected sinews, intent on ripping the strange creature to pieces.

The monitor screen went black. Seconds later, the loudspeaker crashed into life again and Grossman reached hurriedly for the volume switch, turning it right down. The microphones were designed to pick up faint, delicate sounds, not cope with what sounded like half a dozen jack-hammers operating under water. In the ensuing silence, the noise of the ratchet on the cable release jumping out of place cracked out like a rifle shot.

'Jesus Christ!' Flaxman jumped up and made a run towards the cable drum, which was spinning round wildly, paying out snaking, threshing cable over the side of the launch. It was far too dangerous to even attempt to stop the thing. Flaxman could only watch, helplessly, until the supply of cable was exhausted and the drum jerked to an abrupt halt which rocked the small craft savagely.

A loud curse from Grossman announced that he was having problems of his own. 'God dammit, the whole bloody lot has gone dead.' He jumped to his feet, sprinting across the deck to Flaxman. 'Get it up, the whole lot, as fast as you can.'

Flaxman slammed the ratchet into reverse and started up the electric winch. The cable began to wind back on to the drum.

'Good God!' Grossman stared, horrified, at the mangled remains of the sonar equipment swinging gently on the end of the cable. The microphones were gone completely, ripped from reinforced cable which could comfortably support a dead weight of thirty tons. The T.V. camera and infra-red scanner were both crushed like old beer cans, despite the fact that both units were designed to cope with pressures of several thousand pounds p.s.i.

Flaxman trembled nervously, wringing his hands. 'Oh Christ, I'm sorry, Heinz. I really thought I'd locked that brake on securely.'

Grossman continued to stare at the damaged equipment, shaking his head in awe. 'This lot isn't your fault, Charles. There's no way that equipment could get smashed up like this just dropping through water.'

The reassurance did little to soothe Flaxman. In a shaken voice he mouthed the question which both felt uppermost in their minds. 'The point is, what in God's name *was* responsible? What in the name of hell have we disturbed down there?'

Grossman didn't attempt to answer him. He was totally bemused. His sense of guilt went part way to counteracting his fear, but above it all came the awesome knowledge that the matter had just passed beyond his control. There could be no more detached scientific curiosity. Not now that the U.S. Navy was involved. Something had just sabotaged some of their most up-to-date and sophisticated hardware. It would be difficult to view the matter as anything other than a hostile act.

Chapter
Seven

'I'm sorry, sir, but you can't go in there.'

Merton Ellis stared, dumbrounded, at the armed, uniformed naval guard standing outside the entrance to Grossman's laboratory. 'What the hell do you mean, I can't go in there? I own this goddam place.'

He started to move forward, on the momentum of his own indignation. The guard moved slightly back against the wall, his body tensing. The submachine-gun twitched in his hands, the barrel swinging up to line up on Ellis's throat.

'I mean what I say,' the guard muttered in a threatening tone. He jerked his head sideways. 'Move across there. And freeze.'

Ellis stepped back a few jerky paces, his face white with shock.

'You must be Mr Ellis,' the guard said, in a calmer tone.

Ellis nodded, trying to speak, but the words lodged in his throat. The nod sufficed. The guard flashed him a semi-apologetic look.

'Sorry, sir, but I have my orders. I expect Commander Dobey will want to speak to you. I'll just check.'

The guard let the machine-gun swing from his shoulder on its strap, but his right hand stayed in the vicinity of its trigger guard. With his other hand, he unhooked a small walkie-talkie set from his belt, holding it up to his lips. 'Commander Dobey, sir? I have Mr Ellis here. Shall I let him through?'

'Show him in, Lieutenant,' came the terse reply.

The guard replaced the communicator and stepped sideways. 'Please go in, Mr Ellis.'

Satisfied that the threat was over, Ellis turned back to his usual bluster. 'Just what the hell is going on here?' he demanded angrily.

The guard shook his head. 'I'm afraid I can't discuss it, sir. I'm sure the Commander will explain everything to you.'

With an angry grunt Ellis stepped past him and opened the door into the lab. He walked in briskly, but he was thrown temporarily off balance by the radical change which had come over the room. Three more sailors stood rigidly against the walls, also fully armed. Most of Grossman's scientific apparatus had been removed, and in its place were pieces of military equipment. The walls had been adorned with maps, sea charts and complicated-looking graphs. Several office desks had been installed. At one of them sat a U.S. Navy Commander in full uniform.

'Ah, Mr Ellis. Do come and sit down.' Dobey smiled warmly – his standard ploy when dealing with civilians. The smile masked a deep-seated mistrust of anyone in mufti.

Ellis approached the desk warily, accepting the empty chair which Dobey indicated with a casual wave of his hand.

'Well, I expect you're wondering what all this is about?' muttered Dobey, rather too casually.

'You're damn right I am,' Ellis grunted, but his tone was severely chastened.

'I understand perfectly,' said Dobey, flashing the patronising smile again. He placed his elbows on the top of the desk, formed his hands into a cradle and rested his chin in it. This too was a much rehearsed gesture, designed to put people at ease. 'Well, Mr Ellis, the short answer is that this entire complex has temporarily been seconded by the U.S. Navy. Until further orders, you must consider yourself, and all your employees, bound by the rules of martial law.'

'What?' Ellis's mouth dropped open weakly. 'By what right? How in hell can you march in and just take over a private enterprise?'

'It's in the interests of national security. I'm afraid that's all I can tell you.'

'I take it you have the written authority to back all this up? Ellis asked.

Dobey nodded. 'I have Federal warrants issued by the Pentagon, the Select Senate Committee and the President himself. Can I take it that I have your full co-operation, Mr Ellis?'

Ellis shrugged. 'I haven't got a lot of choice, have I?'

'Good. It's nice to understand one another.' Dobey smiled with satisfaction. 'Now, there are a few points I would like to discuss with you.' He clicked his fingers in the air. From another desk a young rating hurried across with a large graph, which he spread out on Commander Dobey's desk top.

Dobey tapped it with the point of a pencil. 'This is a sonar map of the area surrounding this complex,' he explained. 'We have located another underwater structure quite nearby. Can you shed any light on the matter?'

Ellis peered at the unfamiliar graph without comprehension, shaking his head uncertainly. 'Just looks like a jumble of meaningless squiggles to me,' he observed.

Dobey nodded understandingly. To the uninitiated, a sonar map would not make much sense. He summoned his lieutenant again. 'Go and fetch Dr Grossman in here, will you?'

The lieutenant crossed the room, opening the door into the inner laboratory. 'Dr Grossman? The Commander would like to see you.'

Heinz Grossman walked out into the main lab. He looked strained, and ill at ease. 'What is it now?' he asked testily.

Dobey indicated the graph. 'Please explain this sonar map to Mr Ellis.'

Grossman seemed to noticed Ellis's presence for the first time. He nodded deferentially.

Ellis glared up at him. 'Are you responsible for bringing these goons in here?'

'Indirectly, yes,' Grossman murmured apologetically.

'Ellis, I don't give a damn how many million dollars you've got in the bank, you'll show some respect for my uniform,' Dobey cut in angrily. 'I have enough on you to make things awkward, so don't rock the boat.'

Ellis bristled. 'What the hell are you talking about, Commander?'

Dobey started checking off on his fingers. 'One, you get 200,000 dollars' worth of naval equipment all smashed up and then can't explain how. Two, you are privately developing and testing experimental equipment which could be of vital importance to the national defence programme. Three, you protect that equipment with the bare minimum of security which is an open invitation to agents of a hostile foreign power. Four, we find this whole damned area of the seabed bristling with unscheduled structures. Want me to go on? Christ, Ellis, I have enough on you to pull you up before the Supreme Court.'

'I don't know what you're talking about,' Ellis said, in a subdued voice.

Grossman butted in. 'I've already explained, Commander. Mr Ellis knew nothing about that sonar equipment. I borrowed it on my own back. I just happened to have some friends in the supply department at Key West. I worked down there for a time as a civilian attached to the U.S. Naval Research Division.'

Dobey snorted with disgust. 'Well, you haven't got any friends any longer, I can tell you that. Whoever broke out that equipment will be lucky not to get busted out of the service and serve a couple of years in the brig.'

For the first time, Grossman smiled. 'That I rather doubt, Commander,' he said in a quiet voice. 'I have release papers for that equipment signed by Bob Hayes personally.' He paused to let the name sink in. 'Admiral Robert Hayes. You know him, of course?'

Dobey started to say something, then changed his mind. The words were buried under a faint splutter.

Grossman bent over the sonar map and began explaining it to Ellis. 'This is simply a map of the ocean floor all around this area, but it's made up of sound waves. In other words, it's a picture built up from echoes, which gives a precise indication of depths, shapes and heights of any rocks or objects resting on the seabed.' He moved his finger, indicating a particular concentration of lines. 'This is the tunnel. As you can see, the ocean floor drops away quite rapidly at the end of it, continuing to do so for two or three miles. The thing Commander Dobey seems to be interested in is this little concentration here.' Grossman moved his finger, indicating another spot on the sonar map.

Dobey cut in. 'The point is, our surface sonar indicates that there is another undersea structure at that point. It's about two miles south-east of the tunnel, and it's incredibly deep. We can't even get a sub down there to photograph it.' He broke off, staring at Ellis grimly. 'What I need to know, Mr Ellis, is how the hell you built this thing at that depth.'

Ellis looked completely baffled. He shook his head. 'Whatever it is, it isn't anything to do with me.'

Dobey continued to stare him out for several seconds. When he spoke again his voice had dropped to a threatening whisper. 'Do you have any idea of the penalties for withholding this sort of information? I'll ask you again, Mr Ellis, do you have any knowledge of this structure?'

'None at all,' Ellis declared firmly.

Dobey lost all interest in him immediately. He turned away, a bored, dismissive look on his face. 'Lieutenant, show Mr Ellis out and escort him clear of the complex.'

The armed lieutenant stepped over, placing a firm hand on Ellis's shoulder. 'Come with me sir, please.'

Indignation, bordering on panic, rose in Ellis. He was not

used to being summarily dismissed like an errant schoolboy. He was accustomed to administering scorn, not receiving it. It was a sobering, almost frightening experience. Protest rose to his lips, but he could not form the words. He felt the firm, insistent pressure of the lieutenant's fingers on his shoulder. Despite himself, Ellis stood and let the lieutenant usher him towards the elevator.

'Well?' Dobey said, turning back to Grossman as Ellis left the laboratory. 'Suppose you tell me what this goddam thing is.'

'I haven't the faintest idea,' Grossman said quietly.

Dobey jumped to his feet. 'Well it's about time you got some ideas. You're supposed to be a scientist, aren't you? So use some science.'

Grossman took a deep breath, drawing himself upright. 'I'd like to put on record right now, Commander Dobey, that I find your bullying attitude both offensive and unnecessary. May I remind you that I am a civilian, and you have no direct authority over me.'

'You're a civilian under direct military command,' Dobey corrected him. 'As such, you'll take orders from me or my men. And I'll treat you as I damn well please.'

Grossman sniffed with disgust. 'Now you're being childish,' he said cuttingly. He had never attempted to understand the military mind, with its seemingly built-in acceptance of blind obedience.

There was a heavy silence. The tension between the two men was almost tangible. It was a test of strength. Finally, Grossman backed down slightly, as a matter of politics. It was his fault Dobey was involved, and he would have to make the best of it. There was also the fact that he still had a mystery on his hands to be considered. His own efforts to solve it had met with miserable failure. Perhaps, with the full resources of the U.S. Navy, he might fare better.

'All right, Commander,' Grossman said quietly. 'Now let's analyse this thing objectively, shall we?'

They studied the sonar map together for several minutes.

'Whatever it is, it has absolutely nothing to do with this complex,' Dobey said, finally. He stabbed his finger down on the sonar map. 'Are we agreed on that?'

Grossman nodded. 'That's about the size of it.'

'But there can be no doubt that it is a man-made structure?' Dobey pressed.

Grossman smiled gently. 'There's always doubt, Commander Dobey. Science is still not as precise as we might like it to be. We can only deal in probabilities.'

Dobey dismissed the objections with a wave of his hand. 'Look, this underwater structure is big, right?'

Grossman nodded. 'Very big. At least five hundred yards in diameter,' he agreed.

'And it is perfectly circular, absolutely geometrically true?'

Grossman nodded again. 'No, there's no question about the structure, for want of a better word, being a perfect bowl-shaped depression in the ocean floor, clear of all irregular rock formations.'

Dobey raised his shoulders with a slight gesture of exasperation. 'Then why any doubts? It must, surely, be an artefact?'

Grossman sighed. 'It still could be natural,' he muttered. 'An old volcano crater, any jagged edges or irregularities eroded over the years by underwater currents. It might even have been created by a giant whirlpool, or a waterspout. The sonar readings may have been confused by different depths, or false echoes from the surrounding area. Don't forget that we are dealing with incredible depths in an area where normal instruments have been known to behave oddly, give false readings.'

Dobey snarled with impatience. Grossman's hedging was beginning to annoy him. 'Listen, Grossman, cut the crap. What are the chances of this thing being a natural phenomenon?'

Pinned down to a hard and fast answer, Grossman had to tell the truth. 'About one in a million,' he admitted.

Dobey's face cracked into the triumphant smile of a man who knows he has won his case. 'Then it's man-made,' he declared emphatically. 'I don't gamble with those sort of odds. And if it's man-made, and we didn't build it, then someone else must have.'

'You're absolutely sure it's not ours?' Grossman needed to be completely reassured on this point.

'Absolutely,' Dobey answered firmly. 'I've checked with air, naval and military intelligence. With the F.B.I., C.I.A. and N.A.S.A. There is just no way that thing could be of American origin without somebody knowing about it.'

'N.A.T.O.? How about N.A.T.O.?' Grossman asked, clutching at straws.

Dobey grinned, shaking his head. 'Nobody in the Western bloc knows anything,' he said quietly. 'The only other powers with the technology to build that thing are on the opposite side of the fence.'

Grossman sighed. It was obvious that Commander Dobey had made up his mind, believing exactly what he wanted to believe. 'What do you intend to do?' he asked after a brief pause.

Dobey looked up at him in surprise, feeling that the answer to the question was self-evident. 'Why, destroy it, of course,' he said. 'Now, what's the best way of going about it? I take it that conventional depth charges won't be any use?'

Grossman could only gape at Dobey in total amazement. 'What do you mean, destroy it of course? God almighty, Dobey, how the hell can you make a sweeping, irrational statement like that? Here we have something completely new to us, something we know absolutely nothing about. We have no idea what it is, what its purpose might conceivably be, or where it came from. We don't even know if it is an artefact, built by living people who might still be down there. And your simple, straightforward answer is to blow it out of the bloody water. Are you mad?'

'Listen, Grossman, you find something which doesn't belong to you sitting out in your back yard, and you get rid of it, right?'

Grossman shook his head, almost laughing. 'No, that's the very thing you don't do. You look at it, find out what it is, who it belongs to, whether it's useful, valuable, interesting.'

'Not when you're in charge of defending this country you don't,' Dobey said firmly.

'Oh Jesus.' Grossman sighed with frustration. 'God help the first friendly aliens who arrive on this planet bearing the gift of eternal life,' he muttered. 'Commander Dobey will have a sub loaded to the gills with atomic missiles to blow their saucer out of the sky before a single word is exchanged.'

'Now who's being childish?' Dobey countered. 'I have to see this problem in the way my superiors would see it. Failure to take the appropriate action could cost me my career.'

Grossman realised that argument and insults were getting him nowhere. He tried reasoning again. 'Look, let's try to compromise, shall we? Hold off this attack for a while, or at the very least, just drop a couple of small warning charges to see if there is anything down there. The French have got some experimental bathyscapes which can go down far below the maximum dives of our equipment. Surely you could get

67

Pentagon clearance to see if we could borrow them, even come to some joint international exploration agreement?'

Dobey shook his head. 'It's out of the question.'

'In God's name, why?' Grossman's voice rose to a shout as his sense of impotence grew. 'Let me try then, if you're afraid to stick your neck out. I know some of the scientific advisers to the Pentagon. My views should carry some weight, at least.'

Dobey had begun to tire of the argument. He felt annoyed that he had allowed it to develop in the first place. 'This is a purely military matter,' he snapped curtly. 'You will keep out of it.'

Grossman refused to be cowed. 'It's only a military matter because you insist on seeing it as such. If we approached this entire business from the standpoint of scientific curiosity, we could all have a different outlook.'

It was time for Dobey to deliver his trump card and end the pointless discussion. 'You've missed the point, Grossman. Let me spell it out for you. In this immediate area, we have Cape Kennedy and the N.A.S.A. headquarters, the nuclear submarine pens at Key West, the Marine Biology Research Centre, and all our seismological equipment laid along the Ataline fault. Two nuclear subs and five combat aircraft have gone missing in these waters, along with two space satellites. None of them were ever recovered. Add all that up, then consider that there is something down there on the seabed which we did not put there, and is continuing to sabotage our equipment. I have no choice.'

'All right, do something to stir it up, but not destroy it,' Grossman pleaded as a last resort. 'Make a dummy run with enough explosive to provoke some sort of reaction, and then study it. You can have a second load of charges ready if we get a really negative reaction.'

Dobey considered the suggestion thoughtfully.

Grossman added a little incentive, sensing that he had at last got Dobey slightly on the defensive. 'Just imagine, Commander, supposing that thing down there belongs to a previous civilisation, millions of years old. You could be hailed as the man who found Atlantis.'

Dobey hesitated for a few seconds more, seeking a final argument and failing to find it. Much as he disliked it, Grossman had a valid viewpoint.

'All right,' Dobey snapped finally. 'We'll do it your way.'

Chapter
Eight

Commander Dobey was right in one thing, conventional depth charges were no use at all. The answer lay in packing reinforced steel canisters with plastic explosive, dropping them immediately over the target area and then detonating them by remote control from the sub which had delivered them.

With that problem solved, and clearance to order out a nuclear sub from the pens at Key West, Dobey was ready to move in three days. He had compromised with Grossman over the strength of the charges, but he was not prepared to take any further interference. Armed guards followed Grossman everywhere, watching his every movement. He had only to take a couple of steps towards a telephone to be stopped at gunpoint. Grossman realised that his argument had cost him dearly. He was, to all intents and purposes, under house arrest.

Captain James Fliss of the nuclear submarine *Enterprise* supervised the ejection of the last canister from the aft torpedo tubes and ordered the sub out of the immediate blast area. Sixteen canisters had been placed in all, in a roughly elliptical pattern. They were set to detonate in series, to create the maximum disturbance without too much damage.

Fliss had serious misgivings about the whole operation. As far as he knew, no one had ever detonated large quantities of high explosive at such an incredible depth before, so there was no real way of telling what the result might be. He was no expert on geology, but Fliss was well aware that the target was less than five miles from the Ataline fault, and the possibility of setting up an underwater quake seemed a distinct one.

Quite apart from this uninformed worry, Fliss knew that the explosion would set up a steel-warping shock wave which would travel for miles under water. There was no way that the *Enterprise* was going to be within six miles of the blast area when those canisters were detonated. Fliss was not going to take the slightest chance with the safety of his ship and his crew.

Cacha hovered in the water, the dull sheen of his body faintly illuminated by the dim residual light of the Great Chamber. He had spent a lot of time in the Great Chamber during the past few days, for it afforded him the only totally peaceful atmosphere which would allow him the mental concentration he needed. Nah-Ep's revelations had shocked and disturbed him; the challenge facing the liquid world taxed his greatest mental powers. Only through many hours of calm, deliberate meditation could he hope to face, let alone tackle, them.

His delicate sonar system detected the first of the canisters sinking slowly through the waters all around him. Cacha strained his weak eyes to see and identify the strange objects. It was impossible to see them, but intuition told him that they were alien to the liquid world. Concentrating, Cacha picked up the faint but unmistakable throbbing vibrations of the submarine high above him. The two facts tied together neatly. Suddenly, a premonition of danger swamped all other thoughts. With a powerful wash of his tail, Cacha stirred his massive body into movement, instinctively knowing that he had to get as far away from the Great Chamber as quickly as possible.

He swam away and upwards, logic telling him that he was better equipped to deal with danger in the place of light water, where movement was easier and speed of flight could more readily be maintained. His sonar, pulsing out ahead of him, picked up the shape of the submarine and Cacha slowed, keeping his distance behind it. It was moving rapidly, ascending towards the surface on a shallow inclining plane.

Suddenly, behind him, Cacha felt the terrible power of the erupting explosives. The sonics of the explosion struck him first, smashing and blacking out his own delicate guidance system in an instant. Blinded, dazed, no longer with any sense of direction, Cacha could only vaguely sense his mighty body being tossed and buffeted in the water as the shock waves rose up through the water to destroy him. The air was crushed from his lungs in a matter of seconds, leaving only the helpless, hopeless strength of survival instincts to sustain him. Cacha's dying body galvanised into neurotic action, his huge tail threshed wildly in the water, propelling his vast bulk up through the waters at an incredible speed.

Every muscle and nerve numbed, Cacha was mercifully beyond pain as his surging body overtook the submarine and its tall conning tower sliced open the soft underside of his belly. Impaled upon the sub, Cacha died, his seventy tons becoming a dead weight in the water.

Captain Fliss let out a curse and a loud cry of alarm as the *Enterprise* shuddered violently and began to roll over to one side. Thrown off balance, Fliss crashed against a solid steel bulkhead, the impact stunning him and knocking the breath from his body. Unable to move, he could only raise his eyes to the depth gauge as the sub sank rapidly into deeper water, pressed down by Cacha's great weight.

The First Officer did everything he could. He blew all the ballast tanks, brought the lateral rudders full up and coaxed every last erg of power from the engines. Nothing helped. Fliss stared in horrified fascination as the submarine continued to plunge.

As a last resort, to try and free the doomed sub of excess weight, the First Officer gave the order to jettison as many torpedos as the crew could get in the tubes and fire. Half a dozen of the sleek killers left the *Enterprise*, streaking down through the water towards the Great Chamber, where they finally exploded.

Death came to the *Enterprise*, but it was slow and unmerciful. The submarine's armour-plated steel hull held out longer against the intolerable pressures than its designers would have considered possible. The crew lived for several minutes, hearing the grinding and creaking of tortured metal and the shrill, insistent wailing of the warning klaxons. That gut-curdling sound ceased for each man in turn as his eardrums ruptured.

No man on board the *Enterprise* heard the final sound – the shrieking, splintering crunch of metal being crushed like tinplate.

Chapter Nine

Stillness hung in the waters like a plague, a black, oppressive cloud of death. In the blasted, desecrated ruins of the Great Chamber the assembled creatures were numb with shock. The visual images Nah-Ep poured forth enraged as well as saddened them. Horror and disbelief came with every mental bombardment, until their emotional shields crumbled and only the numbness remained.

Cacha the Elder was dead, callously killed by the dry-creature. The ugly debris of the Great Chamber, which had stood untouched since the Time of the First Time, lay all around them. It was the ultimate violation, Cacha's death the supreme act of genocide. With him a whole generation died, for he was the last of the Ancient Ones, the oldest and wisest of the long-lived giant mammals of the liquid world. He would be sorely missed.

Nah-Ep's horrendous outpourings continued. The assembled creatures felt their brains assaulted time and time again as further details of man's savagery came to them in violent images. He killed for pleasure, for sport. He murdered out of greed, for the possession of artefacts which could have no possible bearing upon his life or survival. Man killed for no other reason than that his fellow beings had different coloured skin, or believed in different gods. He killed not only for himself, but for other species of dry-creatures which he kept enslaved and imprisoned and called pets.

Killing was a cancer which seemed inherent in the species. It blighted the creature man, setting him apart from all other living things and leaving him alone and cursed. Now, he had lost control of this cancer, for he had released it into the liquid world, infecting it. Blind, pointless death stalked the seas as man killed through sheer ignorance and irresponsibility. That, perhaps, was man's greatest crime of all. There seemed no way to justify killing through stupidity.

Nah-Ep's revelations continued to pour out in pulsing waves of emotive power. As well as exposing the threat to the liquid world collectively, Nah-Ep directed terrifying instances of man's destructive powers to individual delegates. Rigus, the right whale, learned sadly that once his kind had been many, and now they were few. In a single year, man slaughtered over 70,000 giants of the sea. Delphus and Delia the dolphins learned with dismay that despite their love for the creature man, he continued to decimate their numbers by entangling them in his fishing nets, or smashing open their soft bodies with his ships. Sylph, of the herring family, could hardly accept the figures which Nah-Ep threw at her. It was impossible to conceive that her entire species was facing extinction purely because of man's greed. Tariq, of Nah-Ep's own family the tuna, learned the answer to a mystery which had long been puzzling him. The strange new disease which had spread amongst his kind, rotting their very bones and rendering the females sterile – it was yet another aspect of man's bitter legacy of death. Mercury, a metal which man used and then dumped into the seas when he had finished with it, was the cause of all this misery. It was only one of the deadly poisons which man poured into the oceans in a growing flood.

There were a dozen similar messages of doom, each one accompanied by the clear, unemotional message that it was time for the carnage to cease. Finally, Nah-Ep's horrifying saga was ended. His powerful thought-waves receded, releasing the assembled creatures from his control. Nah-Ep had given out so much of himself that he was totally drained, unable to project another single image, and he could only let the sadness and despair of his subjects flow back into him, drawing it in like a bitter poison. He waited, helplessly, for reaction to break. The last thing the liquid world needed at this time was disagreement and more disruption, yet, somehow, Nah-Ep knew that it was inevitable.

Bluey the blue-ringed octopus launched into the attack almost at once, taking over the spirit of the meeting and infusing it with a new wave of anger. He began to draw upon the Great Legend, repeating long, pointed passages which harked back to the abusive power and greed of man. His refusal to live in harmony with the liquid world, the speed of his growth and the attendant powers of destruction. Each reference was so carefully phrased, so eloquently and passionately expressed, that Bluey's fury began to envelop the Great Chamber, filling everyone with the same hate he himself felt for the creature man. Thoughts of violence swept through the

73

assembled gathering in a hundred different images of retribution. Man could be made to suffer as the liquid world had suffered, for many fish species had frightening powers of mutilation and torture. The stinging jellyfish and venomous creatures of his own species, the slashing, tearing jaws of the great sharks and the sawfish, the numbing shocks of the electric eels and stingrays – Bluey left nothing out. Man could be killed, slowly and painfully. He could be made to suffer an agonising death.

The violent images served to re-awaken a common bond and a new sense of purpose between all the assembled species. Now the numbness and the sense of blind shock were receding, and the spirit of revenge began to dominate.

For a while, Poda the octopus tried to tone down the fervour of the uprising, pointing out that the insane urge to destroy and mutilate belonged to the dry-creature and had no place in the liquid world. As an Elder, Poda commanded respect, but the angry feelings of the meeting had already risen too high. The creatures were attentive to her words, but not to her emotions. Gradually, her objections were fought down, and she retired to the sidelines as members of the shark family began to contribute their own savage ideas of mutilation.

Delphus the dolphin nudged his mate, Delia, gently in the side with his blunt nose. Quietly, in their own strange noise-speech which no other creature could understand, they discussed their own reactions to the tone of the meeting. In clicks, grunts and guttural whistles, they exchanged their fears and forebodings, for Bluey's savage attack on man had been particularly painful to them. Inherent in their species was a deep affection for the dry-creature, despite his evil traits. The dolphins saw man as an integral part of an earth on which neither water nor dry land held sway. There was a link, somewhere, between the two, a hyper-world in which they, the dolphins, lived somewhere on the fringes.

Reverting to shielded thought-speech, Delphus announced his intention to leave the meeting. Now that a semblance of order had been established, the slow process of free democratic discussion would probably grind on for many hours, and the mental barrage of exchanged thoughts and ideas would prevent the two mammals from thinking clearly themselves. Somehow, Delphus communicated to his mate, there had to be an

alternative answer, and as the sole representatives of the tenuous link between fish and man, perhaps the dolphins alone
could provide it.

None of the others took much notice as the two dolphins
rose in the water, swimming slowly and discreetly away from
the meeting. Those who did see their departure simply assumed
that the two mammals were heading up to the surface to fill
their lungs before returning to take part in the discussion.

Soon out of sight in the dark water, Delphus and Delia
cleaved upward, putting on a burst of speed as they neared
the place of light water which they loved so much. Once on
the surface, the bitter and angry exchanges of the meeting
seemed far removed from reality. Up here, free to skim over
the crests of the waves, breathe the cool, clean air and feel
the tingling excitement of water drying on their backs, it
seemed suddenly a thousand times more important to find a
meeting point between land and sea, dry-creature and fish. It
was inconceivable that man could be the deliberately evil
creature he was being made to appear. Communication and
understanding was lacking, that was all, for with that would
come compassion, the joy of shared knowledge and the love
of life itself.

Filling their lungs, Delphus and Delia began to skip across
the foam, heading towards the tunnel. Neither fully understood the strange compulsion which was drawing them in its
direction, yet they seemed to sense, instinctively, that a possible answer lay there. It was there, after all, that the first real
contact had been made. The dry-creature seemed to have made
at least a token attempt to share the liquid world, and the
effort was worthy of consideration.

As the two dolphins neared the tunnel, they locked their
minds together, forging a single, powerful transmitter of
mental energy. They probed deep into the interior of the tunnel
and its connected buildings, seeking out a point of contact.
Thought-waves permeated the water, spreading out like ripples
and gaining strength with every yard.

Suddenly, with a surge of joy, both dolphins felt the first
wispy tentacle of returned mental energy. They stopped
swimming, conserving their full energy for a renewed effort.
In complete rapport, they let out a single, powerful thought-
wave, homing in on the vague reception they had sensed.
Contact came again, slightly stronger now. Redoubling their

efforts, the dolphins began to establish a psychic link with McAllister.

Dobey paced the floor angrily, muttering curses under his breath. At last he stopped, whirling to confront Grossman. 'Dammit, man, you're the marine expert. You tell me what went wrong down there?'

Grossman shrugged calmly. 'I've told you a dozen times, Commander, I haven't got the faintest idea. I'm just a dumb civilian, remember?'

Dobey's face turned red with repressed anger. He waved a menacing finger at the biologist. 'Hell on you, Grossman. I'm not going to warn you again. I'm sick to the goddam teeth of your sarcasm. Now either you start co-operating, or else. . . .'

'Or else what, Commander?' Grossman's attitude was just a shade short of a sneer. His confidence was returning now as Dobey made threat after empty threat, and the man's narrow, military mind became more and more obvious.

His bluff called, Dobey could only change his tone to one of pleading. 'Goddammit, you can't just lose a nuclear submarine and a fully experienced crew. For God's sake, Grossman, we're talking about the lives of nearly 100 men. They may be alive down there somewhere, trapped. In pity's name, you must have some theories about what might have happened to them.'

Grossman's face became a grim mask. Just for once, Dobey seemed to be showing a genuine humanitarian concern. It was time to put personal antagonism aside. Dobey was right; human lives were more important than two individuals with petty differences of opinion. Grossman sucked at his teeth reflectively before speaking. 'Look, Commander, I know little or nothing about nuclear subs. I do know that it went into deep and dangerous waters on a hastily conceived, and to my mind, exceedingly dangerous mission. Those bombs it dropped were untested, their destructive capacity only estimated. On top of that, you had absolutely no knowledge of the structure down there. In blowing it apart, you could have released energy which could cripple or blind a sub. Assuming the best – that it is trapped somehow with the crew still alive – just exactly what is it you want me to tell you? I can't even hazard a guess as to how long they could survive, even what conditions they may be facing. You launched an attack on the unknown, and the unknown has responded.'

The speech did what bluster and argument would have failed to do; it brought Dobey solidly down to ground level, forced him to face the stark reality of his own foolhardiness, and to accept it. Calm, chastened, he spoke quietly and thoughtfully. 'O.K. Grossman, you've made your point. Now let me make mine. Assuming the sub is still semi-operational, the life-support systems should be able to maintain bearable conditions for two to three days on emergency power. It'll take at least that long to get another sub to the area. We need to make the most of that time – locating it, assessing the damage, making rescue plans if they are feasible. Quite simply, you are the only man who can help under the present circumstances.'

Grossman frowned. 'You're asking me to send McAllister down there,' he murmured. It was a statement rather than a question.

Dobey nodded. 'It's our only chance,' he said, quietly.

Grossman looked troubled. He thought for several seconds before answering, hesitantly. 'Look, I understand the circumstances, I fully appreciate your concern . . . but I just don't think I can do it,' he said apologetically. 'McAllister's not right, he's in no fit condition to undertake another dive. I can't put it into words, but I feel that I would be sending him to his death if I let him go down.'

'A hundred other men could die if he doesn't,' Dobey reminded him gently.

Grossman looked even more torn with doubt. 'They may be dead already,' he said flatly.

'True,' Dobey admitted. 'But do you want to have the weight of that assumption on your conscience?'

Grossman considered for several more seconds, answering hesitantly. 'You realise that I can't order him down?'

Dobey nodded. 'I accept that,' he said quietly. 'It will be entirely up to him.'

'Oh, it's all right. I want to go down,' a soft voice said from behind them.

Grossman and Dobey whirled to face the door. McAllister stood just outside, confronting the armed guard with a faint smile on his face.

'Sorry, sir, he just pushed past me and opened the door,' the rating apologised. 'I couldn't open fire, sir.'

'It's all right, sailor,' Dobey snapped. 'Let him through.' The guard closed the door as McAllister stepped into the lab.

'Come here,' Dobey muttered.

McAllister walked towards them. 'I want to go down there,' he repeated in a distant voice. 'My friends are down there, you see. It will be all right.' As if everything were settled, McAllister began to turn away. 'I'll go and get Woodward to connect me up,' he announced, pacing back to the door, opening it and walking out without another word.

Dobey and Grossman exchanged bemused glances. 'Now do you see what I mean?' Grossman demanded. 'There's something funny about his behaviour.'

Dobey looked worried. 'What did he mean about having friends down there? Does he know anyone aboard that submarine?'

Grossman shrugged helplessly. 'I don't think so. I don't even know how he heard about the missing sub. No one has spoken to him for a couple of days now.'

Dobey jerked his head towards the laboratory door. 'Could he have been listening outside for some time before he came in?'

Grossman sighed heavily. 'He could have been listening, but he wouldn't have heard much,' he said in total bewilderment. 'That door is completely soundproof.' On a sudden thought, Grossman picked up the telephone.

'What are you doing?' Dobey wanted to know.

Grossman looked up at him, his finger poised above the dial. 'Can you arrange for a jet to pick up someone from California and fly him here immediately?'

'Well, yes,' Dobey answered cautiously. 'But who? What are you up to?'

Grossman started dialling. 'I'm calling the California Psychic Research Foundation,' he informed Dobey quietly, over his shoulder. 'We should be able to get someone here in time to make the dive early tomorrow morning. Somehow, I just don't think McAllister ought to be alone when he goes down.'

'Alone? Psychic Research?' Dobey was way out of his depth now.

Grossman smiled gently. 'I'd rather you didn't ask me to explain,' he said quietly. 'Somehow, I just don't think you'd be very impressed with the answers you got.'

Surprisingly, Dobey accepted Grossman's vagueness philosophically. 'Well, I leave it all up to you,' he said. 'I assume you know what you're doing.'

Grossman shook his head, smiling sheepishly. 'No, quite frankly, I don't,' he admitted. 'But then I guess there's no better way to open up new frontiers.'

Chapter Ten

Dobey braced himself up against the stern rail of the shore patrol vessel, staring out across the calm sea. A flash of distant movement caught his eye, and he called to Grossman, standing nearby. 'Well, I guess you were wrong, Grossman. All the fish haven't disappeared after all.'

Grossman joined him, lifting a hand to his eyes to shield them from the low glare of the morning sun and peering out across the waters to where Dobey was pointing. Either side of the ship's wake, a pair of dolphins ploughed through the water, their rising and falling movements in perfect harmony.

'Dolphins are not fish,' Grossman corrected Dobey gently. 'They are air-breathing mammals. Distant cousins of ourselves, in fact.'

Dobey shrugged carelessly, refusing to be embarrassed by his own ignorance. 'If they swim, I think of 'em as fish,' he said firmly.

Grossman continued to gaze at the dolphins, fascinated by the sheer poetry and grace of their movements. The beautiful creatures had never ceased to amaze him, even though he had studied them closely for many years. Until the development of his gill-unit, the dolphins had been Grossman's main area of research. There were perhaps only a dozen other marine biologists in the world who knew as much about them as he did.

With this knowledge in mind, it did not seem particularly strange that the two dolphins were obviously following the ship. It had been noted frequently that the creatures seemed to have a rapport with mankind, even to the extent of actively cultivating and enjoying his company. Even so, Grossman mused, this particular pair did seem to be especially dedicated. They maintained an exact distance behind the vessel, and their course did not vary by so much as a single degree.

The patrol boat slowed in the water as the engines abruptly cut off. The captain called down to Dobey. 'We're right over those co-ordinates of yours, sir.'

Dobey pushed himself away from the rail and walked across the deck towards the wheelhouse. Grossman continued looking at the dolphins, who had also stopped and were swimming round in slow, lazy circles on the surface of the water. Reluctantly, he turned away from them, reminding himself that he had more important matters to attend to.

Binsley, the man from the California research establishment, reminded Grossman of a monkey. He was a small, oddly-proportioned man, whose movements invariably seemed awkward and slightly uncontrolled. His wrinkled face was especially simian in appearance, an illusion considerably heightened by his eyes – large, dark brown pools which seemed blank, yet bespoke of a deep intelligence lurking behind them. Grossman had found the man difficult to talk to, since his conversation tended to be conducted in short, explosive sentences punctuated by long pauses, piercing stares and nervous facial contortions. The wide gulf of belief which separated the two men did not help, since Grossman found his standpoint as a rational scientist almost embarrassing, and Binsley seemed to have long accepted that other people naturally regarded him as something of a crank.

With all this in mind, Grossman had left the man alone as much as possible, a condition he seemed to be quite happy with. He had spent a large amount of his time just sitting on the edge of the metal tank which housed McAllister's floating form, apparently muttering to himself. It was only a few minutes previously that Grossman had realised that Binsley was actually conversing with McAllister. Since McAllister could not talk without air in his lungs to vibrate his vocal cords, the two men had to resort to lip-reading. There was no question of them establishing a truly telepathic conversation, since Binsley had freely admitted that his own psychic powers were strictly limited to receiving, rather than transmitting. At best, Binsley could pick up only vague images, snatches of thought. In that respect, Binsley's presence was a bit of a disappointment. Although he had not really expected to see telepathy in action, Grossman had prepared himself to be amazed. In the circumstances he felt much like a confirmed atheist who had prayed fervently, just to see what happened.

Still, Binsley's presence had not been a complete wash-out. He definitely appeared to have exerted a calming influence over the diver. The smile had disappeared from his face and he looked quite serious, as if fully aware of the gravity of the situation he was involved in.

Grossman walked up to the side of the tank, fixing an easy smile on his face as he looked down at McAllister. 'All right?' he mouthed, exaggerating the lip movements so that for a second he looked like a gaping fish.

McAllister held up his hand, the thumb extended. Nodding, Grossman bent over him and placed a communicator in his hand. This time, he was taking no chances. Carefully, he strapped a safety chain around the man's wrist. He glanced up at the two sailors manning the winch. 'O.K., get ready to haul the tank over the side.'

The men stepped forward, clipping the heavy chains into position on the sides of the tank. Satisfied, they stepped smartly back to man the winch mechanism. Grossman checked the connections carefully before nodding his approval. Slowly, the heavy tank began to lift into the air, swinging out over the side of the vessel.

Grossman pressed against the ship's rail, staring down into the water as the steel tank began to sink towards the surface. From the corner of his eye, Grossman noticed the two dolphins begin to move again, swimming in closer towards the ship.

Dobey noticed it too. He stepped back behind Grossman, tapping his lieutenant lightly on the shoulder. 'Give me your gun, sailor,' he murmured in a low voice. Without question, the man responded to the order, quickly unhooking the sub-machine-gun from his shoulder and handing it across with a flourish.

Dobey hefted it up to his shoulder, clicking off the safety catch with his thumb. He weighed it experimentally in his arms, loving the familiar feel of it. His fighting days seemed such a long time ago. A wave of nostalgia hit him, accompanied by that delicious tingle in the gut – a strange mixture of excitement, pleasure, and fear. He brought the gun up to firing position, squinting along the sights as he stepped forward to the ship's rail again.

He drew a bead on the nearest of the two dolphins, a spot

just below the blow-hole, dead centre between the eyes. His finger stroked the trigger gently, lovingly, then tightened with gentle, insistent pressure.

'Dobey!' Grossman's voice shrieked out a split second before he himself flew across the deck, his arms reaching up wildly to grab the gun. Instinctively, Dobey started, half-turning towards the sound. The machine-gun chattered briefly, discharging half a dozen slugs harmlessly into the air.

'What the bloody hell do you think you're doing?' Grossman demanded, his face contorted with fury. He pressed the gun down so that it pointed to the deck.

Dobey grinned sheepishly. 'Thought they were coming a bit close,' he muttered. 'Thought they might get in McAllister's way. I was just going to loose off a few shots over their heads, scare 'em off.'

Grossman's eyes were filled with loathing. 'Lying bastard,' he spat out.

Finally, Dobey held the gun out to his lieutenant, who slid over and grasped it quickly, slipping it back into position over his shoulder. 'Well, shall we get this show on the road?' Dobey said, icily, to Grossman.

They took up a position directly under the winch. The tank was well below the surface of the water now, and McAllister was just beginning to transfer into the open sea. He looked up at Grossman, and his fingers flicked to the communicator. Grossman looked down at his own wrist as the single word flashed up: THANKS.

Grossman looked back at him, mystified, but there was to be no further explanation. With a kick of his flippered feet, McAllister swam free of the tank, propelling himself away from the side of the ship. He swam straight towards the dolphins, who had come together, floating motionless in the water, waiting for him to join them.

'Friends,' Binsley murmured in a soft, distant voice. Grossman glanced sideways at the man. His eyes were screwed tightly shut. He appeared to be concentrating deeply.

Friends they were. As Delphus and Delia closed around him, McAllister accepted their presence as easily as a man accepts the company of his oldest, most intimate companions. Their cool, slightly rough skins rubbed lightly against his own in a gesture of affection. Warm, welcoming images of hospitality swarmed at his brain, overpowering him. The dolphins were inviting him to share their world, and at the same time promising their trust, their protection, their very lives, if need be.

Close to the creatures, McAllister was able to let his mind go, allow pure instinct to flow out to them, embracing them and giving of himself at the same time. What had just been a thought, a doubt, now became a reality. The two universes of land and water should never have been split and left to go their separate ways. All living creatures were bound together, as part of a single indivisible unit. Man and fish, mammal and reptile – all sentient creatures were brothers under the skin. McAllister realised all this now, and the sheer joy of the revelation surged within him.

His eyes prickled with warm tears. Instinctively, he reached out, wrapping his arms around Delia and Delphus in turn, hugging them. A kind of rapture came upon him like a sudden madness and he thrust his body up out of the water, curving his back and performing an acrobatic flip which took him beneath the surface of the waves. He dived, twisting and turning in the water, his body suddenly imbued with a grace and agility which was truly superhuman. Rising, he broke the surface once again, kicking out wildly with his feet so that most of his body left the water for a brief moment. Splashing in again, he swam beneath the belly of Delphus, curled round Delia's tail, tweaking it playfully as he passed.

Despite the seriousness of their mission, the two dolphins could not help themselves as their companion's utter joy infected them, invoking the unplumbed depths of their empathy with man. Clicking happily, they joined McAllister in an aquatic ballet, churning the surface of the water into a foam.

On board the coastguard vessel, Dobey grasped Grossman roughly by the arm, shaking him angrily. 'I told you, for Christ's sake. They're attacking him. The poor bastard's fighting for his life out there.' He pointed out to the disturbance in the water, his finger shaking.

'You bloody fool,' Grossman said pityingly, shrugging off Dobey's grip with distaste. He glanced aside at Binsley, who was beaming happily, even though his eyes were still closed. Grossman looked back towards McAllister and the two dolphins, feeling a sudden urge to dive over the rail of the ship and swim out to join them in their playful enjoyment. Once, frolicking with dolphins had been one of the great joys of his own life. He envied McAllister now.

The play ceased abruptly. McAllister felt a single, intense thought force its way into his brain. It was one of urgency, utter importance. In a flash, McAllister knew that his friends needed his help, that perhaps he was the one human being who could help. There was no hesitation. They had given him so much, he would give everything he could in return. He responded with perfect trust, swimming above Delia's broad back and clasping her dorsal fin with both hands. Bearing his weight with ease, the dolphin thrashed in the water and began to move through the water at nearly thirty knots. Delphus circled once in the water, as though signalling a farewell to the ship which had delivered their new friend, then flashed in pursuit of his mate.

'Follow them,' Dobey yelled at the ship's captain. He ran to the wheelhouse, gunning the powerful engine into life. The ship's screws churned in the water, threshing out foam from its stern. The bows rose slightly as the small craft began to surge after the strange trio.

Chapter Eleven

The Great Council meeting was over. Varying factions of the liquid world community had held sway for brief periods, but Bluey's initial outburst had served to establish the general tone of the meeting. Following closely upon Poda's impassioned plea for calm and continued peaceful resistance, Cuvi the sabre-tooth shark had addressed the assembled company. His message, although couched in more subtle, insidious terms, was basically the same as Bluey's – a move towards direct confrontation, full-scale attack upon the great dry-creature and his hardware.

In the absence of Cacha, with his much respected wisdom, the remaining two Elders had been unable to prevent the meeting from degenerating into an angry free-for-all. Finally, albeit reluctantly, Nah-Ep himself had called the meeting to order and taken a majority vote. In the light of the result, there had been no choice but to approve a course of active resistance and aggression. It was a democratic decision, freely taken. There could be no going back from it.

Orcal the killer whale was the undisputed leader of his pack, and he revelled in the sense of power it gave him. He had wrested power from his ageing father in ritual battle, and had successfully beaten off a half-hearted attempt at resistance by one of his own young bulls. Until another strong young male arose to confront him, he controlled the large herd completely. They would follow him blindly, carrying out his orders without question.

His present herd was a dozen strong, all young males. The females and calves had been left feeding in rich waters whilst Orcal tested out his new powers of leadership. To make fast his point, Orcal threshed through the place of light water, pushing his body to its limits of speed and power to demonstrate his absolute superiority. Behind him, the rest of the herd struggled to keep up, strung out behind his foaming wake in a rough V formation. The tips of their black, pointed dorsal fins just cleaved the surface of the water, like a shoal of sharks, with which they were commonly confused.

Physically exhausted by his efforts to prove himself, and his body still smarting from the wounds of the recent battles, Orcal was in an ugly mood, eager to set upon some other, easier prey which would not defend itself quite so tellingly. Fresh from the Council meeting, the great dry-creature stuck in Orcal's mind as the ideal target. He relished the thought of tearing the soft white limbs from the useless, clumsy body, even though his species did not usually make such attacks.

Orcal slowed himself in the water as his delicate sonar picked up the signals of other large creatures swimming towards him. There were three in all, two of one species accompanied by another, odd creature. He came to a halt as they swam into visual range, the rest of the herd clustering around him.

Delphus and Delia had also located the herd of whales in the waters ahead of them, but had not allowed the fact to alter their course. Under normal circumstances, they would immediately have made a detour, to give the killer whales a wide berth, for they were an erratic, unpredictable species, given to unprovoked attacks upon the dolphin family when they were hungry, or merely felt the need for blood sport. Now, under the emergency conditions which existed in the liquid world, Nah-Ep had banned such petty squabbles between species. Protected by this edict, both Delphus and Delia considered themselves to be completely safe. They swam on, straight into the path of Orcal and his companions.

On board the coastguard vessel, Grossman stood at the prow, the backs of his knees tucked against a capstan for support as he gazed ahead through a pair of binoculars. A chill of fear shivered through him as he picked up the ominous black fins showing above the surface of the water ahead of McAllister and the dolphins. He checked his initial panic, the image of a mass shark attack, and allowed the cold, rationalising part of his mind, which was firmly rooted in marine biology, to establish fact over fancy.

Of course! Grossman's body relaxed. The dark fins were too black, too big, too pointed; they were not the deltoid shape associated with sharks. Not sharks then, killer whales, a herd of killer whales surfacing for air before plunging back into deep water. Despite their name, the whales were not usually of a bloodthirsty disposition. In captivity, they were as friendly and as harmless as their cousins the dolphins. With luck, they would dive again before McAllister reached them, Grossman thought. At worst, they might just want to investigate him momentarily – a trait common to most of the aquatic mammals. A few gentle nudges with their snouts, a cursory inspection of the strange creature invading their watery domain, and they would probably be off, their temporary curiosity completely forgotten. His doubts and fears somewhat allayed, Grossman lowered the binoculars for a moment, turning towards Binsley. 'Picking up anything?' he enquired half-heartedly, still a little embarrassed by his own insistence on the man's presence.

Binsley opened his eyes, blinking owlishly. There was a bemused expression upon his face. He shook his head uncertainly. 'Two distinct images . . . recurring over and over again,' he muttered vaguely. 'Can't quite understand . . . strange, no sense. Fish . . . images of a fish . . . very strong. And a crossroad . . . a signpost. Those two pictures, flashing up time after time.'

Grossman fidgeted uncomfortably, thankful that Dobey was not within earshot. He turned back to peer out over the waters again, bringing the binoculars back to his eyes.

Behind him, Binsley suddenly sucked in his breath sharply.

'No, I was wrong, the images are not separate,' he mumbled incoherently. 'Together . . . one thought, a total concept. Fish . . . with direction, a sense of purpose.'

The words lodged in Grossman's brain without consciously registering. His thoughts were with McAllister.

Orcal viewed the two dolphins with disdain. At the best of times, he and his kind regarded the species with a certain contempt, disliking their highly individualistic behaviour and envying their great speed and manoeuvrability in the water. Now, however, they had made a serious error of judgement which was totally unforgivable. Today of all days to be openly consorting with a great dry-creature, the newly-sworn enemy of the liquid world, slaughterer of the great Cacha; it was a crime which deserved immediate and uncompromising punishment. Blind to any other thoughts, urged onward by rage and the killer instinct, Orcal bellowed out the command to attack.

The herd of killer whales responded to their leader's call immediately, each individual breaking away from the roughly formed group to take up a new, and more formal, position. Soon they had assembled themselves into an almost perfect circle, completely surrounding the two dolphins and their human companion.

Delphus and Delia felt the cold shock of fear as the circle tightened around them, for they recognised the formation for what it was – the ritual pattern of a mass attack. Instinctively, they swam either side of McAllister, closing against him to protect his small defenceless body with their own tough hides. Working in concert, their minds pulsed out a message of alarm, a torrent of explanations.

It was no use. Psychic waves of hate and bloodlust flooded from the assembled whales, drowning out their strongest thoughts. Against the awesome power of blind violence, rational thought was no defence at all. In vain, Delphus and Delia pleaded for a chance to be heard, for the sympathetic dry-creature they had found to act as a go-between. Nothing got through. Only the urge to kill survived above the mêlée, like a rallying call on a crowded, noisy battlefield.

McAllister picked it up too, and his face contorted with disbelief. His new-found world was too fresh, too beautiful to be destroyed so soon. There was so much to do, so many duties to perform.

The circling whales closed in, slowly, inexorably. Orcal made the first move, leading the attack formation. Detaching himself from the circle, he darted forwards, his great blunt snout crashing into Delia's side, thrusting her through the water. Swimming back to take up his place in the circle once again, Orcal watched as one of his companions followed up with a similar sally, surging into the centre of the circle towards the unprotected dry-creature. McAllister's mouth opened wide in a silent scream as the whale's great jaws yawned open, exposing its vicious, razor-sharp teeth.

He felt no pain as the grinding teeth snapped shut over his wrist, meeting again quickly once the puny resistance of soft human flesh and muscles had been overcome. There was only a numbness, a dreamy, detached wonder as McAllister watched the killer whale back off again, dropping the severed hand carelessly into the water. With a sort of idle curiosity, McAllister glanced at the stump of his wrist, appreciating the strange beauty of the coloured patterns that his spurting blood made in the water.

Orcal dived into the attack again, making the end mercifully quick. His tearing teeth ripped at the diver's throat, slashing it open as neatly as a butcher's cleaver.

With that, the formalised attack pattern broke up abruptly as the killer whales let themselves go. In a frenzy, the scent of fresh blood stirring up their primeval instincts, the creatures tore McAllister's body to pieces, their threshing tails churning the surrounding water into blood-flecked foam.

Delphus and Delia could only watch the terrible carnage with heavy hearts, stunned with total horror and the knowledge of the gravity of the mistake which Orcal and his followers had made. There could be no going back now, no chance of establishing a rapport and a meaningful dialogue with the great dry-creature. Any discussion now could be conducted only in a strange and terrible language, with death as its interpreter.

The patrol vessel pulled alongside of the dark pool on the surface of the water. Grossman stared over the side, his tongue in the back of his mouth as he fought to control the retching spasms in his throat. The whales had gone now, their task accomplished. Only the two dolphins remained, mewing and whistling plaintively in mourning for their companion. McAllister's dismembered torso lay belly-down in the water between them, bobbing gently on the slight swell.

Then the dolphins were gone, diving down through the blood into pure, clear water. Grossman turned away from the horror. He stared into Commander Dobey's eyes, holding them with a look of mute accusation.

Binsley had chosen to ignore the sight, refusing to look over the side of the boat. He was as quiet and withdrawn as ever, even appearing to be unmoved by what had happened. Finally, he walked slowly over to Dobey's side. 'It seems that you have started a war, Commander,' he murmured in a quiet voice, then fell silent again.

Chapter
Twelve

Manhito would not give up easily. Not today. The stoical acceptance of bad fortune over the past fifteen days was behind him now, pushed into the recesses of his mind by the growing fear and desperation which seemed to be infecting everybody. Today had to be a fresh start, a redoubled effort to succeed. Before setting out from port at the crack of dawn, Manhito had spent several hours in quiet prayer and meditation, getting his body and mind into a fit and proper state to do his job.

He was a fisherman. It was his life and his livelihood, as it had been his father's and his father's father before him. It was all Manhito had ever been able to do and it remained his one chance of survival. On the tiny Japanese island of Yaku Shima, it was about all there was to do, unless a man was willing to sell his pride and his family heritage and go over to the mainland to work like a slave in some foul factory.

Today he must not fail, for it was his last chance. His employers had made it quite clear: no squid, no contract. If he returned yet again with an empty hold, Manhito would lose his ship, and with it the only chance of feeding his family.

Above his own personal fears, Manhito could quite understand his employers' growing desperation. The total catch of sixteen fishing boats going out from dawn to dusk over the past three weeks had been just five small squid, and they were rapidly running out of their frozen reserves. The entire squid industry was teetering on the brink of collapse, with the grim spectre of bankruptcy staring many people in the face.

Manhito tried to cover his worries with a false air of bravado. Squid there were, and squid he would have. If they had moved away from their traditional feeding grounds, then so would he. He called to his crew, giving them new instructions. In minutes, the sails had been reset and the auxiliary diesel engine persuaded into spluttering life. Turning away from the low, early morning sun, the small fishing boat headed further out into the Togara Straits in search of the elusive gastropods.

Manhito prowled restlessly around the stern of the boat, trying to keep as far away from his crew members as was humanly possible aboard such a small ship. They were edgy and nervous, and Manhito feared that they would become openly mutinous at any moment. He could hardly blame them; for none of the crew members received wages, just a proportion of the catch. As captain, Manhito was directly responsible for their welfare, and he could fully understand that they might be feeling that he was letting them down.

The lack of squid was not the only worry which troubled them all. In the past few days, supplies of milkfish from the mainland had almost completely dried up. There were ugly rumours circulating that the milkfish too had suddenly disappeared overnight without a trace, but Manhito discounted them. It was unthinkable; he preferred to believe that some temporary distribution problem was delaying fresh supplies.

The milkfish were of supreme importance to the eastern hemisphere, providing the major proportion of basic protein needs. Without them, thousands would die, and countless other thousands would suffer from severe malnutrition. Strict regulations protected the industry. Quotas were tightly controlled, and apart from being fished, they were bred in vast inland fish farms. The only trouble was, the wretched creatures steadfastly refused to lay eggs and breed in captivity, so there was a flourishing black market trade in fry, the young baby milkfish. The fish farmers would pay vastly inflated prices to get hold of more than their legal quota, as the fry grew rapidly, and the profit margins were high.

Manhito pushed himself away from the ship's rail, walking briskly to the edge of the catch hold, looking down at the empty floor. Normally, it should be a squirming, slithering mass of life. Now it was still and dead. Even the smell of fish had begun to fade.

Manhito shuddered involuntarily, the faintest sensation of panic creeping up on him. Suppose . . . just suppose that the squid had gone for good? That the sudden dearth was not an unexpected migration, or an unfortunate coincidence? There were already stories going about, frightening stories. A few years back, a foundering freighter had lost a deck cargo of arsenic in these very waters – ten huge steel drums, containing enough of the deadly poison to exterminate eight million people. What if these drums had rusted and burst open now, killing the creatures of the sea in their hundreds of millions?

Manhito clenched his fists, concentrating his mind on dismissing the sense of panic. There was already too much panic about; panic for money, for a job, for sacks of rice to hoard away against famine. The panic grew on the ships, was nurtured in the drinking dens, and from there it spilled out on to the streets. Arguments led to drunken brawls, to wild accusations. In the villages, normal community life was showing signs of strain, threatening to break apart at the seams and start a general free-for-all as each individual fought for personal or family survival.

Manhito walked back to the rail, praying silently under his breath. He gazed blankly out over the still, unbroken waters. A strange thought came to him suddenly : it was over eight days since he had seen a single flying fish or playful dolphin cleave that vast expanse of water.

Certain people no longer worried about hunger and death, for they were already lost, mourned over briefly, and forgotten. in dozens of small Esquimaux settlements, hunched figures crouched over small holes cut into the deep ice, jet-black circles against the white carpet of the surrounding ice and snow. Behind them, the settlements were dark and still, for the oil which kept the lamps and cooking fires sputtering had long since run out, and the squaws huddled together in sleeping groups to keep warm. Only the pitiful squealing of starving children broke the crystal-sharp silence.

Now Tanyuk, too, was dead. For more than a hundred hours he had sat patiently at his ice-hole, his fishing pole clutched tightly in his frozen hands. Weak from hunger, his body numbed by the bitter cold, he had sustained himself on hope alone. The next minute, the next hour, had to bring a bite. This faith, and the desperate need to feed his family, had helped him to maintain his lonely vigil.

He had passed beyond the physical limits of human endurance. Hypothermia, and the intensity of his concentration, had robbed his body of all feeling. Only the human will remained, its entire output concentrated upon that small black hole in the ice which promised everything but gave nothing. It enticed, it hypnotised. Somewhere along the way, Tunyuk's mind had abdicated under the terrible strain. Mesmerised by the hole, he had leaned forward, peering into the black waters beneath the ice, his eyes seeing a fleeting ripple, a sign of life and salvation.

Now his stiffened body lay sprawled out on the ice, his head and arms beneath the water, frozen in the act of snatching up that elusive meal which had been denied him for so long.

Nanpah, his squaw, rocked her fur-covered body to and fro in grief. With the death of her man, she too was dead. With no man to support and feed her, her time was limited. Only the children might survive, for under the strict tribal code of the Eskimo, any other family would take them in readily whilst abandoning their mother to die of starvation.

Nanpah could only pray for the survival of her four children. Sooner or later the seals had to return, the cod had to begin biting again. It had to be, or the entire settlement would die. The pile of frozen bodies was already mounting, the women and children giving in more and more to the racking pangs of hunger which tore at their distended bellies. At most, the village could survive for three more days. There were the dogs still left to slaughter, as a very last resort. After that, there was no hope at all, unless the fish returned.

Buzz Ackerman lifted the last bottle of whisky from the crate and plucked out the cork with his teeth. Taking a deep swig, he cast his eyes around the deckhouse once again, his grim expression reflecting the feelings of the entire crew. Silently, he passed the bottle to Little Porter.

The youngster shook his head. 'No, I'm gonna put the net over the side again. We gotta strike soon.'

Ackerman let out a bitter laugh. 'Talk about the optimism of youth,' he observed, to no one in particular. 'Twenty days out, forty-five tons of crushed ice gone to waste, a bloody fortune in fuel down the drain . . . and the kid's still hoping.'

Al Morin stretched his hand out for the bottle, shrugging his shoulders hopelessly. 'Best of bloody luck to him,' he muttered drunkenly. 'Wish to Christ I had some optimism left.' He held the neck of the bottle to his lips for a good ten seconds, swigging the bourbon down greedily. Wiping his mouth with the back of his hand, he passed the whisky back to Ackerman and pushed himself groggily to his feet. 'Think I'll take a stroll around on deck,' he muttered, following the youngster out of the cabin.

Ackerman gulped down another mouthful, pushed the cork back into the neck of the bottle and laughed again. 'Yeah, why not?' he shouted. 'Let's all go and take in the bloody scenery.'

He staggered out on to the deck, pressing himself up against the side rail and gazing out over the sun-kissed water of the Caribbean. Everything seemed calm and peaceful. The surface of the water was like a blue millpond. A perfect day for fishing, if only the goddamned shrimp would choose to show themselves!

Ackerman glanced sideways at Porter, struggling with the net. 'Forget it, for Christ's sake,' he said in a weary voice. 'It ain't no use. Just as soon as I finish this bottle, we're heading home for port.'

The youngster stared at him for several seconds, soaking in the older man's apathy. Suddenly, his last reserves of hope disappeared. Deflated and demoralised, he gave in, throwing the net to the deck and leaning on the rail, sighing heavily.

The three men continued to stare blankly out over the surface of the sea for several minutes. It was Morin who spoke first. 'Hey, what's that out there?' He pointed towards the horizon.

Ackerman lurched back to the deckhouse, returning with a pair of binoculars. Training them upon the distant speck, he quickly identified the other vessel. 'It's a seiner,' he announced. 'She's at anchor. The nets are hanging over the side, bone dry.'

'At this time of day?' Morin sounded incredulous. 'Jeezus, they on half-time or something, or have they filled up the bloody holds?'

Ackerman moved back towards the wheelhouse. 'Dunno, but I'm sure as hell gonna find out,' he announced firmly. 'I want to have a word with their skipper.'

At three-quarter speed, the 67-foot trawler headed towards the anchored seiner.

Pulling alongside, Ackerman leaned out over the side of the wooden shrimper, holding a loudhailer to his lips. 'Ahoy, there. Anyone on board?'

No answer came. Ackerman and his two companions scoured the deck of the seiner, seeking some sign of life. There was none; the seiner seemed abandoned. At closer sight, it was obvious that the nets draped over the ship's sides had not been used for several days.

Ackerman tried again. 'Do you hear me? Is anyone aboard?' Several more seconds passed, silently. Ackerman glanced aside at Al Morin, a puzzled frown on his face. He placed the hailer to his mouth again. 'Intention to board you,' he shouted. 'Permission to board or I claim salvage rights.'

Still there was no answer. Ackerman dropped the loudhailer to the deck and strolled over to Morin. For the first time in two weeks, there was a genuine smile on his face. 'Jesus Christ, Al, this trip might not be such a disaster after all,' he said happily. 'She must be worth a small fortune in salvage.'

Morin nodded eagerly. 'Could we tow her in?'

'Damn right!' Ackerman said vehemently. 'Even if I have to swim over the side with a bloody rope round my neck.'

'Well, what are we waiting for?' Morin demanded. 'I'll drop anchor and put the tender over the side.'

Minutes later, the two men were climbing aboard the apparently abandoned fishing boat. Their first call was to the hold. It was dry, and empty. Exchanging a grim, knowing glance, they headed straight for the captain's cabin.

The door was ajar. Ackerman pushed it gently with his fingertips. It swung back with a faint creak of salt-encrusted hinges. The two men peered cautiously into the small cabin.

'Dead?' Morin muttered.

Ackerman shook his head. The man sprawled across the mahogany desk was dead drunk, but that was about all. As they stepped into the cabin, the man stirred, groaning faintly, then pushed himself up to rest on his elbows and regard them through slitted, bloodshot eyes.

'You the skipper of this vessel?' Ackerman demanded angrily, furious with disappointment to learn that the vessel was not, after all, going to furnish him with a small fortune in salvage.

The man hiccuped noisily. 'S'right,' he slurred, propping

himself up and sitting back in his chair. 'Welcome aboard, gentlemen.'

Ackerman regarded him with an icy stare. 'Why didn't you acknowledge my call?' he demanded. 'You must have heard me, for Christ's sake!'

The skipper hiccuped again then giggled stupidly. 'Sure I heard you. Heard you real good. Thought you might tow ush back to port, save the bloody fuel being wasted.' He reached across his desk, grabbing a half-empty bottle of Kentucky Rye by its neck and swinging it towards his lips. Taking a deep swallow seemed to sober him up slightly. Pushing back his chair, he tottered unsteadily to his feet and held out a hand. 'Dell Vargas, three and a half weeks out of Port Royal. This is my ship, the *Delaware Darling*.'

Somewhat reluctantly, Ackerman shook his hand. 'Ackerman.' He indicated Morin. 'This is my partner, Al Morin. We're out of Tampa, been looking for shrimp.'

Vargas nodded moodily. 'Bet ya didn't find any.'

'Ain't a lot about,' Ackerman said, cautiously.

Vargas regarded him contemptuously. 'Bullshit!' he spat out. 'There ain't *nothing* about . . . there ain't nothing, no-where.' He nodded towards the cabin door. 'Wanna take a stroll on deck. I need some air.'

The three men walked out on deck. There was hardly any movement in the ship at all. Only a gentle breeze plucked at the loose rigging.

'Nice ship,' Ackerman murmured, more out of conversational politeness than anything else.

Vargas laughed bitterly. 'Yeah, nice, but bloody useless. You and me, we suddenly got ourselves lumbered with the most useless and unwanted thing in the world.'

'I'm not with you.' Ackerman regarded him curiously, not understanding.

Vargas looked back at him with a certain surprise. 'Ain't you been listening to the world news?'

Ackerman shook his head. 'No way. I like to leave all that crap behind the minute I leave port. Just the weather reports, that's all I listen to. Why, what's been happening?'

Vargas shook his head sadly, as if loath to break the terrible news to a fellow fisherman. 'The fish, they're all gone,' he said, his voice still tinged with the disbelief which he couldn't quite shake off. 'All over the goddamned world, the fish have just disappeared. Like I said, we both suddenly got the most

95

useless object in the whole world – a fishing boat when there ain't any fish any more.'

Ackerman stared for a long time at the bottle in the man's hand, then up to his grim face. 'What the hell are you talking about?'

Vargas shrugged. 'Don't take my word for it, you just listen to the news. Any waveband, any language. It's the same story all over.'

Ackerman was rapidly coming to the conclusion that Vargas was insane as well as drunk. 'Where's your crew?' he demanded suspiciously.

Vargas giggled. 'Soon as they heard the news, they demanded I drop 'em off in Jamaica. Wanted to live it up a bit for their last few days. Dropped 'em off two, maybe three days ago. I been kinda losing track of time lately.'

'What do you mean, last few days?' Ackerman asked, with mounting frustration.

Vargas regarded him sombrely. 'Don't you realise what's happening? It's the end of the world, that's what it is. First all the fish die off, next it'll be all the animals. Everything . . . zap . . . all gone.'

For the first time, Ackerman laughed openly, nodding his head towards the bottle in Vargas's hand. 'Wow, man, you really have been hitting the sauce, haven't you?'

Al Morin prodded him discreetly in the ribs, backing away a couple of paces. In a whisper, he said : 'Buzz, this guy's sick. He ain't just drunk. Reckon we'd better take him in tow or something.'

Ackerman nodded. 'Yeah. Maybe you're right.' The two men turned back to watch Vargas as he staggered across the deck to the ship's rail and leaned out over the side. Upending the whisky bottle, he poured a small quantity into the sea. 'Here my fishy friends, a last drink before dying,' he shouted in a cracked voice. Raising the bottle to his own lips, he took a deep swig, then spat it out in a spray. 'Bloody fish!' he said bitterly, as an afterthought.

Ackerman and Morin approached him slowly, one on each side. They took his arms gently.

'Listen, skip, you can't handle this craft on your own. How about you coming over to my vessel and we'll rig up a tow line?'

Vargas shrugged free of them, displaying surprising strength. He stared at them both, wild-eyed. 'You crazy? Who the hell wants to go back to a lousy stinking seaport to die?'

Ackerman flashed him a humouring smile. 'Come on, Vargas, relax. No one's gonna die.'

Vargas sprinted, suddenly, between them and headed for his cabin. He came out again holding a Verey pistol shakily in his hand. He lowered the squat barrel to the level of Ackerman's belly. 'Nobody's taking my ship away from me,' he screamed in a hysterical voice. 'As captain of this vessel, I order you to leave immediately. You ain't gone in thirty seconds, I'm gonna burn your guts out.'

Under a threat like that, Ackerman lost all desire to be a good Samaritan. He exchanged a quick look with Morin, seeing in his partner's eyes the same fear. The drunken Vargas was just crazy enough to carry out his threat. Holding his hands up in a gesture of peace, Ackerman began to back off slowly. 'O.K., Vargas, you have it your way. We're going, right now.'

They clambered down the side of the *Delaware Darling* and rowed away from its side with strong, sure strokes.

Back on board the shrimper, Ackerman headed straight for the radio. The least he could do was to report Vargas's position and condition to the coastguards. They might be able to do something with him. He was just getting through when Little Porter's voice shouted out urgently from topside. 'Hey, skip, come up here, quick!'

Ackerman dropped the radio mike and sprinted up on to the deck, joining the rest of his crew clustered against the side rail. All eyes were on the *Delaware Darling*.

She was foundering rapidly, sinking low in the water and listing heavily to starboard.

'Jesus Christ, the crazy coot's scuppering her,' Morin muttered in a shocked voice. 'He must have opened up the sea-cocks.'

There was nothing they could do but watch as the seiner rolled over, sinking rapidly once water rushed into her holds. She was gone in a few seconds, only a bubbling, frothing disturbance on the calm surface of the sea left to mark her passing. Ackerman trained his binoculars all around the area, looking for a body. There was nothing; Vargas had made sure he went down with his beloved ship.

After a while, Ackerman lowered the binoculars and turned away from the rail. 'Well, I guess it really was the end of the world, for him,' he observed without humour.

He walked purposefully towards the radio room, determined

now to listen to every news broadcast he could tune in to.

In all the major fishing ports of Great Britain, the story was the same. Confusion was giving way to panic, panic opening the path to dissidence and eruptions of violence. The English blamed the Scots for over-fishing, together they blamed the Russian super-trawlers. The packers and dock workers complained bitterly about the laziness of the fishermen and the distributers blamed the dockers.

As always, the housewives took the full brunt of soaring, crazy prices, and collectively blamed the government. Frozen cod reached a wholesale price of £3 a lb., and the lights burned late in the Ministry of Agriculture and Fisheries. Axes were sharpened, and heads began to roll as department chiefs fought tooth and nail to keep their well-paid jobs at the expense of the nearest available scapegoat. The most popular targets were those connected with the Department of Energy, for a creeping, insidious rumour was carefully and deliberately leaked that the fish scarcity was not entirely unconnected with the mushrooming growth of the off-shore oil industry.

Strangely, nobody blamed the fish. In fact, not many people were even really thinking about fish any more. Most of the complaints and arguments were basically economic in content.

From beneath the seething discontent, personal violence made ever-increasing appearances. In Whitehall, a peaceful demonstration of Billingsgate workers was turned into a bloodbath by the sudden and utterly pointless invasion of a National Front contingent. In the small Devonshire fishing village of Brixham, the crew of a Russian trawler forced ashore by bad weather were savagely beaten up and thrown into the harbour. One man died of a fractured skull; two others suffered spinal injuries which would cripple them for life.

In Hull, instances of wife-beating reached almost epidemic proportions as frustrated, frightened fishermen released their tensions upon nagging spouses. In Aberdeen, several trawlers sank in the harbour because of overcrowding, and angry fishermen burned down the harbour-master's office as a protest. The blaze spread to surrounding warehouses, and three hundred firemen fought for three days to contain it. There were two deaths, and the cost of fire damage was estimated in millions.

The British government narrowly survived a crisis vote of confidence, and reverted to their hackneyed ploy of the grand gesture, intended not so much to solve the problem as to set up a gigantic smokescreen around it so that no one would notice it was still there. Diplomatic relations with Russia and Iceland were hastily re-opened, a bevy of E.E.C. officials were despatched to Brussels and the British brandished their very British gifts of diplomacy and level-headedness before the eyes of a confused world.

An international conference was called, to be held under the auspices of a slightly tarnished Britannia.

Chapter Thirteen

Grossman unclipped his safety belt as the small illuminated sign above his head went out with a faint ping. Settling back into the plush upholstery of the DC10's seat, he opened his free copy of the London *Times* and tried to engross himself in it, hoping to push aside his irrational fear of flying. Despite that sense of unease, he felt better than he had done for several days. It was a great relief to get away from Dobey and the claustrophobic pressures that his security precautions had brought upon the Atlantis complex and everyone in it. It would be good to get away, even though the International Fisheries Conference he was flying to attend promised to be an intense and exhausting affair. Glancing through the newspaper, Grossman was deeply surprised to learn the full seriousness of the situation, for he had been so preoccupied with the tunnel and McAllister over the past few weeks that he had paid scant attention to world news.

He finished the main news pages, dropped the newspaper on to the empty seat beside him and picked up a new copy of his favourite wildlife magazine, which he had purchased at the airport. Quite understandably, the entire issue was devoted to investigating the strange phenomenon of the disappearing fish.

The inside front page took the form of a broadsheet, starting out with a quotation lifted from the March issue of *Wildlife*

News, followed by a series of hard-hitting facts about pollution. Grossman settled back to read it, word for word.

'The release of a deadly "Andromeda Strain" of viruses from the Pleistoceine sediments which have remained undisturbed on the seabeds for thousands of years has been described by some scientists as an annihilation spin-off from one of the latest assaults on the sea's resources . . . the mining of manganese modules from the ocean bed. This threat is horrific, but unlikely to materialise. However, other warnings given by scientists about the consequences of the accelerating destruction of the sea's resources is now being referred to as the "marine revolution" and could come true alarmingly soon.

'Upon the development of a sound global policy with respect to the oceans depends the future of this planet as a viable life-support system. Without the living oceans, the earth's ecological system simply malfunctions. It would not be a matter of gradual, scarcely noticeable decay through centuries, rather it would be a matter of days, months, or a very short number of years.

'*Fact:* The oceans absorb forty per cent of man-made carbon dioxide, converting it back into nearly half our life-giving oxygen. This is done by the phytoplankton – minute organisms which absorb energy direct from the sun and provide the first link in the food chain of all marine animals. Pollution is already killing these organisms off. Their complete removal would bring about the immediate termination of all life on this planet.

'*Fact:* Each year, man dumps over 100 million gallons of petroleum product effluent into the sea. In the same period, he dumps 200,000 tons of deadly lead and mercury poisons, hundreds of thousands of gallons of herbicides, pesticides and other killers.

'*Fact:* The oceans currently supply nearly thirty-five per cent of all man's protein needs. We are rapidly over-killing this important source of life-sustaining food. The oceans are vast, but not inexhaustible.

'*Fact:* The shallow areas of the sea receive the greatest proportion of our chemical poisons. Most marine animals need this area for the initial stage of their life-cycles.

'*Fact:* In January of this year, ten drums of deadly arsenic were swept overboard from the Chinese cargo vessel *Chang Tu* when it collided with a Panamanian ship. The arsenic was enough to kill eight million people; it was packed in metal drums which will eventually rust, loosing their contents into the sea. Two months later, a Nigerian-bound ship lost several drums of highly concentrated, dangerous corrosive acid. These are but two isolated instances of accidents which happen all the time.

'*Fact:* When oil rig *Bravo* blew out, directly due to human error, it spouted no less than 12,000 tons of crude oil into the North Sea in eight days, making the previous *Torrey Canyon* disaster seem almost a minor affair.

'Even the most optimistic biologists now agree that there may not be much time before the balance of the oceans is damaged beyond salvation. Many are already saying that the crisis point is passed, and there is no way to reverse the trend already started. If that is true, the *homo sapiens* is already a doomed species. Man will go the way of the dinosaur and the dodo.'

Grossman dropped the magazine. None of the information was new to him, but now, evaluating and assessing it in the light of what was happening, he felt a sense of nightmare unreality. He had found the localised disappearance of fish life around the tunnel disturbing, even slightly ominous. Now, with the knowledge that it was only symptomatic of a world-wide trend, the implications were truly horrific. As a biologist, Grossman could see far beyond the simple human terms of starvation and collapsing economies, terrible as they were. Above and beyond the deaths of several thousand human beings stretched the awesome possibility of planetary collapse, global annihilation.

Earth was a self-sustaining, self-generating spaceship. It was completely self-contained. Nothing existed outside it except the vacuum between the stars. All forms of life which existed upon it survived solely through interaction and interdependence. Viewed against this background, any ecological upset spelled a certain amount of danger. If the ecology of the major part of earth had been totally disrupted, possibly destroyed in a few short weeks, the prospect of a cosmic cataclysm became very real indeed. If the oceans died, then the lands would perish too, rotting like gangrenous appendages on a diseased body. There was no other view to be taken; cold logic told Grossman that earth could not possibly survive such a major shock to its very nature. The seas were the lifeblood of earth, renewing, recharging, revitalising it with every tide.

Grossman's mind rebelled from facing such possibilities. He

was suddenly jerked back to reality as the plane hit an air-pocket, dropping ten or fifteen feet with a stomach-churning jar. He shuddered, suddenly and uncomfortably reminded of how much he hated air travel. Given a free choice, Grossman would have much preferred to make the trip to England by sea. It would have given him more time to relax, collect his thoughts – and even to observe the ocean at first-hand.

He had not been given the choice. The conference was too important, the needs of the world too urgent. Grossman was only one of several hundred marine biologists summoned by their various governments around the world and despatched to make whatever contribution they could to analysing the problem and hopefully coming up with some sort of solution. Indeed, the sense of urgency was so great that Grossman had originally been sent a ticket for the Concorde flight from Washington to Heathrow. He had stuck his heels in over that one, steadfastly refusing to travel supersonic. Not only did Grossman object to being whisked through the stratosphere at twice the speed of sound, he nursed strong objections to the very existence of the aircraft, firmly believing it to pose quite serious environmental threats to his home planet.

Oddly enough, Concorde had already been put forward as a tentative explanation for the disappearance of the fish. Grossman gave the theory no credence at all; it was just one of a hundred different explanations which had already been put forward, varying from the improbable to the frankly crackpot. Even so, it made a little more sense than most, the general suggestion being that the sonic shock waves from the aircraft had somehow passed into the oceans, destroying the delicate sonar systems of whole species of fish. Thus damaged, the fish were unable to control their normal directional impulses towards feeding grounds and migratory breeding routes.

The most popular current theory was that radioactive pollution in the oceans had passed the critical level. A world-wide survey was already under way under the supervision of N.A.T.O. Samples of water from all the major oceans were being collected and subjected to stringent tests. The results would hopefully be known a few days after the conference opened.

Grossman mused idly, considering each of the more credible explanations in turn. The more he thought about the problem, the stronger some buried instinct insisted that there was no simple scientific answer. The feeling defied rational thought, refusing to quite form itself into a definite idea. Binsley's monkey-like face flashed up in Grossman's mind time and time again. 'Fish . . . with direction, a sense of purpose,' the man had said, supposedly relaying McAllister's disturbed thoughts.

Was it possible? Was it conceivable that intelligent thought, rather than some external influence, was affecting the life of the seas? Grossman thought about his earlier work with dolphins, remembering how deeply convinced he had been at times about the power of their intelligence. So many times he had felt on the very threshold of a breakthrough, convinced that he was about to smash through the barrier which separated the two species.

Shaking his head, Grossman returned to his newspaper, not wanting to indulge the wild speculation any further. But it would not be dismissed. Buried, tucked away in the inner recesses of his brain, it lay dormant, taking nourishment and growing like a foetus.

Chapter Fourteen

'Excuse me, Captain, but would you come in here, please, sir?'

Captain Williams of Her Majesty's Submarine *Swordfish* looked up as the voice of his First Radio Officer came over the Tannoy speaker. He pushed away the chart he had been studying and moved to the open bulkhead, ducking through it. He made his way down the companionway to the radio room, walking in after a perfunctory rap on the door. 'Yes, Baines, what is it?'

First Officer Alex Baines nodded towards the main radar scanner, his face creased in a perplexed frown. 'Picking up a very odd pulse echo, sir. Don't know quite what to make of it.'

Williams regarded the scanner briefly. '*Nomad*?' he murmured questioningly. The two submarines were working together, conducting an underwater survey of the German Bite fishing grounds, seeking out the elusive cod shoals.

Baines looked dubious. 'If it is, then she's bloody close,' he observed. 'Too close for comfort, I'd say.'

Captain Williams stared at the radar blip more carefully, finally nodding in agreement. 'Better contact her and get her to confirm her position,' he said quietly. As a secondary precaution, he unclipped the radio mike and held it to his lips. 'Captain to bridge. Hold trim and full reverse engines.' He replaced the mike, putting up a hand towards the nearest bulkhead to steady himself as the sub shuddered to a halt and then began to move slowly backwards.

He waited patiently while Baines contacted their sister ship and established their relative positions. When the radio operator looked up again, he seemed even more puzzled. 'Well, it can't be the *Nomad*, sir,' he muttered. 'According to her, she's exactly in position a good mile away.'

Williams studied the blip again. 'Could it be a large fish shoal?'

Baines shook his head firmly. 'Far too compacted, sir. No, it's a solid object all right.'

Williams thought for a few seconds, sucking at his lip pensively. 'Get back to *Nomad*,' he instructed. 'Ask for a double-check on that position and a full instrumentation check. And while you're at it, plot our exact course, position and depth.'

'Right away, sir.' Baines hastened to comply, as aware as his Captain of the dangers of an underwater collision between two submarines.

Abruptly, the rogue blip disappeared from the screen. Baines cursed under his breath. 'God dammit, it's just gone,' he breathed incredulously.

Captain Williams grabbed the mike again. 'All engines stop,' he barked firmly. 'Hold trim.' He bent over his radio officer's shoulder. 'We'd better get to the bottom of this,' he murmured, in a deliberately calm voice.

Baines nodded, forcing a smile. 'I think you're right, sir.' He began the first of a series of tests designed to check the equipment.

Sibba the blue whale eased her mighty bulk towards the motionless shape of the submarine once again. No sound or vibrations issued from it now, she noted with satisfaction. It meant that her ploy had worked – the great creature had been confused and frightened by her presence and the wave of sonar impulses she had flooded out towards it, destroying its sense of direction. Now, either sleeping or dead, the creature lay helpless in the water, ready for her allies to conduct the next stage of the attack.

Concentrating her thoughts, Sibba sent a rallying call into the black waters beneath her. Moments later, the first of a hundred pilot whales rose up from their hiding place in the depths and began to set about their task. Sibba watched them work with a strange feeling prickling at her mind. Revenge was not an emotion she could normally experience, but since Nah-Ep had released the knowledge of death into the liquid world there were many new feelings which stirred vague instinctive chords. Now, watching the activity around her, Sibba sensed that there was a certain pleasure to be taken in paying back the great dry-creature his own heritage. Sibba had seen her mate and her calf perish, their bodies blown apart by the exploding harpoons of the whaling ships. Retaliation did not lessen the grief of loss, but she took some comfort from knowing that others of her species might now be saved.

Leaving the pilot whales to their work, Sibba swam off, homing in on the sonar impulses of the second invader.

Baines looked up from his instruments, the worry on his face becoming definite fear. 'Nomad reports that all direction-finding equipment is giving false readings,' he said grimly. 'I've checked our own course reports for the past hour and they're also way out. The fact is, sir, we just can't trust our equipment to give us an accurate fix. That blip on the screen may have been Nomad, or it may have been a false echo. There is no sure way of telling.'

Captain Williams regarded his officer in astonishment. 'Are you telling me that both sets of equipment failed simultaneously?'

Baines nodded. 'Looks like it, sir.'

'It's impossible,' Williams blurted out angrily. 'Utterly impossible.'

Baines shrugged. 'That's what I'd have said, sir, but the fact remains that to all intents and purposes both Nomad and ourselves are down here blind – lost, if you like. Not a very healthy thought, sir.'

Baines's last comment was an understatement. Two submarines, in the same area, both without any sense of direction; it was more than unhealthy, it was downright terrifying. At any given moment, they could be on a direct collision course. Captain Williams took very little time to come to a decision. 'There's nothing for it – we'll have to surface,' he announced. He snapped his orders into the mike. 'Ahead dead slow. Blow main ballast. We're going topside.'

He waited for several minutes. Nothing happened. Bristling with irritation, Williams snatched up the mike again. 'Engine room? Did you hear my last order?'

The voice which came back over the Tannoy was apologetic, but also nervous. 'We have a little trouble, Captain. Both screws and all lateral rudders are refusing to respond. She's dead in the water, Captain.'

Williams's temper exploded. 'God dammit, what the hell's going on?' he demanded, of no one in particular. He slammed the microphone down, turning briefly to Baines. 'You get on to the captain of the *Nomad*, explain our position and ask him, on my strict orders, to keep perfectly still. I'm going up to engineering to see what we can do to sort this mess out.'

He stamped out of the radio room, scrambling along the companionway with unusual haste.

The chief engineer greeted him with a grim face. 'We got troubles, sir,' he muttered simply.

Williams glanced up at the depth gauge. The sub was hovering at a depth of 8oo feet. 'Break out a pressure suit,' he muttered to a nearby rating. 'Get a diver out there to inspect the screws and rudders.' He turned back to the chief engineer. 'To think we once had the finest navy on this earth. What else can go wrong with this old tub?'

The answer to that question was not long in coming. The diver had been unable to open the outer hatch on the other side of the airlock. It appeared to be jammed solid.

Williams was really worried now, but he dare not let it show to the rest of the crew. He issued his orders in a quiet, calm voice, only too well aware that he was rapidly narrowing all action down to emergency last resorts. 'Send him out of number one torpedo tube. He'll have to make his own way to the surface once he has located the trouble.'

Able Seaman Graves crawled awkwardly along the flooded torpedo tube, restricted by the heavy diving suit he was forced to wear. Even with the powerful beam of his torch, he could see little. Logic told him that he must be almost at the end of the tube, yet he had no view of the open sea beyond the sub. His fingers encountered the outer edge of the missile launching hatch. He was there. He tried to thrust his hand forward, out into the sea, but something soft yet unyielding restricted him. He fumbled with the torch, thrusting it ahead of him, trying to make sense of what he saw in its beam. The bright light bounced back only dully, hardly reflecting at all from the dark brown, slightly opalescent covering which completely obscured the hatch opening. With a sense of rising panic, Graves waved the heavy torch wildly, attempting to smash through the strange barrier. His efforts were to no avail. The plastic-like substance refused to be shifted.

Switching off the torch, Graves reached up to his helmet, thumbing on his radio. 'There's no way out,' he said, his voice trembling. 'Something is completely blocking the hatchway. It's like a thick plastic film – sheeting material of some kind.'

Inside the sub, Williams choked. He had to make a terrible decision. His heart pounding, he waited several moments before voicing it. He turned to the chief engineer. 'There's nothing for it, we're going to have to try and blast ourselves up to the surface,' he murmured grimly. 'Give the order to blow all emergency ballast tanks at once.'

The engineer's face registered his horror. His jaw dropped slackly open. 'My God, sir . . . that will kill young Graves. There's no way he can survive a sudden pressure change like that.'

Williams clenched his teeth together tightly, hiding his own emotion and the agony of the terrible decision he had made. 'I know that,' he hissed quietly. 'Do you think for a second that I would even consider it if there was any other choice? Damn it, man, not even God could weigh one man's life against this ship and her entire crew.'

The chief engineer paused before passing on the order, racking his brains for an alternative. There was none. Putting Graves in the torpedo tube had been a strictly one-way route out of the sub. The inner hatch doors could not be opened again to allow him back without flooding the whole vessel. Even if they secured the inner bulkheads and let the engine room flood, the extra weight of water taken on would prevent the sub from rising to the surface. Finally, he snapped his heels, saluting his captain. 'With respect, sir, I would regard it as a personal favour if you would give that command direct. This is a request, sir . . . you understand I'm not refusing to obey an order . . .' His voice tailed off uncertainly.

Captain Williams nodded, understanding perfectly. The man

was right, he had no right to pass on an order like that. The responsibility was his alone, it came with the obligations of command. 'Yes, of course,' Williams murmured, reaching for the mike. In a choked voice, he gave the order.

Moments later, the submarine shuddered as the emergency ballast tanks were blown. Both Williams and his engineer looked up hopefully to the depth gauge. It remained static. The sub was not lifting.

'Oh God, we're trapped,' the chief engineer breathed, giving wav to despair. The two men stared at each other blankly, neither able to give or receive any hope.

'No, wait . . . she's shifting.' The chief engineer broke the terrible silence as the nose of the submarine lifted several degrees. Both men gazed at the depth gauge again, with new hope rising in their blood. They felt gentle movement beneath their feet as the indicator needle began to drop back with agonising slowness. *Swordfish* was surfacing!

Captain Williams and his crew were rescued six hours later by a Norwegian minesweeper which came in response to their distress call. Its crew gazed in awe at the grotesque, formless mass floating on the surface of the water, hardly able to believe that the thing could be a submarine. The entire hull of the *Swordfish* was swathed in a slimy green mass of giant kelp – each shiny frond up to a hundred feet in length. The pilot whales had done their job with incredible efficiency, wrapping the giant seaweed tightly around every external projection of the vessel and convoluting it into intricate knots and tangles. Working with oxyacetylene burners, the Norwegians took nearly two hours to free the main hatch, burning through the foot-thick trunks of the weed two and three at a time.

Forty-eight hours later, when the crew of the *Nomad* were known to be dead, they managed to locate its position – two miles from where it should have been and hanging motionless in a thousand feet of water.

Jimmy Bailey surfaced beside the diving platform of the North Sea oil rig *Black Gold II* and scrambled out of the water, throwing himself on to his back, his body contorted with agony. It was several minutes before he could speak.

Smalley, the lead diver, removed his mask and glared down at him angrily.

'You bloody fool,' he spat out. 'You came up too damned

fast. You're lucky you didn't kill yourself.'

Bailey's eyes rolled, exposing the whites. 'Damn right I came up fast,' he managed to grunt out painfully. 'There's a bloody great shark down there.'

Smalley regarded him pityingly. 'A basking shark ain't going to hurt you much, is it?'

Bailey shook his head, despite the pain. 'It wasn't no basking shark,' he yelped out. 'This was a great white . . . I'd swear it.'

Smalley began to laugh. 'Whoever heard of a great white shark in these waters?' he scoffed. 'This is the North Sea, not the bloody Caribbean.'

He passed the story on to the medical officer who came down to escort Bailey to the sickroom. In an hour, it was all round the rig. Everybody had a good belly laugh.

With Bailey out of action for at least two days, Smalley had to go down himself. Algae, barnacles and other crustaceans were building up at a phenomenal rate on the main support pylons. It was taking the full team of divers all their time and effort to keep them scraped clear.

He was down for nearly an hour before his head broke the surface again.

It was only when the first man noticed that it was no longer attached to his body that the panic broke out.

It was only early June, but summer seemed to be descending upon the south-west coast as though it meant to stay. It was the third successive year that the temperature had reached heat-wave proportions. The first year had brought the problem of drought; the second, a holidaymaker overspill which saw people camping out on the beaches and sleeping in their cars by the roadside. This summer, nobody foresaw any great problems at all. It had been a harsh winter, with more than the average rainfall. The reservoirs were full. The overcrowding problem had been avoided by careful checks being maintained upon hotel and guest-house bookings and the provision of large new camping sites and caravan parks. It promised to be a perfect season.

In Torquay, one of the most popular holiday resorts on the coast, that promise appeared to be particularly fulfilled. The beaches were in prime condition, the sands well washed by the surging high tides of January and February, and there had been none of the disastrous oil spillages from the giant tankers which frequently sought sanctuary from rough weather in the bay. Nurtured by the wet winter and forced by the early sun, the palms and sub-tropical shrubs which lent Torquay its unique Mediterranean atmosphere were green and lush, the bright flowerbeds which line the seafront a blaze of colour.

Even the owners of the pleasure boats which filled the inner harbour were no longer worried by bankruptcy. At first, the skippers who usually took holidaymakers on mackerel or shark fishing trips had been worried about the sudden lack of prey. Desperation had driven them to the only obvious solution: to adapt their vessels to other leisure pursuits. Now, instead of fishing expeditions, they offered sight-seeing trips up the beautiful Dart estuary, or night-time floating discos for the youngsters. There were plenty of takers; more than enough to ensure a profitable season for all.

The beaches were comfortably crowded, bright with the rainbow colours of striped deckchairs, beach parasols and bikini-clad bodies. Above the soft lapping of surf upon the shingle, the air was filled with the sounds of childish laughter, the faint scratchings of plastic buckets and spades against sand, and the massed symphonic splendour of a thousand transistor radios. Everything was as it should be, as it usually was.

The jellyfish arrived suddenly, without warning. One moment the splashings in the water were accompanied by squeals of delight, the next by yelps of pain and squeals of terror. Children and adults alike staggered out of the shallows on to the beach, collapsing on the damp sand to writhe in agony, clutching at legs and arms which stung and burned from contact with the poisonous polyps.

In minutes the sea was empty, and a thick wave of frightened and injured bathers retreated up the beaches in panic. In the shallow, light waters, the glistening bodies of the invading jellyfish floated menacingly, forming a deadly, obscene-looking living carpet.

The panic lasted for most of the day, with fleets of ambulances and private cars ferrying paralysed children and cursing adults to the hospitals. The casualty departments were like wartime field hospitals as the overworked staff struggled to keep up with the constant flow of patients. From the nearby town of Paignton, more victims were being offloaded in their hundreds. Many of these were in far worse condition, having trodden upon the highly venomous spines of scorpion and weaver fish which had suddenly found their way to the shore, burying themselves in the sand so that they were virtually invisible.

By late evening the town began to get more or less back to normal. Supplies of anti-toxic vaccines had been brought in from Plymouth, Exeter and Bristol, and most of the victims had been treated and sent back to their hotel rooms. Emergency day beds accommodated the hundreds who required more intensive treatment. The main hospital morgue contained the bodies of seventeen children and five adults who had proved particularly susceptible to the poisonous sea creatures.

Before six o'clock, the Beaches Committee had held an emergency meeting and decided to deter bathing indefinitely. Gangs of Council workmen were commandeered for night-time working, to erect emergency warning notices all round the coastline.

By the time darkness fell, Torquay had regained every outward appearance of normal holiday gaiety. The promenade lights twinkled colourfully, the pubs and nightclubs throbbed with life and the sound of music, and the cleaning trucks moved slowly along the quiet streets clearing up the tons of litter from the take-away food shops and the confectionery purveyors.

On Oddicombe beach, two workmen busied themselves implanting the last warning sign above the high-tide mark. Satisfied that the wooden post was firmly bedded down in the rough, gritty sand, they piled small boulders against it and sat down to smoke a quick cigarette.

Joe Meeker glanced at his watch in the light of the flaring match. 'Jesus Christ, Larry, you realise it's half past ten? Reckon we ought to do all right for overtime out of this little lark.'

His partner chuckled. 'Too right, boy. Could bloody do with it, an' all.' He bent over, cupping his hands around the flame from the match, sucking at the cigarette in his mouth. He inhaled a deep lungful of smoke, exhaled it again and breathed deeply in through his nose, savouring the night air. Suddenly, he coughed harshly, making retching noises in his throat.

Meeker laughed. 'About time you gave up smoking,' he observed jokingly.

Larry Jenks shook his head, still choking. He fought to control his heaving chest so that he could talk clearly. Finally he managed it. 'Ain't the smoke,' he managed to blurt out. 'Blimey, didn't you get a whiff of that stench?'

Meeker sat up, sniffing the air cautiously. At first he smelled nothing unusual, then the light breeze changed direction momentarily and a foul odour wafted to his nostrils. 'Oh Christ, I see what you mean,' he muttered to his companion, wrinkling his nostrils in disgust. 'Right bloody pong.'

Jenks scrambled to his feet. 'I'm not staying around here,' he muttered, firmly. 'Must be a batch of rotten seaweed or something, just drifted up on the tide.'

Meeker rose to join him. He shook his head. 'No, it isn't coming from the sea,' he muttered, testing the wind direction with a moistened finger. It's coming from over by the harbour wall, where the drainage outlet is.'

The two men walked quickly up the beach, climbing the concrete steps which made up the protective sea wall. On the top, they walked along a few paces until they were directly above the suspect drainage outlet. Meeker bent over slightly, taking a very tentative sniff. 'Ugh,' he muttered in disgust, as an even more powerful smell assailed his nostrils. 'You're right – it is coming out of here.'

Jenks grunted. 'Well that's up to the sanitation boys,' he muttered. 'We can mention it in the morning. Certainly wouldn't want to be on this beach tomorrow if it keeps up.'

'Right,' Meeker agreed with a slight laugh. He turned to move away, then stopped suddenly as a faint scratching sound came to his ears. 'Listen,' he hissed, clutching at his companion's jacket sleeve.

Jenks pricked his ears. Below him, a strange slithering, scraping noise echoed out of the mouth of the drainage outlet for a few seconds, then faded away again.

'What the hell do you reckon on that?' Meeker asked, puzzled.

Jenks shrugged. 'God knows,' he said, somewhat carelessly. 'But like I said, drainage problems are down to the sanitation department. Come on, let's get going. We got time for a pint before going in and clocking off.'

Meeker stopped worrying about the odd sounds abruptly. The immediate prospect of a drink seemed much more important. The two men moved away along the sea wall to gather up their equipment.

Less than half a mile away, in the small secluded cove which adjoined the Oddicombe beach, a young couple finished making love and lay back on the fine pebbles, breathing heavily.

After a while, the boy stood up, adjusting his trousers. He began to walk away, his shoes crunching noisily against the shingle.

The girl looked up in alarm. Surely he didn't intend leaving her here on a dark, deserted beach, now that he had managed to get what he wanted. 'Hey, where are you going?'

The boy stopped in his tracks, looking back at her with a grin on his face. 'I'm just going behind the rocks for a pee,' he informed her without embarrassment.

He continued to walk towards a large clump of rocks some fifteen yards away. Satisfied, the girl relaxed again, lying full length on the beach and staring up into the clear night sky. After a few moments, she heard the faint splashing of a stream of urine against the rocks.

Suddenly a louder, sharper sound came out of the darkness. She sat up with a start, straining her eyes through the gloom towards its source. Across the dark beach, vaguely illuminated by the pale quarter moon, something darker seemed to be moving – a black, shapeless mass which seemed to heave and writhe up and down and from side to side as it made forward progress towards her. The girl began to scramble to her knees, her mouth opening to scream as the formless shape closed the distance between them.

The scream surfaced as the shuddering, rippling mass surrounded her, and she saw dozens of pairs of tiny, blood-red eyes glinting wickedly. Her shrill, ululating cry of terror continued as the first of hundreds of the loathsome creatures broke over her, pushing her back on to the pebbles. Their claws tore and scratched at her partially clothed body as the pack of rats surged in a blind wave over her, oblivious to any such minor obstacle in their path.

The scream finally died in her throat as the girl passed mercifully into unconsciousness.

By the next morning, the rats had been sighted everywhere. Early-morning shoppers and holidaymakers froze in the streets, screaming in terror and fainting on the pavements as hordes of the sleek, furry bodies poured out of drains and sewerage vents.

Behind them came the filthy, mind-assaulting stench which had driven them from their underground lairs. Above the drains, yellowish tendrils of gas could be seen hovering in the air before being wafted away by the breeze and dissipated into the surrounding atmosphere.

By mid-day, when the temperature had soared into the high seventies, the lower part of the town was uninhabitable. The harbour was completely deserted, with shops locked up tightly and windows firmly closed and bolted. Huge packs of rats swarmed along the beaches and the main seafront promenade. The smell of sewage hung in the air like a wispy fog. It spread insidiously throughout the day, creeping up from the harbour area into the higher parts of town, driving the rats ahead of it. By mid-afternoon even the residential areas were affected, and the roads out of Torquay were a bedlam of traffic jams and road accidents as thousands of frightened and disgusted holidaymakers tried to get further inland.

The problem took two days to identify, but would take a lot longer to solve. Intense concentrations of giant Japanese seaweed had established themselves in the off-shore sewerage outlets, propagating at an unbelievable rate and quickly spreading up through sewer pipes into the drainage systems. On the undersea outlets crustaceans had built up, layer upon layer, until they formed an impervious wall which prevented the waste-matter escaping into the open sea, forcing it back where it rapidly built up dangerous concentrations of noxious gases. It was this smell which had forced the rats out of their normal habitat. As the rodents retreated, the weed moved in, adding its own unpleasant odour to the general stench

Suction drain-cleaners were useless. They soon became hopelessly clogged with the clinging, sticky weed. It began to show itself in the streets, the odd tendril curling up around drain gratings and starting to climb wastepipes.

Man was suffering another bitter lesson in revenge from the sea. For years he had pumped his filth into the open waters; now he was having it forced back upon him, along with rodent infestation and the perils of disease.

Chapter Fifteen

The first day of the International Fisheries Conference was drawing to a close. For more than six hours the assembled delegates had been bombarded with facts, scientific data and inexplicable puzzles. Now it was time to start drawing a few conclusions.

Dr Stuart Bell, head of the Lowestoft Research Centre, held the chair for the final address. He stood stiffly as the projector was switched off and the auditorium lights turned up.

'Well, gentlemen, you have seen the problem. Now we have to come up with some answers.' He paused briefly before carrying on whilst the various translators in the building conveyed his words to the non-English-speaking delegates.

'The fish have not disappeared, they have merely moved into deeper water,' Bell went on. 'Whole species have become geographically displaced, and individual fish and aquatic mammals have been reliably reported in places many thousands of miles from their natural habitat. What this conference must do is to ascertain the reasons for this unprecedented change, and then decide what we, as an international body, can do about it. I hardly need to remind you all that the problem is a global one, affecting us all. It can, therefore, only be tackled on a free-sharing, humanitarian basis of global co-operation.'

With a final nod of his grey head, Bell sat down. The first day was over. The delegates had a lot of data to mull over and consider before meeting again to discuss theories and possible solutions.

The auditorium was still for several seconds whilst the delegates sat in hushed silence. The realisation that all the talking was over for the day dawned slowly. Finally, with each national group striving to preserve international protocol, it became obvious that the motion to disperse must come from the rostrum. Bell rose to his feet again somewhat awkwardly, leaning forward to the microphone. 'That will be all, gentlemen. This conference will reconvene at 10.00 hours tomorrow morning.'

The ensuing silence was quickly broken by the squeaking

and scraping of chair legs upon the bare wooden floor of the Lowestoft Town Hall. It was far from being an ideal venue for the conference, but it had been decided to conduct at least the initial few days of discussion in a place where the most relevant data and equipment was at hand. Virtually all Great Britain's fishery and marine research was carried out at the Lowestoft Centre. The Town Hall had been the largest place available.

Heinz Grossman shuffled out of the hall behind the other members of the United States contingent, his head bowed in thought. Purposely, he let his companions go ahead of him. For the moment at least, Grossman did not wish to become involved in any further group discussion. He wanted to come to terms with himself first, formulate some purely personal, objective viewpoint upon which he could build any argument or discussion.

He walked down the front steps of the Town Hall, lifting his face gratefully towards the gentle evening sunshine. He took a deep breath, savouring the strange, exhilarating smell of English air. After the dry, heavy heat of Florida and the sterile air-conditioned humidity of the tunnel, he found the moist thickness of a small island nation's air particularly refreshing.

He strolled thoughtfully through the town for nearly an hour, not wanting to return to his hotel. Coming to a small green area of public park, he chose an empty wooden bench and sat down to marshal his thoughts.

There were so many different aspects to the problem, it was difficult to lump them all together. Quite apart from the incredible problems of protein deficiency which the elusive fish posed, there were all the strange and disturbing side effects and sub-issues which had sprung from the inexplicable changes in the seas of the world.

From the corner of his eye, Grossman saw a small girl taking her pet puppy for a walk. He fixed his attention on her, captivated by her prettiness and the colours of her simple summer dress. A wistful smile came to his face as he realised that even that child's simple pleasure and love for her pet was in danger of being spoiled by one of the very side effects he had been considering.

The puppy, no more than ten weeks old, would soon grow into quite a large mongrel, Grossman estimated by the size of its shaggy paws. It would have to be fed. At present, the vast majority of pet foods came from whalemeat and offal. For this reason, it was reasonably cheap and reasonably plentiful. Quite obviously, if the fish by-products dried up, pet food would become an expensive scarcity. If there was less protein to feed the starving humanity of the world, then luxuries like pet animals might well become both socially unacceptable and economically unviable.

It was a disturbing thought. Grossman looked at the little girl's face with a new sadness. Her obvious pride and love for her appealing little puppy was obvious in the smile which shone from her face, the fierce determination with which she gripped its thin red leather lead.

A harsh, squawking cry suddenly broke the peaceful quietness of the park. Grossman glanced up, quickly, into the sky, as a small flock of seagulls swooped and dived into the area of the park. They circled for a few seconds, then plunged towards the ground.

Grossman leapt from the bench like a coiled spring as the child's coloured dress was suddenly obscured in a wild flurry of white wings and snapping yellow beaks. Hardly believing what he was seeing, he ran towards her as her first terrified screams tore through the air like a jagged knife.

Waving his arms wildly, Grossman threw himself into the flock of birds, feeling their savage beaks peck and tear at the backs of his hands as they retaliated. The little girl held her hands tightly closed over her face, either in an instinctive reaction of self-protection or because she did not want to see the horror of what was happening. The puppy, cringing and whimpering with fear and bewilderment, was already bleeding from half a dozen deep wounds where the slashing beaks of the big gulls had torn into its back and sides.

Abruptly, they were gone, wheeling away into the sky again with strident calls of danger. Grossman held the child in his arms, speaking softly. 'It's all right. Everything's all right now. They've gone. The nasty birds are gone.'

The child dropped her hands, peering up at him through tear-filled eyes. Sobbing, she looked down at her injured puppy, shaking her blonde head in bewilderment. 'They wanted to eat Footle,' she muttered, accusingly. 'They wanted to eat her up for dinner.'

Grossman stooped to pick up the puppy, running his fingertips gently over its furry body. It would be all right. The cuts were not deep, and the bleeding would soon stop.

He held the puppy out in his arms. 'She'll be fine,' he assured the child. 'But I guess we'd better take her to a doctor, eh?'

The child nodded gratefully. 'Thank you. You're a nice man.'

Grossman smiled. 'Thanks. And you're a very pretty little girl. What's your name?'

'Samantha,' the child announced proudly.

'And where do you live, Samantha?'

She gestured to a row of houses bordering the far side of the park. 'Over there.'

'Fine.' Grossman nodded. He began to walk slowly. 'We'd better get you home to your mummy and daddy before I take your doggie to the animal doctor, O.K.?'

'O.K.,' the child murmured trustingly, falling into step behind him.

As they neared the house, a woman rushed out from the front gate, shouting loudly in a tone which betrayed both fear and anger. 'Samantha! How many times have I told you not to talk to strange men.'

She pushed past Grossman with a glare of mistrust, gathering the child up in her arms. Samantha broke into a babble of explanation, aware in her childish way that her benefactor was being wrongly accused. 'The nasty seagulls tried to eat me and Footle for their dinner, and the nice man rescued us,' she announced. 'He's going to take Footle to the dog doctor.'

Her mother looked up at Grossman, puzzlement in her eyes. He smiled reassuringly. 'A flock of birds attacked the puppy,' he murmured quietly. 'I drove them off, that's all.'

For the first time, the woman noticed the bleeding puppy. She looked at Grossman again, also noticing that his hands were bleeding slightly. She became immediately concerned. 'You're hurt,' she said gently. 'You'd better come into the house and let me clean up those scratches.'

Grossman nodded in agreement. The beaks of seagulls were not the most sanitary things to have piercing the skin. 'A little disinfectant would be a safe precaution,' he muttered. He followed the woman into the house.

After swabbing and lightly bandaging Grossman's hands, the woman ushered him into the lounge. 'I'm sure my husband will want to thank you,' she said, having gained the full story from Grossman, with a few garrulous interruptions from her daughter.

Grossman shrugged. 'It was nothing.'

'No . . . please,' the woman tugged gently at his sleeve. With another faint shrug, Grossman followed her into the room.

Her husband rose from his easy chair as she explained what had happened. He held out a hand to Grossman. 'You certainly have my thanks and gratitude, Mr . . . ?'

'Doctor,' Grossman corrected gently. 'Doctor Heinz Grossman.'

'Clive Frazer,' the man responded, shaking his hand firmly. 'My wife, Dorothy, and Samantha I think you've already met.'

Grossman grinned. 'I sure have. She's a beautiful child.'

Frazer nodded with the embarrassed pride of a parent. He glanced back at Grossman. 'Canadian?'

'American,' Grossman said.

'You over here for the conference?'

Grossman nodded. 'I'm a biologist. Marine life is my speciality.' He suddenly remembered the dog. 'Look, I really think you ought to take that pup down to the nearest vet. The cuts aren't deep, but seagulls are scavengers, and they can carry some nasty germs.'

Frazer nodded. 'Yes, you're right. There's a surgery not far from here. I'll go now.'

'I'll stroll down with you,' Grossman said. 'I'd like to find out if there have been any other attacks like this.'

Frazer shook his head as he pulled on his shoes. 'Not attacks as such, as far as I know. But the gulls have been a particular nuisance lately – raiding dustbins, flocking around the rubbish tips and that sort of thing.'

Grossman nodded absently. 'Yeah, it figures,' he mumbled under his breath. He moved to the door as Frazer put on his jacket. He waited for Frazer to pick up the puppy then followed him out of the house. The two men strode briskly down the road towards the veterinary surgery.

'I'm sorry, but the vet is terribly busy right now. It'll be at least three-quarters of an hour.' The receptionist smiled apologetically, nodding at the puppy. 'If you like to leave it here and come back later, I'll look after it for you.'

Frazer thought for a moment, turning to Grossman. 'Look, that's not a bad idea. There's a pub across the road. I reckon the least I can do is buy you a drink to show my gratitude.'

'It's not necessary.'

Frazer grinned. 'I know that, but it's a damned good excuse for a drink, anyway.'

Grossman also smiled, responding to the man's infectious good humour. He was warming to Frazer quickly. 'Yes, I'd like that,' he said, simply.

'Good.' Frazer clapped him on the back. 'I'd welcome the chance to chat with you, anyway. It's not every day I get to meet an American biologist. Hopefully, I might learn something.'

'That's important to you? Learning something?' Grossman asked.

Frazer led the way out, pausing on the pavement before crossing the street. 'Of course. Shouldn't it be to everybody?'

Grossman smiled. 'Well, yes. It's just most people don't see things that way. The urge to learn is a dying one, I fear.'

'Don't I know it,' Frazer said emphatically. 'I battle every day with minds gradually sinking into a state of atrophy.'

They crossed the street and entered the pub. Walking up to the bar, Frazer ordered a beer for himself and turned to Grossman. 'What's yours?'

'I'll try an English pint. I'm told it's very good.'

'Not as good as it used to be, I'm afraid,' Frazer said with a touch of nostalgia. He ordered another pint of Double Diamond and motioned to an empty table. 'Want to sit down?'

'Sure.' Frazer led the way to the table, and the two men sat down, sipping their beers.

After a while, Grossman said: 'What did you mean just now, about minds sinking into atrophy? You a teacher?'

'Lecturer,' Frazer said. 'Languages, but my particular field is semantics. Not something there's a great call for any more. The whole world is becoming totally dependent on visual images rather than the spoken or written word.' He broke off to sip at his pint. When he looked up again, there was a serious frown creasing his forehead. 'This seagull business, it's all part of the same thing, of course?'

'You mean the fish business? Yes, it is,' Grossman agreed, following Frazer's drift at once. 'They're starving too – no fish to catch near the surface, no scraps left behind by fishing boats or around the harbours. They have to come inland to find other sources of food wherever they can. It could get a lot worse, I'm afraid. Gulls are a very voracious species. They'll eat several times their own weight a day, given the chance.'

'Have you formed any theories yet?' Frazer asked, casually.

Grossman shook his head. 'It's too soon for me. I haven't even sorted out all the data yet,' he admitted. 'How about you?'

Frazer looked rather embarrassed. He regarded Grossman

with a curious stare for several seconds. Finally he spoke, in a rather distant tone. 'Are you a religious man, Dr Grossman?'

Grossman was guarded. 'I'm a scientist. Science is a demanding mistress. She doesn't leave a lot of time over for theological speculation.'

Frazer shook his head. 'No, don't get me wrong,' he said hastily. 'I'm not talking about Jehovah, Buddha, Mohammed – a wise old grey-haired gentleman in the sky. Not any of the pretentious man-made images of God. I mean religion as an abstract, but nevertheless pure, concept. Surely, as a biologist, you must accept that this world runs to some kind of order, under some form of intelligent control?'

Grossman thought carefully before answering. 'If you mean do I believe in the balance of nature, then the answer is yes. If you're asking if I consider it to be a free-thinking intelligence form, then I can't really answer.'

Frazer smiled. 'You're copping out,' he accused, gently.

Grossman laughed, beginning to enjoy the discussion. 'No, I'm not,' he countered. 'All I'm saying is that it is far too easy to confuse natural phenomena with conscious action, and animal instinct with intelligence.'

'All right . . . take those seagulls,' Frazer said in a quiet voice. 'It's surely not instinctive in the species to attack animals. Yet, deprived of their normal food supplies, those birds somehow managed to figure out that a supper of fresh puppy would suffice. Doesn't that suggest at least a faint intelligence, an ability to make a definite decision?'

Grossman fell silent, sipping at his beer thoughtfully. It was some time before he spoke again. 'Just exactly what are you hinting at?'

Frazer had lost his embarrassment now and was well launched into his argument. The fact that Grossman wasn't a rigid sceptic encouraged him. His face brightened. 'Look, if you deliberately and systematically illtreat an animal, almost any animal, sooner or later it's going to fight back, or at least defend itself, right?'

'Agreed,' Grossman muttered.

'O.K., so we, and when I say we I mean man in general, have been mistreating marine life for years now. We've poisoned and polluted their environment, we have massacred whole species to the point of extinction and radically interfered with the natural ecology in a hundred different ways. Do you accept that?'

Grossman nodded.

'So accept that nature is fighting back,' Frazer said with disarming simplicity. 'You mentioned the balance of nature yourself – that's exactly what it's doing right now, balancing things up, tipping the scales back in favour of the normal order of things.'

Grossman grunted thoughtfully. 'But you're saying a lot more than that, aren't you?' he asked, penetratingly. 'What you are really suggesting is that fish in general are acting in a deliberate, and therefore intelligent, manner?'

'Am I?' Frazer asked, grinning. 'Or have you just followed this argument through to that conclusion yourself?' He stood up, draining his glass. 'Want another one?'

Grossman pushed himself to his feet, reaching for his wallet. 'No, let me get these.'

'Nonsense.' Frazer laid his hand upon Grossman's shoulder, pushing him gently but firmly back into his seat. 'I owe you for my daughter's happiness, perhaps even her eyesight. Those gulls could have gone for her eyes if you hadn't dived in.'

'Oh, I don't really think so,' Grossman murmured.

Frazer glanced down, his face grim. 'Don't you?' he asked, in an icy voice. 'Birds take food where they can find it. Can you really imagine them sitting back and letting themselves become starved into extinction?' With this chilling thought he walked away to the bar.

Grossman sat back in his seat, deep in thought. Frazer's arguments had brought echoes of his own doubts to the surface, making him confront them head on. He thought back to McAllister's death, Binsley's cryptic comment: 'Fish . . . with direction, a sense of purpose.' It had cropped up again, that nagging, niggling suspicion buried deep in his mind. Maybe a sense of purpose was overstating things. But some driving force, perhaps, giving direction to their behaviour? The balance of nature . . . doing with man what she did, impassionately, with every other species, keeping them in check, manipulating the ecology to maintain the status quo. What made his worries even more acute was that an educated, intelligent man had seriously voiced such an argument. Not a wild-eyed crank or a fanciful idiot, but an apparently rational, sane man like Clive Frazer.

He was still frowning when Frazer returned with the fresh drinks and set them down on the table.

'I see I've managed to give you some food for thought,'

Frazer observed, smiling with a sense of satisfaction.

'Yes, you have,' Grossman murmured. He paused for a few seconds. 'Do you believe in the possibility of telepathy, Mr Frazer?'

The man laughed explosively. 'Ah, now you're going beyond me. That's really into the realms of fantasy – sheer rubbish.' He broke off suddenly, realising how he had blundered into a verbal trap in exactly the same way Grossman had. He grinned sheepishly. 'Point taken,' he murmured. 'We all have our blind spots.' He leaned over the table, impulsively. 'Listen, Dr Grossman – I'd really like it if you could come home and have supper with us. It would be nice to chat some more; I think we could become friends.'

'Heinz,' Grossman suggested gently. 'Yes, I think so too. I'd love to accept your invitation, if you're sure it would be no trouble for your wife.'

Frazer shook his head. 'She'd love to have you,' he assured Grossman. He sat back, smiling contentedly. 'Good. That's settled then.'

Chapter Sixteen

The next few days of the International Conference produced little except further evidence that International Conferences invariably produce nothing. Time and time again, Grossman found himself shaking his head in total bewilderment and frustration as it became increasingly obvious that his fellow delegates seemed absolutely incapable of even conceiving the problem in global terms, let alone making any concerted effort to deal with it. There were far too many vested private interests, too much nationalistic posturing, too many fears and prejudices.

Delegates from the smaller nations felt helpless and under-privileged, jealous of the technological resources of the major powers. Time-consuming motions of censure, points of order and petty wrangles constantly interrupted the discussions, breaking up any continuity of dialogue which might, conceivably, have led somewhere. The leading world powers were hamstrung by their own security fears. No one present doubted that the Russian delegates were being less than frank about their own research data, for the scientist delegates were effectively gagged by the presence of K.G.B. agents who had been infiltrated into their midst. The American delegation were equally wary about pooling information, and Grossman suspected at least two of his countrymen of being directly answerable to the C.I.A. As hosts to the conference, the British were fiercely and openly protecting their own interests, and their territorial rows with Iceland and Norway were rarely out of the arguments.

Theories and speculations continued to abound, each new idea triggering off a pointless or time-wasting new research project, or heated arguments between dissenting factions. A general re-mapping of the earth's magnetic force lines was born out of the theory that the world had shifted slightly on its axis, causing a change in the Gulf Stream and disruption of migratory routes. Observatories all over the world were ordered to recalculate lunar cycles, just in case the moon was causing tidal changes.

By the end of the fourth day, Grossman was thoroughly depressed – a fact which he openly confided to Clive Frazer. Their evening drink had become a regular habit, and their friendship had already become firmly established.

Frazer smiled understandingly as Grossman gave him a brief rundown on the petty squabbles of the day. 'Sounds like the fish have got a better organised policy,' he observed drily. 'At least they're consistent.' The gentle jibe evoked nothing more than a moody grunt from his companion.

'Surely to God, you'd imagine that a gathering of such learned and intelligent men would be able to come to some integrated decision, start taking some sort of positive action?' Grossman asked, after a couple more beers.

Frazer shrugged philosophically. 'Maybe you ought to be thankful they aren't taking any action,' he said, strangely. 'Have you seen what some of the local authorities are up to?'

'No,' Grossman admitted. He had been so completely tied up with the conference that he had tended to neglect the news over the past days.

Frazer pulled a daily newspaper from his pocket, indicating several passages, 'Just look at this,' he muttered. 'This blocked sewage problem has spread to over a dozen coastal towns now, and some of them are really under siege from the seagulls.

And what are the authorities doing? They're tipping Christ knows how many gallons of acid down the public drains, and dumping poisoned garbage out for the birds. Some action, eh? We don't even seem to have as much sense as the birds themselves. Poison, corrosive chemicals? Jesus Christ, even a bloody bird has the basic common sense not to shit in its own nest.'

Grossman sighed heavily, glancing at the accusing paragraphs. 'Funny you should mention it,' he murmured. 'Somebody suggested something like that at the conference today – large-scale dumping of poisonous chemicals into the oceans, to stun or kill the fish so that they would float to the surface where they could be scooped up.'

'You're joking.' Clive Frazer looked utterly shocked.

Grossman shook his head grimly. 'I wish I was,' he said. 'One of my illustrious countrymen even maintained that we have the right chemical to do the job – a cute little nerve gas called PCDD 24. Something our humanitarian scientists dreamed up for use in Vietnam, the general consensus of opinion being that it was slightly more sporting to paralyse your enemy's central nervous system than blow the top of his head off with a machine-gun or burn him to death with napalm.'

'They wouldn't dare,' Frazer breathed in awe. 'Anyway, what the hell use are poisoned fish?'

Grossman shrugged. 'They have a bright theory about that as well, of course. A couple of biochemists at Princeton reckon that it might be possible to process the fish in such a way that any harmful residue in their bodies is neutralized, thus rendering the protein fit for human consumption.'

'Wow!' Frazer gulped at his pint. 'Let's hope that little idea ends up at the very bottom of some bureaucratic waste-paper basket.'

Grossman sucked at his teeth. 'I have a sneaking suspicion that it has already gone past the pure theory stage,' he murmured. 'There's a strong rumour about that they have already started carrying out limited field tests.'

As he finished speaking, Grossman drained his pint. Frazer looked across at him with sudden concern, aware that his companion was drinking more than usual. 'Listen, Heinz, are you sure you ought to be telling me all this?' he murmured quietly. 'You know – security, secret information and all that?'

Grossman looked at him, a mischievous twinkle in his eyes. 'Damn security,' he muttered vehemently. 'I happen to think it's about bloody time the man in the street started knowing about the sort of damned thing that goes on around him all the time.' Grossman leaned over the table, clapping his hand on Frazer's shoulder. 'And you, my good friend, are a man in the street, so I'm telling you.'

Clive Frazer looked awkward and embarrassed. 'Well, a man in the pub, at least,' he said, trying to turn it into a joke.

Grossman smiled. 'Yes, of course. Fancy another drink? I'm going to have a double Scotch. Tonight, I intend to get rotten stinking drunk.'

Despite his suspicions, Grossman was still stunned two days later when a jubilant colleague announced proudly to the entire conference that the initial tests with PCDD 24 had been a resounding success. In a rare gesture of international bonhomie, the formula was even going to be made available to the Russians, so that they could conduct their own experiments in home waters.

It was the first real sign of international co-operation. To Grossman, it was the first faltering step away from stupidity and on to the path of total and utter insanity.

He got drunk again that evening.

Chapter Seventeen

Cuvi the sabre-tooth shark glided through the light water, circling aimlessly in search of a single remaining sign of life. There was none. Beneath him, the entire coral city was dead — a total eco-system virtually wiped out overnight.

Where once the delicate waving tentacles of the sea anemones had spread out like the petals of beautiful coloured flowers, now only collapsed, shapeless jelly-like lumps remained, already rotting with decay. The coral itself was dead, and would soon crumble away into fine debris to be dispersed by the underwater currents. The sea-fans and coloured weeds were dark and limp, their roots exposed like torn, shredded nerve endings. The fish — those who had survived the initial onslaught — were long gone, for their very survival depended on the constant living balance of the coral city which fed them, housed them and gave a focal point to their existence. It was a system which could only be maintained under perfect conditions of clean, fresh, life-filled water. The slightest trace of pollution was the kiss of death to the whole chain.

The poisonous chemicals had dispersed now, absorbed into the surrounding waters and diluted to a comparatively harmless level. Like a terrible, silent plague, they had risen up from the depths of dark water, bringing instant annihilation with them.

This then was the death of which Nah-Ep had spoken, the pointless, evil heritage which man wore like a black mantle. Recognising it for the first time, Cuvi felt a strange feeling surge inside him, triggering off a lust which even the greatest time of hunger could not match. Hate, and the terrible yearning for revenge, drove him away from the decimated coral reef towards the places of broken water where he knew the great dry-creature could be found.

Poda the octopus unfolded her arms quickly, causing swirling eddies in the water around her. They plucked at the thick clutch of eggs she had been jealously enfolding against her body, sweeping them away into the black water.

She let them drift away, knowing that she was losing nothing which had not already been stolen from her. The eggs would never hatch now – some deep maternal instinct told her that they had been dead from the moment the strange sleeping water had washed over her, blanking out her mind.

Poda did not question her own survival. She noticed only that the waters around her were strangely still, bereft of life. Only her tight purchase upon a rocky crevice had kept her in place while the other fish had floated up like ghosts all around her, white and silver bellies upturned towards the places of light water which claimed their bodies.

Still groggy, Poda spread her tentacles, gathering them together again awkwardly as she called on reserves of strength to expel water through her body, jetting away in search of fresh water and the reassurance that life still existed in the liquid world. As she fled the place of death, she knew it to be the work of the great dry-creature. With every fibre of her being, she ached to release the strange heat which burned within the icy coldness of her sorrow.

Quench the crayfish had also felt the touch of death, but his tough, armoured body had afforded him some degree of protection against the terrible burning waters which poured from the dry lands into the places of broken water.

The outpourings of corrosive acid had all but stopped now, as the last, most persistent growths of weed in the sewerage systems shrivelled and dropped away. Even so, the effects upon the tidal dry lands had been disastrous. Entire colonies of shellfish had been wiped out, rock pools along the shore had become fuming hell-holes of death, pouring forth the stench of dead and rotting matter – both fish and vegetable. The turning tides did little to bring even a vague hope of replenished life.

Now Quench saw yet another horror. With each gentle wave breaking upon the shore, more death from the liquid world was deposited upon the dry lands. Out in the places of dark water, the great dry-creature was using another weapon of destruction, detonating huge caches of explosive deep beneath the waves to kill fish in their millions. Man could never hope to harvest even a third of those he slaughtered. With the incoming tides and shoreward currents, the surface of the water became thick with the mutilated carcasses of marine creatures, spewing them up on to the beaches where they piled upon each other and began to decompose in the heat of the sun.

Bristling with fury, Quench gathered all his powers as an Elder, relaying a thought-message into the shallow waters around him. It would travel on every ripple, spread with each tide, radiate out around the tidal dry lands of every country and every continent until the living knew that they had to avenge the dead.

In all the liquid world the call was essentially the same: the great dry-creature had surpassed himself in his savagery and had now to feel the wrath of Nah-Ep as he had once before. A state of war existed between the liquid world and the dry lands – a war which was totally uncompromising, rooted in cosmic survival itself.

Earth would survive – with either or both her two worlds. The most basic of natural laws, locked in the very fabric of all matter, insisted that it should be so.

Like all natural laws, it swung into operation smoothly, automatically and with infinite power. Even Nah-Ep could not have resisted it, and in his great wisdom he did not try. He watched, dispassionately, as his ocean kingdom erupted into blind, instinctive action.

There could be no more warnings, no more sanctions to

be imposed upon the great dry-creature. The Elders of the liquid world had seen the death and destruction in the very heart of their domain, and their inestimable sadness flowed throughout all the waters like a disease, infecting everything which lived there. After the sadness came despair, the terrible knowledge of frustration and an overpowering, all-consuming dread. So much fear, so much concentrated negative energy had only one natural release. After sorrow, after desperation, came anger – an intense, seething, self-generating anger which was almost a collective madness.

Even the most naturally aggressive species of the liquid world could not fully understand the fury which gripped and guided them. There was only the deep inner conviction that there was no alternative way, other than to lie back and wait for annihilation. The great dry-creature was nothing more than a brute, insensitive force, without the saving grace of a collective intelligence. It was bent on destruction, of itself and everything around it. Now out of control, that force could only be stopped by another of equal or superior strength.

Around the globe, in every ocean and sea, every harbour and estuary, the creatures of the liquid world arose to repay death with death, to exterminate the great dry-creature and release the earth from his destructive grip.

Man would know the absolute anger and power of the sea. He would be confronted, and ultimately beaten, by the very forces of nature which he had so arrogantly sought to control throughout his puny existence. As a species, he had reached the point at which he was no longer a viable proposition or a tolerable hazard. Like the mighty dinosaur which had preceded him, man now threatened the balance of the environment. He could be as summarily dismissed from existence, for no single species really mattered. They were the experiments of a capricious, ever-inventive creation. Inevitably, there were mistakes, evolutionary failures. They had always been hastily scrapped in the past. Nature, if lacking any real sense of humour, was at least perfectly tidy.

And man, after all, was a very young and very recent experiment. The sea remained the womb of life, the original drawing-board of creation. If nature had any maternal instincts, they surely lay there.

Chapter Eighteen

Kraka's huge body and flailing tentacles boiled over the surface of a calm sea like an underwater eruption from the depths. Surfacing a few yards from the side of the small ship, he fixed unblinking eyes upon it with a cold contempt. It was such puny prey, almost unworthy of his attention, but it was the only target in the immediate vicinity, and it would suffice – for the present.

The 38-foot Bermudan sloop *Dolores* bobbed violently on the turbulence caused by the sudden surfacing of the giant squid. Its captain, engrossed with his sharp fishing line, glanced nervously over his shoulder as the vessel shuddered and keeled over on to one side. The scream of terror which rose to his lips was stifled abruptly as the tip of one mighty tentacle coiled around his throat, the deadly barbed suckers tearing lumps of flesh away from the underside of his soft, flabby jowls. As the sloop rolled back into the trough of a wave, his plump body was plucked out of its seat and waved in the air like a tiny rag doll. Kraka flicked the tentacle like a cracking whip, breaking the man's neck without effort and flinging his limp torso clear across the sloop's deck and into the sea with one smooth movement.

Kraka's two long front tentacles snaked up into the rigging, tearing the flimsy sail away from the mast and bringing spars and ropes crashing down on to the deck. Coiling around the stripped mast, they began to pull the vessel over on to its side, where Kraka could enfold the fibreglass hull in the vice-like embrace of his remaining eight arms.

The stricken vessel began to ship water through the open hatchway, flooding the inner cabins. As the sloop became heavier in the water, Kraka eased his bulky body down into the depths, dragging his prey with him. Slowly but surely the giant squid pulled the sloop beneath the surface of the sea.

It was all over in a few bubbling, frothing moments. Kraka released his hold upon the sunken craft, watching it fall away beneath him, plunging into the inky depths below. He paid scant attention to the three pathetic little figures that struggled briefly in the water and then became still. He allowed the dry-creatures to float away, knowing that they were dead and having no further interest in them. They were not a food he wanted to ingest. Some other scavengers of the sea could have them, to suck and tear their flabby white flesh from their ridiculous and ungainly inner bones. Perhaps the barracuda might care to sharpen their razor-like teeth upon the skeletons, once they had been picked clean. Some fiddler crabs might like to make a juicy feast out of their eyeballs. Perhaps the bodies would just bloat with water and sink to the bottom, gradually rotting into the living debris which fed those creatures at the very fringe of the life-chain. Whatever happened, the dry-creatures would now serve to sustain the liquid world in some way, rather than continue to destroy it.

Satisfied with this thought, Kraka propelled himself through the water in search of a larger and more demanding kill.

Lasar the great white shark smashed his way through the flimsy net which was supposed to keep him and his kind clear of the Californian beaches. Through the gaping hole, he led a mixed pack of killers towards the resort centre of Santa Monica, flattening himself against the seabed so that his tell-tale fin would not show above the surface and serve as a warning.

It was a planned, cold-blooded attack. Hammerheads, nurse sharks, tiger sharks and even the odd large barracuda were heading in towards the beach with the express purpose of killing and maiming as many bathers and surfers as possible. There would be plenty of targets. It was a Saturday, and the resort was jam-packed with weekend trippers.

Lasar reached the shallows unnoticed. The water was no more than eight feet deep – usually crystal clear, but today a heavy swell broke the surface, masking the incoming sharks from the eyes of swimmers and people on the beach. A dark shadow passed over him. Lasar turned in the water, tilting his head to peer upwards to the surface. A small two-seater paddling raft was just passing over him, bearing two small spawn of the great dry-creature.

Lasar threshed his tail, surging up through the water towards it. His solid bulk smashed against the underside of the frail raft, splitting its twin hulls and throwing the two boys into the sea. As they splashed into the water with shrill cries of alarm, two hammerheads set upon them at once, seizing flailing arms and legs between their savage teeth, grinding through bone and muscle.

Lasar swam on, disregarding the carnage behind him. Only the strong smell of fresh blood tickled his senses as the two hammerheads played a savage game of tug-of-war with one of the children, finally declaring a draw when they each tore off a leg and ploughed apart from each other, leaving trails of blood hanging like dark red smoke in the water.

Lasar was in the thick of the swimmers now, in less than five feet of water. Already, panic had descended upon the bathers, and Lasar could see the surface being churned into foam as dozens of dry-creatures struggled to reach the safety of the beach. With powerful flicks of his tail, Lasar darted amongst them, his great jaws opening and snapping shut time after time, severing arms and legs from bodies, tearing huge soft chunks of flesh from plump bellies to release streaming entrails into the water like a knot of writhing crimson snakes.

The water was dark with blood now – a misty, opaque redness through which Lasar found it almost impossible to see each new target. It hardly mattered, for he was fully immersed in the frenzy of blood-lust and instinct guided each clash of his huge jaws, which invariably closed on a piece of prey. Some pieces of flesh he swallowed whole, others he spat aside in case the action of eating should stop him tearing another limb from its owner. In an orgy of destruction, Lasar threshed the water behind him, leaving a grisly trail of dismembered bodies, severed arms and discarded chunks of bleeding flesh.

The killing went on until there were no more living targets to attack. For a few minutes more, the other sharks toyed with the human debris littering the water, shaking them from side to side in their savage jaws as if trying to shake new life, and new sport, into them.

Slowly, Lasar's frenzy subsided. He slowed to a graceful glide. Then, with one powerful thrust of his tail, he propelled his huge body up through the water and into the air, displaying himself to the survivors on the beach. As he splashed down into the water again, he turned back towards the open sea, leading the killer pack away. There were many hundreds of such beaches in his vast territory. The day was only just beginning. The pack would pick up other members on the way, and lead them to fresh arenas of sport.

Behind them they left a horrified, numbed crowd, a huge circular red patch floating upon the surface of the water, the golden sands gradually becoming stained with pink. The waves continued to lap gently on the shore, one of them bringing with it the first severed human foot, which lay grotesquely upright like an abandoned shoe on the sands.

Off the coast of Japan three fishermen whooped aloud with delight as they strained to haul in their heavy net. Their weeks of patience had paid off at last, as they had known it must. Although others had long since given up even attempting to fish, these three had kept faith with the sea, respecting her strange ways and trusting her to deliver up her riches again when she felt like it.

Now, they felt like naughty children who had been punished and forgiven. Their net was full again, after so many long and hungry days. The excitement and relief lent new strength to their arms and backs as they pulled the bulging net up the side of the small boat and on to the deck.

Cries of joy quickly changed to screams of fright and disbelief as the net discharged its squirming contents at their feet. The mass of writhing tentacles spread out across the wet, slippery wooden deck boards like flowing oil.

There was not a single squid in the net! The creatures now slithering across the deck were small, but deadly, blue-ringed octopuses – hundreds upon hundreds of them. The three fishermen turned to run as the glistening, jewel-like creatures flowed across the deck towards their sandalled feet. Each of the fishermen had seen the creatures before, although never in such massed numbers. A single specimen could deliver a poison sting which would cause almost intolerable pain. A severe sting could bring unconsciousness, even several days of comatose sleep.

Too late, each fisherman realised that his initial surprise had cost precious time. Even as they lifted their feet to sprint away from the danger, the slithering mass washed over their sandals, the sucking tentacles of the small creatures clamping on to their bare ankles like limpets. The initial pain from a half-dozen stings seemed nothing compared to the fiery agony which surged up their legs as the venom flowed into their bloodstreams. The men collapsed, writhing in pain upon the wet deck as more of the terrible creatures swarmed on to their bodies, on to their necks and faces, stinging as fast as they could clamp themselves in position.

Leaving three twitching, barely conscious men dying upon their drifting boat, Bluey crawled back across the deck, leading his avenging pack to the edge of the boat and dropping off into the water with a faint plop.

By the time the last octopus had plunged back into its home environment, the three fishermen were dead. Their contorted bodies lay still now, six sightless eyes pointed up into the sky, where a flock of scavenging gannets had begun to wheel, slowly, above the silent vessel.

The birds began to drop, squawking excitedly. Their vicious beaks chattered as they homed in upon the tempting titbits that a generous nature had seen fit to drop in their way.

The sound of the band playing in the ballroom on 'A' deck drifted up to the bridge of the S.S. *Fiesta*. They were playing much louder than usual, strictly on Captain Milton's orders. The sound of music helped to drown out the insistent moaning of the foghorn; a sense of gaiety would prevent the passengers from becoming too alarmed about the increasing roll of the cruise liner, and also prevent them from realising that the ship was helpless, out of control, and in deadly danger.

Milton gazed out into the blackness of the night and the swirling grey fog. His mind raced as he tried to cope with the facts which confronted him. It was unthinkable that a ship carrying six hundred passengers should be waiting to die, yet only a miracle could save them.

It was nearly half an hour since the first 'Mayday' call had gone out. Even under ideal conditions, the nearest rescue vessel would take two hours to reach the *Fiesta*. In the fog, without navigational lights and in the teeth of a force 10 gale, that figure might easily be tripled. The *Fiesta* could not hold out that long.

Milton tried desperately to understand, and failed. So many weird, improbable coincidences, all coming together as though they were planned. All the navigation lights and buoys had gone, swallowed up by the sea. Captain Milton could not possibly know that every marker in every shipping lane, every warning beacon above every wreck, every reef and sandbar all over the world had suffered the same fate. Millions upon millions of small crustaceans had piled up on them, building themselves up in layer upon layer until sheer weight dragged the floating buoys beneath the surface of the waves.

In dangerous waters, with the storm about to break, the *Fiesta* had been making only a quarter speed when the collision occurred. Something had struck the screws and rudders hard — hard enough to put them out of action. Milton had assumed a submerged reef, or perhaps an uncharted wreck. In the fog, no one had noticed the smashed bodies of the two right whales who had sacrificed themselves to cripple the ship.

Both port stabilisers were also out of action. Helpless, the huge liner wallowed in forty-foot waves, drifting at their mercy towards a known danger area where jagged reefs could rip the bottom out of the vessel within minutes.

There was no escaping the unthinkable but incontrovertible fact. The *Fiesta* waited to die all right; there was no hope of salvation. Milton struggled with his conscience, aware that he ought to be thinking of his ship and its six hundred passengers, and feeling guilty because he was thinking of his wife and children instead.

Chief Engineer Branson took a last look at the oil rig as the rescue chopper lifted off, climbing up and away from the abandoned hulk. Six million quid's worth of hardware and technology, and creatures no larger than his little finger had rendered it useless. It was crazy!

Even if the rig had held out, it was doubtful if the men would have been able to go on much longer. Two weeks of living under a virtual state of siege had sapped their nerves. The quiet yet relentless fear of death had not let up for a moment, driving them all to the verge of hysteria. In a few more days the men would have been at each others' throats.

It had taken three terrible deaths before the remaining divers flatly refused to go over the side any more. The perils of going too deep, coming up too fast, or of equipment failure were the accepted hazards of their jobs, the reasons they were so well paid. Sharks, manta rays and deadly sea-wasps were not. There was no money in the world which could tempt a man to flirt with a death like that.

So all normal maintenance work had ceased abruptly. The rig became a tiny island in the middle of a vast, alien ocean, cut off from the outside world. Its population of thirty-eight men was at the mercy of the sea and the elements — and both seemed to be conspiring to destroy them. An infestation of sea-lice had moved in, the tiny but amazingly strong creatures eating their way into solid steel as if it were rotten wood. The bracing cables, the main pylons, the decking supports – anything below the surface of the water became a target for the voracious, destructive little pests.

Eight days of rough weather played upon the structural damage to turn the whole rig into a deathtrap. Another five men died horribly from being literally torn in two by snapping, whiplashing cables, or crushed as sections of deck collapsed beneath them. The rescue helicopters had come only just in time. It could only be a matter of hours now before the entire rig began to break up and sink beneath the dark waters of the North Sea.

Chapter Nineteen

It was a Saturday. The conference had broken up for the weekend to give the exhausted delegates a chance to relax a little. Grossman was looking forward to a long lie-in, possibly followed by a late lunch and a leisurely walk in the country-side. Instead, the telephone in his hotel room rang shrilly at eight in the morning. He reached out to the bedside cabinet, lifting the receiver. 'Yes?' he muttered, a little testily, into the mouthpiece.

'Dr Grossman?' The enquiring voice sounded gently apologetic. 'Sorry to disturb you, Doctor.'

The voice was vaguely familiar, but Grossman could not quite place it. 'Who is this?' he demanded.

'Dr Bell, from the Research Centre. Look, Grossman, I know we're all supposed to be having a rest, but I would like to talk to you – on a more confidential basis, if you know what I mean. Do you think you could come over here to the Centre a little later this morning?'

Grossman's irritation evaporated. His tone softened, for he had respect for Bell as a senior scientist, and the man came across as a gentle, genuine humanitarian, if a little less force-ful than he could have been. 'Yes, of course,' he answered. 'Is there anything in particular you wanted to discuss?'

'I'd rather not talk about it over the phone, if you don't

mind,' Bell said softly. 'Shall we say about nine-thirty?'

'Nine-thirty sharp,' Grossman confirmed. The line went dead with a faint click.

With a slightly puzzled frown, Grossman replaced the receiver, swung his legs over the side of the bed and walked towards the shower. He had heard Stuart Bell making his normal addresses to the conference, and had exchanged perhaps three or four polite pleasantries with him in informal company. The scientist had never before expressed any personal interest in him. Why now? Shrugging philosophically, Grossman dismissed the worry, reminding himself that he would find out soon enough. Slipping off his pyjamas, he stepped into the shower.

'Dr Grossman. I'm glad you could come.' Bell stepped forward as Grossman was ushered into his private office, extending his hand and beaming warmly.

Grossman shook his hand. 'It's an honour, sir,' he murmured politely. Englishmen of Bell's old-world, suave manner still tended to throw him a little off balance. Grossman could never quite make out how they expected to be treated.

'Tea? Or would you prefer coffee?' Bell moved to his desk, extending a finger to his intercom.

'Oh, tea would be fine,' Grossman replied, smiling. 'I've developed quite a taste for it.'

Bell fingered the switch. 'Miss Eldritch, would you bring in tea and biscuits for two, please.' He turned back to his guest. 'I expect you're wondering why I asked you to come?'

Grossman nodded. 'I am,' he said simply.

Bell gestured to a reclining leather chair. 'Please sit down, Doctor.' He waited until Grossman had settled himself comfortably before going on. 'I'm sorry if I sounded a little mysterious on the telephone,' he apologised. 'It's just that . . . well . . . we've had the security wallahs in here over the past couple of days. You know, secret service chappies and all that. It seems we are all under some additional security precautions – very strict rules about telephone conversations and things like that.' He broke off to smile. 'Bit paranoiac, some of these chaps, to be truthful. Seem to think the Russians or the Red Chinese have every telephone in England bugged or something.'

Grossman smiled back, remembering Commander Dobey and the tunnel. 'Yes, I know what you mean,' he murmured.

A light tap on the door announced the secretary bringing in the morning tea. Bell remained silent while she poured two cups, handed them out and left the room again. He sipped at his tea, eyeing Grossman over the rim of the cup. 'I hope you'll accept that anything I say to you must, of course, be in the strictest confidence?' he murmured, after a while.

'Of course.' Grossman nodded firmly.

'Good.' Bell placed his cup gently in the saucer and lowered it to his desk. He scratched the lobe of his ear somewhat nervously. 'It will not be any great revelation to you if I say that the conference has been something of a failure,' he said flatly, without apparent emotion. As Grossman opened his mouth to utter a polite denial, Bell waved his hands, gently, halting any argument. 'Seriously, Dr Grossman. We're scientists, we can afford to be frank with one another. We both know full well that the conference has achieved virtually nothing. It is going to break up in the next few days, I'm quite sure. Which brings me to my first question: what are you planning to do in the immediate future?'

Grossman thought for a few seconds. 'Well, at present, I'm seconded by my government to attend this conference,' he said, hesitantly. 'If it breaks up, I'm not quite sure of my exact position. If that obligation is then over, I'm still under a term of contract to the Ellis Corporation.'

Bell smiled gently. 'I don't think you need to worry unduly about that,' he murmured. Picking up a copy of the *Wall Street Journal* from his desk, he passed it across to Grossman. 'Sorry to have to be the one to break it to you, but it seems you're out of a job.'

Grossman took the magazine, glancing at the headlines: '*ELLIS EMPIRE CRUMBLES: Panic Selling Sets Shares Tumbling.*'

'I'm afraid your ex-employer is virtually bankrupt,' Bell went on. 'Like everything else which has any connection with maritime industry, or infringes upon the sea, his Atlantis project is the kiss of death to investors at the moment. He should have stayed in aero-space – that appears to be booming again.'

Grossman tossed the journal back on to Bell's desk. Surprisingly, he did not feel even slightly disappointed. There was even an undercurrent feeling of relief. 'Things are really getting bad, then?' he said quietly.

Bell nodded gravely. 'Worse than you might think,' he said. 'The media have been under considerable censorship for some weeks now. If the full truth leaked out there could be international panic. Civil shipping is almost at a standstill. The list of maritime disasters is appalling. Lloyds are virtually wiped out. The loss of ships and lives is already greater than the total at the end of the last war. The fish are back, but no one wants to go after them any more. Quite frankly, the whole world is landlocked.'

'Why are you telling me all this?' Grossman asked.

'I've studied your researches and your personal file very thoroughly,' Bell said. 'You're not a dogmatist . . . on the contrary, you have always displayed a very open mind, you've never been afraid to hold out, and stick to, your own theories in the face of criticism, even ridicule. Your most recent notes suggest to me that you are one of the few serious biologists in the world who are more or less ready to accept, realistically, what appears to be scientific heresy.'

Bell was being wary, skirting carefully around the central core of the matter and trying not to say anything too definite. Grossman saw through his oblique references and brought the matter out into the open.

'You mean, of course, that we have to start accepting that man and marine life are involved in a major evolutionary upheaval?' he said, throwing the words down like a challenge.

Bell smiled thinly. 'Yes, I knew I was right about you,' he mused quietly. 'Although even I am not quite ready to state the matter in quite such definite terms. I prefer to say that I feel natural forces are at work, in a way we do not quite understand at present.'

'But on a scale of intensity unprecedented in human history?' Grossman put in, pressing his point.

Bell coughed nervously, betraying a certain embarrassment. 'You're trying to put words into my mouth, Dr Grossman.'

Grossman shook his head. 'No, I'm not, Dr Bell. I'm using my own mouth to phrase the words you are thinking. That's slightly different.'

On the defensive, Bell laughed awkwardy. 'You're being pedantic,' he accused gently.

Grossman shrugged. 'Perhaps,' he conceded. 'But we are both being evasive, as well. To quote your own words of a few minutes ago, we are both scientists, we can afford to be frank with one another.' He paused for a moment. 'Well?'

Bell capitulated. His shoulders slumped slightly. He looked both ashamed and apologetic. 'Yes, of course, you're right.'

Grossman smiled faintly. 'Scientists are like children, playing with the building-blocks of matter,' he murmured quietly. 'But unlike the child, we lack a sense of wonder, an open-ended curiosity. The child learns by direct experience, without the inhibitions of preconceived ideas and limitations. Perhaps, if we made ourselves more willing to be the same, we might also learn.'

'Playing with the building-blocks of matter,' Bell repeated, savouring the words. 'I like it. A quotation?'

'A personal reflection,' Grossman muttered. 'Nothing terribly profound, I'm afraid.'

'But a sobering thought, nevertheless,' Bell said. 'Go ahead and make your point, Dr Grossman.'

'Right.' Grossman settled himself more comfortably in his chair before going on. 'Firstly, let's accept that we are facing some extreme contradictions here. Primarily, the fish appear to be acting in a definite, concerted manner which would ordinarily suggest at least a guiding intelligence, at most, free, rational thought. Now, as simple laboratory dissection will corroborate, fish do not possess brains as such. The higher marine mammals, yes; fish, most definitely no. However, we can also be equally positive that a plant has no brain either, yet there is now serious scientific evidence that most plants are able to register simple emotional responses.'

Bell broke in, interrupting. 'You're referring to Cleve Backster's experiments of the late 'sixties, of course?'

Grossman nodded. 'And all the intensive research which has gone on ever since,' he added. 'The Backster findings threw us a real curved ball. We're still trying to track it. Even the most optimistic explanation remains at a basic cellular level. On this basis alone, we can surmise that a rational brain is not absolutely necessary to gestalt, or group intelligence. No serious biologist would credit a single ant with much of a brain, yet the workings of a complete colony remain a miracle of science. Agreed?'

Bell nodded, his face serious. 'Agreed.'

Grossman spread his hands in a gesture of frustration. 'That's about as far as I can go,' he said. 'Somewhere, within that contradictory framework, I feel we must seek the answer. We are dealing with a group force, which demonstrates all the outward criteria of directive intelligence, without the slightest trace of individual participation. Now, as scientist to scientist, freed from prejudice and strictly off the record, am I close?'

Bell sighed heavily. 'Very close,' he admitted. 'You have more courage than I have, Dr Grossman. I have not dared to voice the similar thoughts which have plagued me these past few months. However, you and I are no longer lone voices whispering in the wilderness. There are others. The whisper is growing into a quiet, but ever more insistent voice.'

'So what's the pitch?' Grossman demanded.

'Pitch?' Bell's face clouded over with puzzlement at the unfamiliar term. Finally, he brightened. 'Ah yes, forgive me. I'm not too well versed in these neo-Columbian colloquialisms. The pitch, as you put it, is that the conference, in its present form, has to be disbanded. In nearly two months it has done nothing but go round in circles. What I want now is to gather a smaller number of hand-picked scientists into a concentrated study group, based right here in the Research Centre. You are one of that number, Dr Grossman. I would like you to join us.'

Bell fell silent, regarding Grossman quizzically. 'There is no pressure upon you, of course. However, should it colour your decision in any way, I have already taken steps to clear it with your government, just in case.'

Grossman didn't have to think about it for very long. Without the financial resources of the Ellis Corporation behind him, his work at the tunnel was finished. There seemed little else to rush home to, and over the past seven weeks he had developed a strange attachment to the English way of life. Above all, Bell was offering him a chance to become part of a most exalted scientific team, engaged on perhaps the most fascinating and challenging field of research ever. There really seemed to be no choice at all.

He nodded curtly. 'I'd consider it a privilege to join the team, Dr Bell,' he said, firmly.

'Splendid.' Bell seemed relieved. 'It will be a privilege to have you. I'll arrange for the necessary contractual papers to be drawn up at once. Hopefully, we can disband the conference and get down to work within the next three or four days.'

'That's a long time,' Grossman murmured. 'Have you any up-to-date data I could be studying in the meantime?'

'You're a keen man, Dr Grossman.' Bell was impressed. He glanced over his shoulder to the safe behind his desk. Looking back at Grossman, he smiled apologetically. 'I cannot let you take the material out of this building, of course.'

Grossman shrugged. 'Of course. I hadn't planned anything for this morning anyway.'

Nodding thoughtfully, Bell pushed back his chair and stood

up, bending over the safe. Opening it, he extracted a thin red folder, handing it across to Grossman. 'This should give you some food for thought,' he said. 'It's not much, but it will serve as the bare bones of the matter.'

Grossman took the folder, sitting down again to open and study it. He was engrossed in its contents for the next hour and a half.

When he had finished reading, Grossman tossed the folder back on to Bell's desk and let out a long, quiet whistle through his teeth. 'You're right, it is much worse than I had imagined,' he said grimly. 'This is all the data you've assembled so far?'

Bell shook his head sadly. 'I only wish it were, even though that's more than enough,' he murmured. 'No, that folder contains only the material we have been able to check and process in the last two weeks. There's probably three times as much material still to be sorted and categorised.'

'Good God!' Grossman looked down at the brief notes he had scribbled on a pad. He ran his eyes down the list of disasters, hardly daring to take them seriously. Over a thousand small craft known to have been attacked and scuppered by giant squid; several hundred more missing with no survivors to tell the tale. Entire fishing fleets smashed to pieces by marauding whales, crews stung to death by poisonous jellyfish and other venomous aquatic creatures. Report after report of full nets being slashed to pieces by saw-fish thousands of miles away from their home waters. Cargo ships wrecked in their hundreds, lured on to rocks and reefs by huge shoals of fish and the marine leviathans confusing the ships' sonar scanners.

All around the world, playground paradises were deserted, golden beaches empty. No one wanted to go anywhere near the sea any more. Shark attacks, mile-wide armadas of poison jelly-fish which seemed to come from nowhere – these alone had taken a terrible toll in human lives. From remote Japanese and Polynesian islands there were hair-raising rumours of octopuses and giant coconut crabs crawling out of the sea at night, making their way overland to villages and shore communities and attacking the natives as they slept. Light-ships and drilling rigs which mysteriously sank overnight with the loss of all hands; gas and oil pipelines blocked; telephone cables ripped apart. The list seemed endless.

Grossman looked up at Bell. The two men's eyes met with a shared chill of fear. 'We're under attack,' Grossman said.

Bell nodded gravely. 'And where real fear ends, superstition begins,' he added. 'It's not in that file, because it's not scientific fact, but reports of mythical sea monsters are widespread, all over the globe. You name it – from the Kraken to sirens and mermaids – they're all awake again in the human mind. It's as if we have suddenly dropped back three thousand years to primitive savages who live in fear and awe of the sea.' He inclined his head on one side. 'Contagious hallucination?'

Grossman shook his head. 'More probably just folklore,' he ventured. 'A terror of the sea has never been buried very deeply in the human psyche. All the basic phobias – fire, water, height, snakes – they're still quite real and recent fears to a comparatively helpless ape who dared to leave the safety of the trees.' He paused, briefly. 'What are the various world governments doing about it?'

'Well, I can't speak for other nations, but we are putting merchant shipping under control of the military as quickly as possible,' Bell answered candidly. 'Civilian mariners don't want to know any more. Even the Royal Navy is hearing the grumble of mutiny. At best, we can just about hope to maintain shipping at a basic survival level.'

'Long-term contingency plans?'

Bell shrugged. 'A lot of wild ideas, at present. There's talk of paroling non-violent criminals provided they will serve a quarter of their existing prison terms on board Navy-controlled vessels. A similar scheme has been suggested with regard to foreign immigrants. The basic idea, I believe, is that a one-year period of service in the merchant marine or the fishing industry will be a strict condition of entry to this country. Private industry is already recruiting mercenary forces; our public sector prefers slightly more subtle methods. The idea is also being considered by your own government, I believe, who are applying it to Mexican and Puerto Rican labour.'

'We'll be back to slavery and press-ganging before we know it,' Grossman breathed.

Bell nodded in agreement. 'Survival breeds savagery in all species,' he murmured quietly. 'Yes, it could well come to that. The veneer of our so-called civilised society is a very thin and brittle one indeed. It will not take much strain to shatter it. It can only be a matter of time before the major powers are forced to call a halt to what they will term "non-essential exports". No doubt these will include all grain and basic food supplies to the underdeveloped nations of the world. Shipping will be cut back to the very minimum to sustain economic survival. The strong nations will survive, the weak will perish.'

Grossman's voice was unsteady. 'You're saying that millions upon millions of people will die.'

Bell sighed heavily, his head drooping. 'Yes, Dr Grossman, that is exactly what I am saying, unless we can come up with some kind of a solution . . . and fast!'

Grossman fought off the feeling of despair which threatened to engulf him. Grave as the situation appeared, if there had ever been a time when hope, however desperate, was needed, then this was it. 'How many of us will there be?' he asked, quietly.

'Five,' Bell said flatly. 'You, myself, Professor Vaksilov of the U.S.S.R., Herr Graunglich of West Germany, and Dr Jossen, the noted Swedish biophysicist. You have each been chosen not only because you represent the scientific cream of your nations, you are all also individualists, not tied to dogmatic political creeds and party lines. All of you are first and foremost humanitarian scientists, with the needs of the world, not a specific country, in mind. You will have to take my word that although this research establishment is under the control of Her Majesty's Government, our work will in no way favour the government of this country or, indeed, of any political or social bloc. We will be working for mankind, Dr Grossman . . . I hope that does not sound too pretentious.'

Grossman shook his head. Under any other circumstances, such a statement could well have sounded trite, sickeningly altruistic. Try as he might, however, Grossman could detect nothing but a deep and convincing tone of humility in Bell's voice.

He extended his hand across the man's desk. 'You will have my fullest co-operation, Dr Bell,' he muttered as the two men shook hands again. 'I just hope to God we can succeed.'

A thin, ironic smile passed fleetingly across Bell's thin lips. 'Odd, isn't it?' he murmured. 'That He should still seem important to us . . . we who have dedicated our lives to disproving His very existence?'

Chapter Twenty

Delphus and Delia trembled with anticipation. Their request for a private audience with Nah-Ep had been granted at last. Despite the terrible disappointment over McAllister, despite all the waiting and doubt of the time which had passed since, the dolphins had remained quietly sure of themselves, their hopes and aspirations unabated. They carried within themselves the painful zeal of the apostle, knowing they were lone voices crying out in an alien, hostile wilderness, yet totally convinced of the truth of their mission. Now, at last, they would perhaps get a real chance to put those beliefs to the test, for Nah-Ep, in all his wisdom, must surely have the eyes to see the light of truth.

It seemed to the dolphins that all living creatures fell into two distinct and apparently irreconcilable groups. There were those whose limitations of personal belief started and ended within themselves. In conflict, they could only think of 'an eye for an eye, a tooth for a tooth'. Unfortunately, these made up the vast majority. Against the mass, there were the struggling few whose optimism conceived the evolution of life at its highest, and whose efforts took firm root in a conscious struggle to reach it. Perhaps they would never know how, or even clearly recognise their eventual goal, but they tried anyway. Nah-Ep must surely recognise and sympathise with this, for he had already transcended mortality and emerged as a god.

The two dolphins allowed themselves to be ushered into Nah-Ep's mighty presence, dropping all thought-shields so that he would know the purity and unselfishness of their motives.

After a while, the two dolphins felt waves of empathy and compassion rippling around them. The sure knowledge of Nah-Ep's understanding was like bright golden strands wrapping themselves around their bodies, sustaining and strengthening them.

Nah-Ep himself felt a renewed sense of wonder in the powers greater than himself, and a fresh new hope for the future. These searching, sensitive creatures had been created out of his wrath, yet they responded only with a love which could encompass both the liquid world and the dry lands. Such devotion, however naïve, deserved reward. Hope the dolphins already had; Nah-Ep need not give them more than that. But power he could give them, new strength to sustain them upon their lonely journey and help crown their desperate effort with success.

Their bodies throbbing with the strange new sense of destiny, the two dolphins swam upwards towards the place of light water to bathe for a while in the clear light and gentle warmth of the sun. They would rest, concentrating their newly-given powers before putting their plan to work. When they were ready, the others of their species would join them and share in the joy of Nah-Ep's blessing. Together, the dolphins could use his benign blessing to begin their work. Hopefully, an end to the bloodshed of the past dark months was in sight. If optimism was the essence of success, then they would succeed. It would only take the great dry-creature to play his part, match their efforts. Somewhere, there must be others like McAllister. There had to be other dry-creatures who were sensitive enough to establish contact, a rapport. Given that, the dolphins could become the living bridge between the land and the sea, on a mental as well as a physical level.

Their first efforts were daunted, for few dry-creatures now cared to venture out upon the surface of the sea. Undeterred for long, the massed dolphins headed in towards the place of broken water, congregating within clear sight of the dry land itself and concentrating their mental energies upon the creatures who lived there.

All through the remaining hours of daylight and on through the night, the dolphins kept up their lonely vigil. It seemed at times that even the powers which Nah-Ep had extended to them were being sapped needlessly, for the great dry-creatures they so desperately sought seemed to be deliberately blocking their attempts at contact. Everywhere, their thought-shields were firmly up, locked in position. Their minds were cordoned off, cocooning each dry-creature in a little world of self, which admitted nothing new.

By daybreak, the dolphins knew that they had failed. Weak and exhausted from the intense mental effort, they turned away from the dry lands and moved sluggishly back into deeper waters. The sum total of all their efforts had been a few fleeting tickles of tenuous contact with sleeping minds. In dreams, or nightmares, a scattered handful of the great dry-creatures had known the dolphins, then rejected them along with other fantasies of Morpheus.

Drained of all energy, without even their optimism left to sustain them, Delphus and Delia were morose and filled with gloom as Nah-Ep summoned them to report upon the outcome of their mission. In hesitant, apologetic thoughts, they relayed the dismal extent of their failure.

Even through their sinking consciousness, it quickly became apparent to the two dolphins that Nah-Ep did not share their dismay. This revelation came as a shock to them both, jolting them out of their state of self-pity and awakening them yet again to take in power and mental energy from Nah-Ep's shimmering aura. His penetrating flashes of thought pierced their gloom, illuminating their minds anew.

Nah-Ep had given them his blessing to go ahead, knowing that they would surely fail. This strong, paradoxical thought registered with both dolphins simultaneously, confusing them. He had allowed them to make the attempt because he wanted them to understand that it was not enough to live on hope alone. There had to be firm guidance to back up a vague ideal, a course of planned action, seen right through to its conclusion. The mind of the idealist needed the mind of wisdom.

Now, as they remained in Nah-Ep's presence, the two dolphins learned this, and many other things. His aura glowed even more brightly in the water, emitting crackling, luminescent bolts of energy which crossed the gulf of water, charging their tired minds and bodies with a new and even greater sense of determination. They had proved themselves in Nah-Ep's eyes, and now he was repaying them a dozen times over. Strange memories of far-off days crowded in upon their minds. The two dolphins felt the dry lands beneath legged bodies once again, sensed the smell of the jungle air, the feel of rain and wind against soft and delicate skins, glossy with fine hair. In a moment, millions of years fell away. The dolphin and the great dry-creature were as one again, brothers and not merely distant cousins. All that had come between the two species to part them dropped away, sloughed off like a discarded shell.

The moment of revelation passed. The dolphins returned to the consciousness of their present bodies, their place in the liquid world. It had been enough, that glimpse of knowledge. Now they fully realised how close they had been, how close they would have to be, if the great dry-creature was to be reached at all. Their vague hope had not been enough. Now that Nah-Ep had given them something of himself, and shown them the right path, there was a real chance at last. This time, they would not fail.

Chapter Twenty-One

Dorothy Frazer waited patiently outside the infant school as the children began to trickle out in twos and threes. Samantha would be one of the first to clear the gates, she always was.

Dorothy bent to scoop up her daughter as the child came bounding happily towards her. 'Hi, darling. Have a nice day?'

Samantha nodded, her blue eyes nearly popping out of her head. 'Miss was in a good mood,' she announced. 'It's always a nice day when Miss is in a good mood.'

Dorothy smiled quietly, kissed the child on the forehead and dropped her gently to the pavement, clasping her small hand.

'Are we going to the shops?' Samantha demanded.

Dorothy nodded. 'Yes, darling. I've got to buy something especially nice for tea. Uncle Heinz is coming to see us.'

Dorothy looked down as she spoke, expecting to see the child's face light up at the news. She had become very fond of Heinz Grossman, as, indeed, they all had.

She was surprised to see that Samantha accepted the information without apparent pleasure. Her small face was almost grave as she spoke again. 'Good. If we're going to the shops, you can buy me some more water-paints.'

Dorothy chided her gently. 'Now you don't need any more paints for a while, darling. You still have plenty left in that last box I bought you.'

The child shook her head defiantly. 'No. I used them all up the other day,' she said. 'I need some more . . . honest, Mummy, I do.'

Dorothy frowned, thoughtfully. Only two hours previously

she had been cleaning out her daughter's room. The box of watercolours, and three fresh brushes, had been lying in full view on top of her play-box. It was not like Samantha to forget things so easily. It was not usually in her nature to tell lies, either.

Gently, Dorothy adopted a more forceful tone. 'Now you mustn't tell fibs, Samantha. I saw your paints this afternoon. You have plenty left. You can't have forgotten about them.'

The corners of Samantha's mouth trembled as she pulled her lips into a sullen pout. 'You can't have seen them. I used them all up the other day,' she maintained, defiantly.

Dorothy stopped dead in her stride, glaring down at the child. Her voice took on a hard edge. 'Now I know you're telling fibs, Samantha, and that's very naughty.'

Caught out, the child changed her tack. With the faintest suggestion of a sob in her voice, and the first glistenings of impending tears in her eyes, she spoke again. 'Well there aren't many left. Not enough, anyway. I need some more. I've got some work I have to do.'

'Work, darling?' Dorothy didn't understand. The children never had homework – except perhaps some research or project ideas suggested as an extra-curricular activity. 'Who said you had to do work at home?'

The child became evasive. 'I just have,' she muttered sullenly, under her breath.

Sighing philosophically, Dorothy recognised the mood. Samantha was not a stubborn or badly-behaved child, but she did have a strongly determined streak in her which sometimes came to the fore. Dorothy had always put it down to her Arian horoscope. She turned to continue walking towards the car. 'All right, we'll get some more paints, if you really think you need them,' she said, giving in because it seemed the path of least resistance.

Samantha brightened immediately, her face shining with happiness. 'I'm glad Uncle Heinz is coming to tea,' she announced suddenly. 'They like Uncle Heinz.'

'They . . . who's they?' Dorothy enquired absently.

'My friends,' Samantha answered.

It did not occur to Dorothy to press the matter any further. Had she been thinking about it seriously, she would have remembered that Heinz Grossman had never met any of her school friends. Climbing into the car and buckling Samantha into the safety seat, Dorothy drove to the shopping centre, her mind on the spiralling cost of living.

'That was a superb meal, Dorothy.' Grossman rose to his feet, dabbing at the corners of his mouth with a napkin. He turned to Frazer. 'I tell you, Clive, if ever you turn your back for a moment, I'm going to whisk that wife of yours off to Uncle Sam before you can say "abduction".'

Frazer grinned good-naturedly, reaching up to clasp his wife around the waist as she cleared away the dishes from the table. 'No chance,' he said fervently, squeezing her.

Dorothy detached herself gently from his embrace, smiling at Grossman. 'Mind you, if you can get sirloin steak over there for less than £5·50 a pound, I'll come with you, willingly.'

Frazer whistled through his teeth. 'Good God. Is that what it's up to now?'

Dorothy nodded. 'The papers are hinting that it will go even higher in the next few weeks. Honestly, the price of meat at the moment is crazy.'

'Spendthrift hussy!' Frazer chided her jokingly. 'To pay for tonight's little extravagance, we'll have to eat fish fingers and beans for the next three weeks.'

Dorothy laughed. 'Believe me, I would feed you on them if I could get them,' she joked back. 'Fish has disappeared from the shops completely now. I think it's that which is jacking up the price of meat.' She walked away from the table towards the kitchen.

Frazer glanced across the table. 'Seriously, Heinz, when are you going home? Now the conference is over, there can't be much to keep you here.'

'Well, I have a few personal things to tidy up at the Research Centre,' Grossman said guardedly. He did not like lying to his friend, but he had sworn a strict oath of secrecy about his real attachment to the Centre. He grinned, turning it into a joke. 'Why, are you that anxious to get rid of me? Yanks go home, and all that?'

Frazer smiled back. 'On the contrary. We shall miss you,' he said, genuinely. He turned to his daughter. 'Shan't we, Samantha?'

The child nodded vaguely. All through dinner she had seemed unusually withdrawn, preoccupied. Now that the meal was over, she looked openly bored. 'Can I leave the table now?' she enquired politely.

'Of course, darling,' Frazer murmured. 'Something on the telly you want to watch?'

Samantha shook her blonde head. 'No, I want to go up to my room,' she announced. 'I want to do some painting.'

Frazer grimaced. 'Well, that's an encouraging sign,' he muttered. 'Maybe we have a budding artistic genius in the family. When television takes second place, I begin to see hope for the next generation.'

'Can I go, then?' Samantha displayed absolutely no sense of humour. She looked quite intense.

Frazer looked puzzled, briefly. Then his face brightened into a smile. 'Of course, darling. You run along. You have a couple of hours before bedtime.'

The child walked off without another word. After she had left the room, Dorothy walked back in to clear the remaining dishes. Frazer looked up at her, concern showing on his face. 'Is Samantha all right, darling? She's not sickening for something, is she?'

Dorothy shook her head. 'She's fine, as far as I know. Why?'

'Oh, nothing,' Frazer said, dropping it.

Dorothy replaced the plates she had just picked up. Her maternal curiosity and concern were aroused. 'Why did you ask me that, Clive?'

Frazer shrugged. 'I just thought she seemed a little out of sorts, that's all. Probably nothing to worry about. You haven't scolded her about anything today, have you?'

As his wife shook her head, Frazer turned aside to Grossman. 'How about you, Heinz? Did you notice anything unusual in her manner this evening?'

'No, not really,' Grossman muttered. 'A little quieter than usual, perhaps . . . but that's all.'

Frazer was tired of the subject, and slightly embarrassed because he had brought it up in the first place. There was nothing more ill-mannered, he thought, than playing the proud, concerned parent in front of guests. He dismissed the whole affair with a last joke. 'Oh, well, that can't be bad, can it?'

With a faint shrug, Dorothy picked up the dishes again and went back to the kitchen. The incident was forgotten. Frazer and Grossman retired to the lounge to enjoy a drink and a game of chess. After nearly an hour and a half of concentration, Grossman had only one pawn and a hopelessly trapped rook to guard his king. He reached out his forefinger, tipping the king sideways. 'I concede,' he murmured quietly. 'You're too good for me, Clive.'

'Nonsense. You weren't really trying,' Frazer accused. It was the first time he had ever beaten Grossman.

'You're being modest,' Grossman answered, but he knew it was true. He was finding it increasingly difficult to push aside the worries of the day each evening. Every morning brought fresh news of disasters, clearer indications that civilisation was being nudged, gently but insistently, back towards the dark ages. This morning alone he had sifted through no less than sixty-five reports of Loch Ness monster sightings. The madness was spreading. It was becoming impossible for people to look upon any stretch of water without succumbing to some ancient, primal fear.

What was even worse was the fact that he and his fellow scientists were rapidly coming to the conclusion that there was absolutely nothing they could do about any of it. World shipping trade was dying. Small, dependent islands like Great Britain would go under first. The larger continents would fare better for months, maybe years to come. Last of all, the self-sufficient landmasses would survive by closing ranks and jealously guarding their resources. Strife and wars would be inevitable. In the final analysis, it had to boil down to the ultimate confrontation between the two largest and most powerful nations on earth. The journey towards Armageddon was beginning. They were probably warming up the missile silos already.

Dorothy's voice broke into his reverie. 'Samantha's finally decided she'll go to bed,' she announced. 'She wants you to go up and say good night to her.'

'Sure.' Grossman rose from his chair, smiling.

Frazer started to get up as well. Dorothy shook her head. 'No, just Uncle Heinz. I have strict orders. She wouldn't even let me into her room to tuck her in.'

Frazer groaned. 'Dammit, I knew there was something funny about that kid tonight. She's in a funny mood all right.'

Dorothy smiled. 'Growing pains,' she said. 'We can both go in and kiss her good night when she's asleep. Right now, only Heinz gets that honour.'

Grossman looked across at his friend uncertainly. 'Sure you don't mind?'

Frazer laughed. 'You get used to things like this with kids.

Six months ago she refused to call either of us by anything except our first names. That lasted for two weeks. I expect this is another little fad – Sammy trying to show us how grown-up she is. You go ahead.'

'Right.' Smiling broadly, Grossman stepped out into the hall and began to walk up the stairs. The door to Samantha's bedroom was slightly ajar. He pushed it gently, stepping into the small box-room.

The tiny attic window, covered with a blue curtain, threw little light into the room. As Grossman walked in, it seemed dim, even gloomy. He looked towards the bed, picking out Samantha's blonde, curly hair draped across the pillow.

Heading across to her, Grossman suddenly stopped dead in his tracks, uncomfortably aware of many pairs of eyes staring at him. A brief, irrational shiver of fear shook him. Slowly, he turned on the balls of his feet, staring round the walls of the dimly-lit room.

Everywhere he looked, there were fresh paintings. Samantha certainly had been busy. Grossman stared at each picture in turn, feeling a strange sense of unease. There was something about the paintings which was not quite right, didn't quite tie in with the child's age, or natural artistic ability. It was not the technique so much as the subject matter, and the obvious intensity of concentration which had gone into the production of the pictures. There were at least ten of them, every one almost exactly the same! It was as if an obsessive urge had come over the child, sending her immature brain into a repetitive, blindly obedient cycle.

Every painting portrayed a dolphin. Even through the child's crude, washy watercolours something inspired shone through. The bodies of the dolphins were static, somewhat grotesque in terms of shape and proportion, but recognisable nevertheless.

It was the eyes which fascinated Grossman. They seemed to glow from each painting, looking out of place against the childish background, for they showed the undeniable quality of an advanced artistic expression.

The overall impression was quite eerie. He tiptoed over to the bed, anxious to ask the child why she had devoted her entire evening to the strange drawings.

'You've been a busy little girl,' he murmured, running his fingertips through her curls. 'Has all this painting made you too tired to say good night to Mummy and Daddy?'

Samantha didn't answer. Instead, she looked up at him with a quizzical expression. 'You're quite old, aren't you, Uncle Heinz?'

Grossman smiled. 'Oh yes, positively ancient,' he agreed. 'Why?'

'Do you remember living in a tree?' the child asked, strangely.

The question threw Grossman for a moment. Then he remembered his childhood, the woodlands just outside the small township where he grew up, and the many unsuccessful attempts to build a tree-house for his younger brother. 'Oh, you mean making a tree-house, when I was a little boy?'

Samantha shook her head. 'No, I mean when we all lived in the trees. When there weren't any houses or motorcars.'

Grossman laughed out loud, suddenly falling in. 'No, darling, I'm not quite as old as that. That was a long, long time ago. Thousands of years, millions. Nobody alive today can remember that far back.'

The child suddenly smiled secretively, inwardly happy to have caught a grown-up out, put something over on him. '*They* can remember,' she announced proudly, waving a hand at the pictures on the walls.

Grossman shook his head, still amused. 'No, sweetheart, I think you're a little mixed up,' he said gently. 'Dolphins never lived in trees.'

Samantha nodded emphatically. 'Oh yes, they did,' she said. 'We all lived together, once upon a time.'

Grossman laughed again, bending over the bed to plant a light kiss on the child's forehead. 'I think you're tired, Sammy. I guess it's time you got to sleep.'

Samantha threw her arms around his neck, hugging him tightly. 'I feel funny, Uncle Heinz,' she said in a plaintive voice.

Grossman was concerned at once. 'You mean you feel sick, sweetheart? Shall I go and fetch Mummy?'

Samantha shook her blonde head. 'No, I don't feel sick . . . I feel *funny*.'

Grossman gently detached her entwining arms and laid her small head back on the pillow. 'How do you mean, funny?' he asked.

'I don't know,' the child complained. 'Just funny, that's all. How can you be happy and sad at the same time, Uncle Heinz?'

Grossman smiled wistfully. Now he thought he understood. For a child, coming to terms with the complexities of growing and developing human emotions could be puzzling, even frightening. 'Oh, we can all feel like that sometimes. If you love somebody, love them very much indeed, you can feel very happy . . . and yet sad because you might lose them one day. Do you understand?'

Samantha's puzzled expression faded. She smiled again. 'Yes, I do now. That's how they feel.' She pointed to the pictures again. 'They keep telling me, and that's what makes me feel funny inside. I like it when they make me feel happy, but not when they make me feel sad.'

The child's eyelids began to droop heavily. Grossman wanted to question her, but she was obviously very tired. Reluctantly he straightened up and began to back away from the bed. As he reached the door, Samantha's voice whispered to him, the words slurred and heavy with encroaching sleep. 'You will help us, won't you, Uncle Heinz?'

'Sure, sweetheart, sure,' Grossman whispered back, pacifying the child without fully understanding. He looked up again at the dolphin paintings, fascinated. The more he looked, the more the strange eyes haunted him. It was almost as if the child's obsession was contagious. Finally, shaking his head in bewilderment, Grossman backed out of the room and closed the door quietly behind him.

He walked down the stairs, deep in thought. Inexplicably, he kept flashing back to McAllister, and his troubled, withdrawn state of mind after he had come back from that first dive.

'How is she?' Dorothy Frazer asked as he re-entered the lounge.

'Oh, fine,' Grossman lied. 'She's fast asleep now.' He didn't want to worry Dorothy and Clive with any details of their daughter's odd conversation, and even odder behaviour.

Chapter
Twenty-Two

Grossman walked towards town from the Research Centre, his tread heavy with fatigue and despair. His face was drawn and tense, a nervous tic displaying itself from time to time at the corner of his mouth. For the twentieth time, he pulled the evening newspaper out from under his arm and gazed at the front page through dull eyes. The headline screamed out at him with its challenging question: 'IS MAN UP FOR THE CHOP?' Luridly written and poorly researched as it was, the accompanying article got chillingly to the nitty-gritty. Everything pointed to the harsh but inescapable fact that mother nature appeared to be getting ready to phase homo sapiens quietly out of existence.

Grossman's mounting sense of anger and impotence finally got the better of him. With a savage sweep of his hand, he cast the newspaper into the gutter, gritting his teeth and kicking out at a lamp-post. A jolt of pain shot up his leg.

'Damn it, I'm beginning to crack up,' he thought, making a strong effort to pull himself together. He straightened his shoulders, drawing in a deep breath and lengthening his stride. He tried hard to search his brain for some sustaining grain of optimism, but there was nothing.

It had been one hell of a day! First of all, Professor Vaksilov had been hastily recalled to Russia by his government, serving to throw even more gloom and depression upon the remaining scientists at the Research Centre. They were all already at their lowest possible ebb, for it was increasingly obvious that their combined efforts were getting absolutely nowhere. The loss of a brilliant mind like Vaksilov's would only hamper them even more.

Later in the morning, a promising field of research into controlling fish movements by mild electrical currents had come to a dead end. The idea was feasible enough in a laboratory tank, or even in strictly localised conditions, but the computer had shown, without the faintest shadow of a doubt, that it was not commercially viable. There was no point in extending the experiment any further. The failure hit everyone hard.

To cap it all, a secretary had brought the evening newspaper into the lab around four o'clock. It had proved to be the final straw. There could be no further hope of imposing strict censorship upon the news media without lengthy government legislation. The full truth was about to burst upon the general populace like a tidal wave. In its wake, there would be mass panic, wild speculation, a wave of hysteria which would rock the world to its foundations.

Grossman strode on, his mind locked in a cage of his own fears and doubts. The only conscious thought surfacing was the desire to get to the pub where he was meeting Clive Frazer, and get a few drinks into his drained system. False as it was, the stimulus of alcohol might just make him feel vaguely human again. At the moment, he felt like a mechanical toy whose batteries had run down. He could hardly function on even a basic emotional level. His brain was numb.

He was passing the gates of a primary school. Something suddenly screamed out in the deepest recesses of his mind. Grossman stopped dead in his tracks, a sudden shock paralysing him. He stared, somewhat incredulously, down at the pavement and the images that had triggered his reaction.

For a good twenty feet on either side of the school gates the pavement was completely covered in chalked drawings of dolphins! Grossman stared at each picture in turn, a chilling feeling creeping up on him. Although the pictures had obviously been executed by older, more capable children, they were virtually identical to the paintings produced by Samantha only a couple of nights previously. There was no mistaking the similarity of the pictures, for the posture and the basic definition was identical in every case.

Even more disturbing was the haunting, hypnotic quality of the dolphins' eyes. Grossman had sensed something quite eerie about Samantha's crude daubings. These chalked pictures were a dozen times more powerful, almost sinister.

Those eyes . . . Grossman stared at the pictures again, his mind assaulted by a barrage of confused emotions. It was almost as if they had been drawn on the pavement specifically for him, for the eyes of the dolphins seemed to stare upwards to hypnotise him, command him to study them. Behind the chalk eyes lay something else – an expression, a need to convey something which could not quite be defined or stated. Behind an understanding of the expression, Grossman sensed that there was also a message of some kind, something which had to be converted from one dimension into another, so that a human mind could understand it.

Still staring, Grossman fought to capture an elusive wisp which darted about inside his brain. It defied all his efforts to trap it and analyse it, staying a ghost-like prisoner of his subconscious, unable to quite break free into the realms of rationality.

The eyes . . . baleful, almost. Accusing . . . without anger. It was the mute plea of some terribly tormented soul staring up from the pavement at him, Grossman thought, in a flash of clarity. The eyes were at once both accusatory and forgiving; stern and yet infinitely sad at the same time. Grossman felt his own brain straining, flexing unexercised powers to jump some etheric gap to understand, to communicate across a strange void.

It was not to be. In an instant, something inside his mind switched off. The inner robot of rationality cut in, smoothly taking over again, re-establishing control and putting things into an acceptable perspective. The chalked drawings were no more than crude, childish scribblings. There must be some local craze going around the area amongst the kids, like hula-hoops or yo-yos. On sane reflection, there was no particularly outstanding feature about the chalked eyes. Perhaps some trick of the evening light had caught them for an instant, imbuing them with special significance.

The mood broken, Grossman walked on, shaking his head. Fifty yards down the road he found another dolphin symbol, sprayed with aerosol paint on a rotting fence. He smiled to himself faintly. If it was a new craze, then it was, at least, a slight improvement. Graffiti in the form of dolphins was preferable to obscene slogans or declarations of violence. Grossman quickened his pace, eager to keep his appointment with Clive Frazer.

Frazer was already seated at a table when Grossman strolled into the pub. He too looked worried, a little tense. A copy of the same evening newspaper was spread out on the table in front of him. He glanced up from it as Grossman tapped him lightly on the shoulder.

'Hello, Heinz.' Frazer started to get up.

Grossman pushed him gently back into his seat. 'I'll get a round in,' he announced, walking away to the bar. A few minutes later he returned with two full glasses and sat down, forcing a cheerful smile for his friend.

It was greeted with an equally strained smile in return. Frazer nodded his head at the paper. 'What's all this rubbish about, Heinz? Just what the hell is going on?'

Grossman sipped at his beer. 'Just journalistic sensationalism,' he lied, after a few seconds. 'They'll print anything if they think it'll sell a few extra copies.

Frazer turned on him with a weary anger. His nerves were all jangled up. 'Don't bullshit me, Heinz,' he said with quiet vehemence. 'If anybody knows what's happening, it's you. I'm asking you, as a friend. Dammit, I've got a right to know, haven't I? We all have a right to know what is happening to us . . . to our world.'

Grossman stretched his arm across the table, clasping Frazer's shoulder. 'Hey, Clive, ease up, feller. Cool it,' he murmured in a quiet voice. The man was trembling violently, his lips twitching. Frazer was in a bad state.

'Look, what is it? What's upset you?' Grossman enquired, gently.

Frazer's words poured out in a torrent, his voice broken on a sob. 'For God's sake, Heinz . . . I'm frightened, dammit. I'm bloody frightened, and I'm confused, and I'm all mixed up. These things . . . this force, whatever it is . . . it's taking over my kid, for God's sake . . . don't you understand? It's taking over all the kids . . . eating into their minds, turning them into bloody zombies. I'm seeing my daughter turn into . . . something else . . . right under my damned nose, and I can't do a thing about it.'

Grossman punched him lightly on the chest. 'Come on, Clive, pull yourself together. Let's talk about this. We're intelligent men, let's talk some sense into the situation . . . what do you say?'

'Yeah.' Frazer shook his head violently, glancing round quickly with embarrassment in case anyone had noticed his outburst. No one apparently had. Slightly calmed, he turned back to face Grossman, who winked. 'Right?'

Frazer nodded. 'Yeah. Right.' He sipped at his beer for a couple of seconds until his trembling stopped. 'Sorry about that, Heinz. It's just that you feel so bloody useless, impotent. You're damned lucky, you know that? Being a parent can be sheer hell at times.'

Grossman clucked sympathetically. 'I can believe it.' He leaned across the table, his face calm and serious. 'Now tell me, what's wrong with Samantha?'

Clive Frazer drew in a deep breath. 'It started the other night, when you came round for dinner. She'd been acting a little oddly . . . you remember, I asked you if she seemed strange to you?'

'Yes, I remember,' Grossman said gently, nodding.

'Well, those damned paintings,' Frazer went on. 'They're an obsession, Heinz. There's some power at work, and it gets stronger and stronger every minute. The morning after, Dorothy went up to wake her for school and her bedclothes were all over the floor. It looked like she'd been tossing and turning all night, like with some terrible nightmare or something. Dorothy made a joke out of it; she said, "What do you think you were doing?" and do you know what that kid replied?'

'No, what did she say?'

' "I was swimming," for Christ's sake. In a dead serious voice, she said she'd been swimming. Not dreaming about swimming, or pretending to be swimming . . . but *swimming*.'

Grossman shrugged slightly. 'It could have been a dream. Kids of that age often can't quite distinguish between dreams and reality. That's why they sometimes invent such weird and improbable stories.'

Frazer shook his head. 'No, there's more, much more,' he insisted. 'For the past couple of days she has withdrawn further and further away from Dorothy and me, from everybody. She looks like she's in some kind of a trance. Her eyes are glazed, blank-looking. Every second is spent painting those same damned pictures . . . over and over and over. They're on the walls, under the bed, on the furniture. Everywhere you look, there's another painting of a dolphin. Well, this evening I went up to the infant school, to ask her teacher if she knew anything. And it's not just Sammy, Heinz. It's every kid in the school, in the whole damned town! They're all acting exactly the same, drawing the same pictures, looking spaced out of their minds. The teachers are worried sick about it. None of the children will do any work. As soon as they have a pencil in their hand, and a handy exercise book, they just start doodling dolphins again.' Frazer broke off, cradling his head in his hands. 'Something weird and horrible is happening to the children, Heinz, and it frightens me silly.'

Grossman was silent as his friend paused. He was deep in thought, racking his memory for the elusive clues he knew to be there, somewhere. Dolphins . . . there was a continuity, a definite flow of events which must determine how the pieces of the jig-saw fitted into the puzzle. He cast his mind back to the day of McAllister's death, analysing the events which had preceded it in minute detail.

Tiny snippets of information, disregarded detail – taken in context, they began to show a significance which Grossman had overlooked at the time. Dobey . . . the gun. Remembering, Grossman realised that he had been looking out over the side of the boat when Dobey had tried to shoot the two dolphins. There was no way he could have seen the man taking aim. So how had he known? What made him turn to Dobey and knock the gun into the air?

Then, immediately after – McAllister's communicator, flashing up that single word, 'Thanks'. Binsley's monkey-like face, that dreamy expression, his cryptic comment, 'Friends'. McAllister, playing with the mammals in the water, his obvious exultation . . . before the killer whales struck.

Grossman's mind dug into the subject, at last having a focal point for speculation, reflection. He delved back even further into memory, sifting through a mass of trivia for the tiny things of importance. Back in the early days of studying dolphin behaviour – the thrill of beginning to suspect he was dealing with an intelligent, rational life-form which had a language, the capacity to pass on acquired information. A pretty, female face flashed up in Grossman's brain. Marcia . . . Marcia Hope. A trainer, a girl who seemed as at home in the water as on land. She'd had a particularly close relationship with the dolphins. It was a love, deeper, more meaningful than just the self-indulgent love of a human for an appealing pet. Something greater, on a higher emotional level.

Grossman dismissed the memory of the brief love affair he and Marcia had shared. That was of no importance now, it was in the past, finished. It was something else that needed to be remembered.

It came, suddenly. A picture of Marcia's face, serious, yet with a perplexed, unsure smile lurking underneath. 'Sometimes, Heinz, I get this incredible feeling that they anticipate my commands before I actually voice them. It's uncanny, really . . . just as if they know what I'm going to say before I say it.'

Frazer's voice cut into his thoughts, snapping him back to the present. 'It's just one thing on top of another, Heinz. I can't cope. It's all too much.'

'Sorry, I was thinking about what you said, about the children,' Grossman apologised, feeling slightly guilty because he had temporarily forgotten about his friend and his problems.

'The thing is, I have to go away for a few days,' Frazer carried on. 'I have to take some students down to London for a seminar, I can't really get out of it. That's one of the reasons I felt so upset, I hate the thought of leaving Dorothy and Sammy alone at the moment. I was going to ask you a favour, Heinz – you're the only person I feel I can trust.'

'Of course, Clive,' Grossman said softly, pulling himself together. 'Anything I can do, you know that.'

Frazer smiled gratefully. 'I'd like you to keep an eye on them for me, while I'm away. Perhaps you could pop round to the house in the evening, just to see they're all right.'

'Of course.' Grossman nodded absently, his mind wandering again. The dolphins . . . mental influence . . . it was making a kind of sense, if not logic. He phrased his words carefully as he addressed Frazer again. 'Look, Clive, this obsession, which is affecting Samantha and the other kids. I don't quite know how to say it, but it may not be as sinister and evil as you seem to think. I can't tell you exactly what's happening, because I don't know, but I just have a personal feeling, an instinct, if you like, that the children are not going to come to any real harm.'

Frazer looked far from convinced. 'God, I wish that I could believe that,' he moaned.'

'Look, I promise I'll keep a close eye on Samantha for you,' Grossman reassured him. 'When are you leaving?'

'Tomorrow morning,' Frazer said.

'All right. Now just try to relax . . . and trust me,' Grossman said. 'And don't let wild newspaper articles start getting to you.'

'Yeah. O.K.' Frazer breathed, feeling a little better.

Grossman dreamed that night. He dreamed of Marcia, of warm Florida summer nights, walking hand in hand past the outdoor pools, listening to the faint splashings of the captive dolphins.

He dreamed of Marcia swimming in the aquarium, riding on the backs of the dolphins, laughing at their child-like sense of fun and mischief.

The dream image misted and blurred, changing like trick photography. The dolphins melted into an amorphous mass, their bodies transmuting into something else.

Children . . . laughing, playing, irrepressible children. Marcia playing with them, loving them, lavishing maternal love upon them. He watched, from the side of the aquarium, sharing their joy and knowing that they were all a part of himself. Marcia, children, his children. He wanted to dive in, swim with them, share their happiness completely.

Then the dream misted over again, changing back. Grossman stood watching the children which were not children, the dolphins which were not dolphins, a Marcia who was turning her back on him, swimming away for ever.

An inexpressible sadness washed over him as the pool changed into an open beach, the ocean stretching out to meet the horizon at the point of infinity. He watched them go, leaving him stranded upon the beach, cursing the two pathetic sticks of legs which rooted him to the land, setting him apart from those he loved.

He turned back towards the promenade, dragging himself across the sand. The figure of Commander Dobey was silhouetted against the night sky, a gun in his hands. He pointed the muzzle out over the dark sea, squeezing the trigger. 'I'll catch them for you . . . I'll get them back.'

Then desperation swelling up inside him. Running blindly towards Dobey, knowing that he had to get to the man before he pulled the trigger. Closing the distance, lungs bursting, legs aching . . . and heart sinking, realising that he could never make it in time. The gun beginning to chatter death out across the dark water. No time left, no time at all. Falling, tripping on the loose sand and sprawling head first on the beach, knowing that it was all too late.

He lay there for a long time, crying with bitterness and frustration as the turning tide crept up to the beach to engulf him, wash over his prone body and drag it gently back across the shingle into the sea.

Grossman jolted awake, sweating heavily and tasting salt water in his throat.

Chapter
Twenty-Three

Grossman arrived at the Research Centre early in the morning, seeking out Dr Bell in his private office. Despite the protestations of the scientist's private secretary, Grossman burst through the outer defences and penetrated the inner sanctum, rushing in without knocking.

'Dolphins,' Grossman said, excitedly. 'The answer lies with dolphins, I'm sure of it. How soon can we get a couple down here to study?'

Stuart Bell looked up in amazement. 'Are you feeling quite well, Grossman?'

The man's English sang-froid failed to put a brake on Grossman's exuberance. With the words tumbling over each other, Grossman blurted out a condensed version of his suspicions, fantasies and thin sheaf of facts. McAllister, Dobey, Marcia, the children. And lastly, the revelation which had come, suddenly, in the moment of wakening from a nightmare.

Bell shook his head slowly. 'I've been intrigued by this dolphin obsession myself, but what you're saying is nothing more than a wild theory, is it?' he asked, when Grossman paused for breath.

For the first time, Grossman collected himself, taking a deep breath and marshalling his thoughts. He nodded, seriously. 'Yes, of course . . . you'll want proof. I'm sorry,' He fell silent for a while. When he did speak again, he seemed to be his normal, cool, analytical self. 'Can you let me have a private room, a telephone, and a couple of hours?' he requested politely. 'If I'm right, that should enable me to give you all the proof you need.'

Bell smiled thinly. 'I should think so, Dr Grossman. We've spent the last weeks clutching at thinner straws. I'll arrange it with my secretary at once.' He reached for his desk intercom.

'Thanks.' Grossman turned, striding towards the door.

It took much less than the two hours Grossman had asked for. In just over ninety minutes he was back in Bell's office with a handful of hastily scribbled notes and a new, more resolute sense of enthusiasm. He threw the notes down on to Bell's desk. 'There you are,' Grossman declared triumphantly.

'That should be enough proof to satisfy anyone.'

Fascinated, Bell begin to riffle through the papers as Grossman went on to explain what he had been doing.

'I telephoned schools all over the country,' Grossman said. 'One thing became clear almost at once – this sudden childish obsession with dolphins is not confined to Lowestoft. It has hit every coastal town all over this country, more or less simultaneously. I tried further afield, Europe, the U.S.A., Australia. Everywhere, the story is exactly the same. Kids from the age of five to fifteen have spontaneously become totally fixated by dolphin images. It's absolutely impossible for it to be a natural fad, spreading throughout the world virtually overnight. Therefore, there can only be one possible explanation.'

'And that is?' Bell needed Grossman to put it into words for him.

'Telepathy,' Grossman said flatly. 'Dolphins, arguably the most intelligent creatures on earth next to man, have somehow established mental contact with children, for some reason. I can only surmise that the reason is that they need to communicate with us, and that the message they have for us is a critical and desperately important one.'

Bell looked bemused. Despite the weight of evidence staring him in the face, he hardly dared to believe. 'But why children?' he murmured weakly.

Grossman shrugged. 'Obviously young minds are more receptive. They're not so conditioned, filled with rigid preconceived ideas. And don't forget, for many hours of each day they are concentrated together at schools. All in close physical proximity, their minds all attuned to the accepted process of receiving information. Don't you see? It would work better that way. Mob violence, mass psychosis – all emotional or mental unheavals spread and proliferate much more readily under crowd conditions. Hitler made maximum use of that fact at the Nuremberg rallies. So did Jesus Christ, for that matter.'

'Two pretty diametrical examples,' Bell said heavily. 'What do you suppose we are dealing with in this case, good or evil?'

Grossman shook his head. 'At this precise moment, I don't know,' he admitted. 'But I can't help feeling a strong sense of optimism, rather than foreboding. Either way, I think that it is imperative that we start concentrating our efforts on dolphins, and the sooner the better. Something tells me that there may not be very much time.'

'I agree,' Bell said. 'As a matter of fact, while you were on the phone I did a bit of investigating myself. I rang a private dolphinarium in Great Yarmouth. They are having a lot of trouble with children there as well, apparently. Dolphins have suddenly become so popular that hundreds of kids are staying away from school and mobbing the place. Good for business, but then once they get inside, they refuse to leave. They weren't too keen to lend us a couple, but we eventually came to a financial arrangement and they are going to send two dolphins down here immediately. They should arrive late this afternoon. Meanwhile, what do you plan to do?'

Grossman smiled thinly. 'I think it's about time I went back to school. Do you think you could get me clearance to spend a few hours at the local secondary school this afternoon? I'd like to interview some of the brighter twelve- to fifteen-year-olds.'

'I'll see what I can do,' Bell promised. 'And anything you think you might need – tape recorders, film equipment – please feel free to requisition it.'

'Thanks,' Grossman said gratefully. 'I just hope I can come up with something worthwhile.'

It proved to be a forlorn hope. Despite searching questions, Grossman learned virtually nothing from the children he spoke to. They seemed more or less as confused as he was about the significance of their sudden strange obsession. The one thing Grossman did learn was that the older the children were, the less they had been affected. It was the younger children who were doing most of the drawing, but they could not explain their motivation. Even the most eloquent pupils could only shrug and mutter vague phrases like 'pictures in my head', 'silent voices'. It confirmed Grossman's suspicion that some form of telepathy was at work, but brought him no nearer to knowing what it was meant to communicate.

The afternoon appeared to have been fruitless. As he left the school, Grossman realised that he should have concentrated on a primary school rather than a secondary. He would do that tomorrow. Thinking of younger children suddenly reminded him of Samantha, and he felt a flash of optimism again. The day need not be wasted after all. He could go round to see her later in the evening, thus fulfilling his promise to Clive Frazer at the same time. The strength of Samantha's images, plus the fact that she was emotionally close to him, made Grossman feel that she might well be his best hope.

He returned to his hotel to enjoy a pot of coffee in the lounge. It came up on a tray, complete with an assortment of biscuits and a copy of the local evening newspaper, neatly folded.

Grossman shook the paper open, fully expecting another diet of screaming sensationalism. He was not disappointed. It hadn't taken reporters long to pick up the dolphin story. The front-page headline read: DOLPHIN MANIA!

With a slightly sinking feeling, Grossman read the accompanying article. It was much more highly informed than the previous piece of rubbish, suggesting that journalists were taking the whole matter a lot more seriously. That much was to the good, Grossman thought, then sank into a depression again when he read the postscript about the two dolphins being transferred from Great Yarmouth. Somebody must have leaked the information during the afternoon. Grossman cursed under his breath; he had wanted to keep the whole thing as quiet as possible until they could get down to some serious research. He finished scanning the paper gloomily, finished his coffee and ordered an early dinner in his room.

Afterwards, he took a quick shower before dropping round to see Dorothy and Samantha. They both seemed pleased to see him, although Samantha had a mischievous smile playing behind her blue eyes. Later in the evening, when he took her aside and began to question her gently, he realised what it was. Sammy would say nothing at all to him about the other evening, or answer any direct questions concerning dolphins. She was playing a teasing, childish game with him. She had a precious secret which she knew taunted him, and she was going to get the maximum of childish pleasure from the fact. Afraid to alarm Dorothy by upsetting the child, Grossman reluctantly let it drop. Depressed, he stayed until the child had been put to bed, then said good night to Dorothy and returned to his hotel to get an early night.

Sleep came surprisingly easily. Grossman hadn't fully realised how tired he had become over the past few days.

The harsh jangling of the telephone woke him at a few minutes past midnight. He shook himself awake, snapping on the bedside lamp before holding the receiver to his ear.

Dorothy Frazer's distraught voice tumbled out of the earpiece. 'Heinz, something terrible has happened. Samantha . . . she's disappeared.' She broke off with a racking sob.

Grossman was suddenly wide awake, his tone firm and

authoritative. 'Listen, Dorothy, pull yourself together. Now, calmly . . . what has happened to Sammy?'

'I couldn't sleep, there was a door banging. I looked out on the landing. Sammy's bedroom door was ajar . . . she's gone, Heinz, she's not in the house. I've looked everywhere.'

'All right. Now keep calm,' Grossman urged. 'Have you phoned the police?'

There were several choked, gulping sounds before Dorothy answered. 'I've tried, a dozen times. They're always engaged. I couldn't think of anyone else to turn to, Heinz . . . I'm desperate.'

Grossman was already clambering from his bed, throwing on his trousers with one hand whilst keeping the telephone to his ear with the other. 'Look, Dorothy, you keep trying to get through to the police. I'm on my way over now. Just try to stay calm.'

He slammed the receiver back into the rest, finished tucking in his shirt, and then lifted the phone off the hook again, dialling the night porter. 'Get me a taxi round to the front entrance as soon as possible.' He finished dressing quickly, grabbing a raincoat as he heard the sound of heavy drizzle tapping against his window. Half a minute later he was waiting outside the hotel as the minicab pulled up at the kerbside. Grossman threw himself into it, barking out the address to the driver.

Dorothy greeted him at the door as he arrived. She was standing well inside the porch, so there was no mistaking the tears coursing down her face for rain. Grossman offered her a pair of friendly, comforting arms, which she fell into gratefully. 'Thank you, Heinz, you're a true friend,' she sobbed, pressing her damp cheek against his shoulder.

Grossman gripped her gently by the arms, disengaging her and staring into the tear-filled eyes. 'Now don't worry. Everything's going to be all right,' he assured her in a soft voice. 'Did you manage to get through to the police?'

Dorothy shook her head soundlessly.

'O.K. So we go round there,' Grossman said. 'Give me your car keys.'

'It's all ready. I got it out of the garage after I phoned you.' Dorothy pulled the door closed behind her and stepped out on to the drive, fishing in her handbag and extracting a bunch of keys. She pressed them into Grossman's palm and led him around the side of the house.

'Good girl,' Grossman murmured, soothingly. He opened the

passenger door, ushered her in, then ran round quickly and settled into the driving seat. He took a few seconds to familiarise himself with the controls, then started the engine. With a slight initial fumbling with the unfamiliar manual gear-change, he edged the car out into the road. 'Which way?'

Dorothy jerked her head to the left. 'Straight down the road and third on the right,' she murmured. She was pulling herself together now, displaying remarkable self-control, Grossman thought.

He followed her directions, peering ahead through the rain-lashed windscreen in search of the telltale blue light of the police station. Just before the third turning on the right, a jumble of cars announced a hopeless traffic jam. There were vehicles slewed across the road, some left empty with their headlights on and engines running. All around, there were people running to and fro, women screaming, horns blaring.

Grossman slewed the car into the kerb and pulled up the handbrake. He switched off, darted out and round the front of the car, wrenching the passenger door open. 'Come on, we'll have to make it on foot,' he urged, helping Dorothy to scramble out of the car. Running, they joined the growing crowd of people converging on the police station around the corner.

The forecourt of the police station was a solid mass of distraught people, pushing and shoving each other in a blind panic to accost the nearest policeman. Above the general hub-bub of noise, Grossman heard the same phrases shouted out over and over again: 'Where's my baby?' 'My child is missing.' 'Where have the children gone?'

'Oh my God.' Dorothy Frazer began to collapse into hysterical tears again.

Grossman rounded on her, grasping her shoulders and shaking her roughly. Suddenly, he knew where the children were, and what they were doing. Why hadn't he thought of it before?

'Dorothy, it's all right,' he shouted, above the screaming crowd. 'I promise you, it's all right.' Satisfied that he had her full attention, he lowered his voice. 'I know where Sammy is, love . . . where all the children are.'

Dorothy's sobs subsided. 'Take me to her, Heinz, please,' she begged.

'Yes, in a minute.' Grossman dragged her behind him, push-ing through the crowd towards the nearest uniformed figure. Reaching the young constable, he grasped him by the arm.

'Listen to me, please . . . I'm a doctor, I'm pretty sure that I know exactly where all these missing children are.'

The policeman looked at him sharply, confused and suspicious.

'Please, listen to me,' Grossman urged. 'I know what I'm talking about.'

The young policeman came to a decision. 'You'd better come with me, sir.' He turned, and began pushing a way through the crowd towards the station entrance. Inside, he ushered them to the station sergeant's office.

'Bloke here reckons he knows where all these missing kids are, Sarge,' he announced.

'Oh, he does, does he? Better show him in then.' As soon as Grossman was in the office, the sergeant turned on him aggressively. 'What the hell's going on then? You know something about this madness?'

Grossman nodded. 'Listen, you've got to get those people out there calmed down,' he said breathlessly. 'Someone's going to get hurt any moment.'

'Never mind them,' the sergeant cut in rudely. 'Where are the kids?'

'You know the Marine Research Centre?' Grossman said. 'Well I'm pretty sure that's where the missing children will be.'

'I see, sir.' The sergeant looked at him uncertainly for a few seconds. 'All right, sir, we'll look into it. Do you mind telling me your name, and exactly what your connection with this business is?'

Dorothy tugged at Grossman's sleeve. 'Please, Heinz . . . take me to Samantha.'

'Yes, of course.' Grossman turned back to face the sergeant. 'My name is Grossman. I'm a scientist working out at the Research Centre. Now, please, I think we ought to get to those children. Is there a back way out of here?'

'Yes,' the sergeant replied, gesturing vaguely with his hand. 'Look here, sir, if you work out at that place, perhaps you ought to show a couple of my men. I'll get a patrol car laid on.'

'Fine,' Grossman said.

The sergeant crossed the office, opened the door and barked out orders. Minutes later, Grossman and Dorothy Frazer were being driven towards the Research Centre at top speed, the police siren wailing mournfully.

'Slow down here,' Grossman called out to the police driver,

as the car approached the outer security fence.

The car cruised up to the main gates and pulled to a halt.

'Got a searchlight?' Grossman asked.

The driver shook his head. 'Just a couple of torches.'

'All right, just turn the car around and put your headlights full on,' Grossman suggested.

The driver complied without question. There was something about Grossman's tone which was utterly authoritative. As the car wheeled slowly round, Grossman peered out to where the blackness was sliced open by the twin beams of the headlights.

'There,' he shouted, suddenly. In the glare of the lights, a bizarre sight greeted his eyes.

All along the perimeter of the mesh fence, children sat cross-legged on the wet ground, neatly spaced out in orderly rows. They seemed oblivious of the cold night air and the rain beating down on their soaked pyjamas and nightdresses. Their small bodies rocked slowly and rhythmically to and fro as their eyes gazed blankly through the metal fencing towards the pool containing the two dolphins.

Dorothy let out a little cry and fiddled with the door handle. She threw herself out of the car, shouting Samantha's name. Grossman jumped out after her and seized her hand, squeezing it. 'Quiet, Dorothy,' he urged.

As she fell silent, Grossman pricked his ears. A strange, guttural chant was echoing across to them from where the children sat. Grossman felt a slight shiver of apprehension as he tried to listen to it. It had a strange, unearthly quality, an uneven resonance which suggested that the children were not really familiar with it. Yet, unmistakably, there was a definite pattern in the sound, a kind of mnemonic phraseology which indicated a meaningful structure.

Both Dorothy and Grossman started to run towards the assembled children, searching for Samantha's small blonde head. It seemed hopeless, like searching for a needle in a haystack.

The strange maternal instinct of a female for her offspring came to the rescue. As a seabird chooses its own nest from thousands upon a cliff-face, Dorothy's eyes were guided through the mass of children to the tiny, hunched body of her daughter. With a sob she pulled free from Grossman's hand and ran forward, stumbling over other children in her urgency to get to Samantha. Behind her, Grossman ran a little more carefully, stripping off his jacket to throw around the soaking child.

Gathering Samantha up in his arms, Grossman carried her back towards the police car as the first of dozens of pairs of car headlights began to curve down the slight hill leading to the Research Centre. The patrol car had obviously radioed back to the station, and now a whole convoy of cars were bringing distraught parents to collect their offspring. The strange chanting faltered and died as the roar of car engines shattered the night.

In Grossman's arms, Samantha began to shiver violently as the cold and wet seeped into her tiny body. Dorothy tucked the jacket more tightly around her, muttering soothing noises, but the child did not even seem to recognise her.

Grossman looked at her little face carefully. The child's eyes had a dull, glazed look, and her lips were still moving silently, phrasing the strange chant.

Grossman slapped the child across the cheek with the flat of his hand. The lip movements ceased abruptly. With a shudder which rippled right through her body, Samantha began to cry.

'She'll be all right now,' Grossman murmured. He had seen enough people snap out of hypnotic or somnambulistic trances to recognise the signs. He handed the well-wrapped bundle across to Dorothy as Samantha held out her arms and began to scream for her mother.

Cuddling the child to her breast, Dorothy also gave vent to the pent-up feelings inside her. She abandoned herself to deep, shuddering sobs of relief. Grossman nodded to himself, content that she too was coming out of a state of shock and returning to normal. He threw his arm around the woman's shoulder. 'Come on, love . . . let's get back and get her into a warm, dry bed.'

They transferred to Dorothy's car at the police station and drove home. Grossman ran the car straight into the garage and switched off the engine. He glanced across at Dorothy, smiling reassuringly. 'Everything's fine now.'

Dorothy nodded absently, a mute plea glistening in her eyes.

'What is it?' Grossman asked gently.

Dorothy spoke hesitantly. 'Heinz, you've been wonderful; I don't know how to thank you, let alone ask any more of you . . .'

Her voice tailed off. Grossman understood. 'What is it, Dorothy?' he prodded, gently.

'I don't want to be alone,' she blurted out. 'Would you stay with us, Heinz . . . please!'

He smiled. 'Of course. Let's just hope that Clive understands when the neighbours start gabbling.'

Dorothy gripped his arm, smiling back. 'Thank you, Heinz. It won't take me a minute to make up the spare room. God bless you.'

Grossman turned in his seat, reaching over to pick up Samantha. She had been completely silent on the journey back to the house. He had supposed she was sleeping.

His body froze. Without looking back, he hissed to Dorothy, 'Quickly, have you got a pen or a pencil in your purse, and a slip of paper?'

'I think so.' Grossman heard the click of the catch on her handbag opening, and the faint rattle of loose change and articles of make-up. 'Here,' Dorothy said, finally, passing him an eyebrow pencil and an old shopping receipt.

Grossman rested the paper on the back of the car seat, staring past Samantha to her childish squiggles on the rear window. Traced on the misted-up glass, by one pudgy finger, was the unmistakable outline of a dolphin, but it was not this which had grabbed Grossman's attention. Beneath the drawing there was a line of curious hieroglyphics. Scribbling furiously, Grossman tried to transfer the symbols to paper before they disappeared.

'What is it?' Dorothy asked.

Grossman found it impossible to keep a note of excitement out of his voice. 'I may be wrong,' he muttered, 'but I think this may be what we have been waiting for.' He finished transcribing the signs, then checked his copy against the original. Satisfied that he had reproduced them as faithfully as possible, he tucked the piece of paper into his pocket and scooped Samantha up from the back seat.

Dorothy led the way into the house, ushering Grossman into the lounge while she took Samantha upstairs to be dried off, clad in a warm woolly nightgown and tucked safely back into bed. When she returned, Grossman was staring silently at the cryptic hieroglyphs.

'What does it mean?' Dorothy asked, looking over his shoulder.

Grossman shrugged. 'I don't know,' he admitted. 'But it just might be a message of some kind.' He stared again at the meaningless symbols, suddenly thinking of Clive Frazer. He looked up at Dorothy. 'When's Clive due back?'

'Monday,' she answered. 'He's staying in town over the weekend.'

'Damn.' Grossman cursed softly under his breath. 'That's too long to wait.' He looked up at Dorothy again, his face serious. 'Look, Dorothy, I'm going to ask you to do something for me . . .'

'Anything, you ought to know that,' she answered at once. 'We owe you, Heinz.'

'Do you know where Clive is staying?' Grossman demanded.

Dorothy nodded. 'I have the name and address of the hotel, yes.'

'All right. I want you to telephone now, this minute, and tell Clive that it is important that he get back here first thing tomorrow,' Grossman said. 'I know I'm asking him to risk his job, and probably cause him a great deal of inconvenience, but I really think it's important.'

Dorothy glanced at the mantel clock. It was nearly two in the morning. Still, she didn't argue. There was something in the urgency of Grossman's voice which told her that he would not have asked lest it had been vital. 'I'll go and call the hotel now,' she said in a soft voice, crossing the lounge and going out into the hall. Minutes later, she came back. 'He'll catch the very first train in the morning,' she announced. 'He should be here by noon at the very latest.'

Grossman relaxed with relief. 'Good,' he murmured. He handed the slip of paper to Dorothy. 'Keep this in a safe place. I want you to give it to Clive as soon as he arrives home and ask him if it makes any sense at all. Ask him to ring me at the Research Centre as soon as he's had a chance to have a look at it.'

Dorothy took the scrap of paper, nodding firmly. 'I will, I promise,' she vowed. 'I hope for your sake it means something helpful.'

'I hope for all our sakes,' Grossman said quietly, and he meant it.

Chapter
Twenty-Four

The butterfly phone purred softly. Grossman lifted it to his ear. 'Grossman.'

'Heinz, it's Clive,' came Frazer's voice down the line. 'I've just arrived back.'

'Sorry to call you back like this, Clive,' Grossman apologised. 'It's a terrible imposition upon a friendship, I know, but . . .'

Frazer cut him off abruptly. 'Rubbish, Heinz. Dorothy has told me what you did last night. Now, how can I help you?'

'Those symbols, do they mean anything to you?' Grossman asked. 'I could only think of you in a hurry, you're the only language expert within immediate reach.'

Frazer's voice sounded dubious. 'It's not a language, Heinz . . . at least, not any language I've ever come across. At first sight, it appeared to be just meaningless signs, but there is a definite repetition of the old Greek symbol epsilon, and a bastardised form of the symbol gamma. If I'm not mistaken, it is a composite text, made up of crude Mycenaean, cuneiform derivatives and what appear to be straightforward visual hieroglyphs. If there is anything at all to be read into it, I'm going to need time, and some help. I'll need to go down to the university building, bone up on some old texts and run whatever I can dig up through the IBM, on a sort of code-breaking basis. Can you give me until this evening?'

'However long it takes, Clive,' Grossman answered. 'And thanks.'

'Forget it. See you this evening.' Frazer hung up.

Grossman replaced the receiver and sat back in his chair, crossing his fingers superstitiously. Idly, he gazed across his small office and out of the window. It had a perfect view over the main gates into the Research Centre. There appeared to be some sort of a disturbance going on. Grossman saw two or the guards running about, waving their arms and shouting. Curious, Grossman rose from his chair and walked across to the window for a better view.

He saw the guards' problem at once. A group of some two dozen children had congregated just to the right of the gate, and some of them were attempting to climb the high wire-mesh fence which protected the Centre. As Grossman stared, fascinated, more children appeared from the direction of town, converging on the Research Establishment in a repetition of the scene the night before. In a matter of minutes, the two dozen had become two hundred, and the children had lined themselves up all around the perimeter fence, faces pressed close against the mesh, peering in as though seeking something.

Grossman glanced at his watch. It was half past twelve. It explained how the children had arrived at the Centre, since it would be their school lunch hour. He marvelled yet again at the inexplicable but incredibly powerful mental force which was at work amongst the young.

The weird chant began to drift to his ears, diffusing through the glass of the window. Turning away quickly, Grossman headed for the door, eager to be on the outside, where he could observe the phenomenon at closer quarters.

'Well, did you get anything?' Grossman asked, the second Clive Frazer admitted him to the house that evening.

The man nodded. 'Surprisingly, yes,' he answered. 'But it doesn't make any sense, I'm afraid.'

Grossman sighed heavily. He had been hoping for some clear message, a definite clue which he could work upon. Feeling deflated and disappointed, he followed Clive Frazer into the lounge.

Frazer rummaged through a sheaf of papers and books on the coffee table, finally extracting a single sheet of paper and handing it to Grossman. 'That is the rough translation,' he murmured. 'I don't know if it will mean anything to you . . . it certainly doesn't to me.'

Grossman stared at the message which was printed on the sheet. 'When the Great Fire burns in the frozen waters, only the mountains shall be free.' He turned back to Frazer, shaking his head in puzzlement.

'No, I didn't think you'd make any more of it than I did,' Frazer said miserably. 'Sorry it wasn't any more promising.'

'Is there any other possible translation, even transposition of words or symbols which would make a clearer statement?' Grossman wanted to know.

Frazer shook his head firmly. 'If there is, then it is too complicated for an IBM 360 computer to work out. No, I'd say that was it, such as it is.'

'Have you asked Samantha about it?' Grossman asked.

'Yes. I've read it to her several times, and asked her if it means anything.'

'And?' Grossman prompted.

Frazer shrugged. 'She just bursts into tears,' he said. 'And when I say that, I mean real tears, not just childish tantrums. It's as if she really feels a deep, terrible grief. It takes five or six minutes to calm her down again.'

Grossman's eyes opened wide. 'Then it *does* mean something to her,' he exclaimed.

'It would appear so,' Frazer admitted. 'But why the hell can't we see it?'

Grossman did not reply. Instead, he gazed deeply at the words again, trying to open his mind to them, let the cryptic message speak for itself inside his head. Nothing came. Just the words – oddly archaic, faintly poetic, yet meaningless.

Conceding defeat, he dropped the paper back on to the table with a sigh. It was obvious that he would have to try another approach. He thought about it carefully for several minutes. Finally, he looked up at Frazer. 'How are you on phonetics?'

'O.K., I guess,' Frazer replied. 'It's not my specialist subject, though. I get by, I suppose.' He regarded Grossman curiously. 'Why?'

'I've had a couple of dolphins brought down to the Centre. I want to have another serious crack at making a communication breakthrough. I also took a tape recording of children chanting this dolphin-inspired thing of theirs. I'd like you to see if you can make anything of it.'

Frazer shrugged. 'I'll do what I can, of course,' he said willingly. 'But don't expect any miracles.'

Grossman smiled wryly. 'I don't,' he said flatly. 'But I'll settle for a good old-fashioned fluke.' For the first time, Grossman realised that Samantha and Dorothy were missing. 'Where is Sammy, by the way?'

'Upstairs in her bedroom. I asked Dorothy to take her out of the way so we could talk,' Frazer said. 'Do you want to see her?' He moved towards the door.

'No, wait,' Grossman said suddenly. He regarded his friend seriously. 'Listen, Clive . . . I want to ask you another favour.'

'Go ahead,' Frazer said.

Grossman paused thoughtfully before going on. 'I want to take Samantha into the Centre,' he said slowly. 'I want to observe her with the dolphins at close hand, maybe try to

prise her mind open a little. I know I'm asking a lot, more
less wanting to use your child as a human guinea-pig. It n
be very upsetting for her, of course. I really don't know, w
fighting in the dark.'

Frazer's face clouded. He chewed at his lip pensively
several moments. 'Do you seriously think it might help?'
asked, after a while.

Grossman shrugged. 'I can't answer that. It might.'

Frazer seemed torn with indecision. He had seen his daugh
disturbed enough already, yet he realised they had to expl
every possible avenue as soon as possible. 'Look, let's see h
she reacts to the idea,' he suggested. 'If she appears to tak
all right, then I'll agree.'

'O.K.,' Grossman said. 'Fetch her down here.'

Frazer walked to the door and called up the stairs to
wife. Moments later, Dorothy walked in holding Samantha
the hand. The child's face was emotionless, devoid of expr
sion. Only her eyes seemed to betray any feeling. They w
blue, mysterious pools which seemed to hold incredible dep
of sadness and misery. She looked at Grossman with
recognition.

'Hi, Sammy,' Grossman said brightly, smiling broadly. 'A
how are you today?'

The child did not answer. Dorothy looked into Grossma
eyes, a mute plea in her own. She looked drawn and worri
The child's increasing detachment was having a terrible dra
ing effect upon her natural vitality.

Grossman tried again. 'Listen, Sammy, how would you l
to come and see the dolphins with me tomorrow?' he ask

For the first time, Samantha seemed to come to life. In
instant, her little face was transformed. The blue eyes spark
the pink lips curled into a childish laugh of joy. She nod
eagerly.

Then, just as suddenly, her face became blank again. Fo
moment, tears pricked at the corners of her eyes. Looking
her, Grossman thought that he saw an expression of terri
misery cross her face, an expression so intense it belied
child's tender years. Grossman tried to capture its quality,
failed. He felt only a deep psychic shock, a chilling fee
in his stomach. It was as if, for a second, he had seen
face of the whole world suffering, had been given a glim
of a million years of sorrow.

The strange image fled his mind as Samantha threw her

against him, wrapping her small arms around his waist and hugging him tightly. She spoke for the first time, in a sobbing, frightened voice. 'Please, Uncle Heinz, you won't let all the people drown, will you?'

She drew away again, lapsing into the blank stare. Dorothy embraced her protectively, easing her away towards the door. 'Come on, darling, I think we ought to go to bed,' she murmured. Without protest, the child allowed herself to be led away.

'Well?' Grossman confronted his friend.

'She smiled, Heinz. Just for a moment, she smiled again, dammit.' Clive Frazer seemed quite excited. 'Yes, of course you can take her into the Research Centre. It might be just what she needs to jolt her back to normal.'

Grossman smiled thinly, disguising his real feelings. He could not quite share Clive Frazer's enthusiasm, for he alone had seen that other expression which had followed the brief smile. Her impassioned plea haunted his thoughts, stirring up deep, primal fears.

Chapter Twenty-Five

Grossman had a hard time persuading Dr Bell to open up the Research Centre on a Saturday, let alone allow him to bring in a civilian and a five-year-old child. His initial request was met with a polite but blank refusal. Grossman was not to be beaten, however. Undeterred, he telephoned his two fellow scientists, hoping to get them on his side.

The slim evidence he had already uncovered fascinated and excited them both. With Jossen and Graunglich firmly behind him, Grossman had no further trouble. Bell capitulated, giving him more or less carte blanche to use the Centre and its facilities.

Several children had already gathered outside the perimeter fence as Grossman arrived with Frazer and Samantha. Like the previous day, they pressed themselves up against the wire mesh, peering hopefully into the Centre even though the dolphins were housed in a pool behind the main administration building, out of their field of vision.

Passing through the security gates, Frazer stopped, listening to the children's strange chant. It was the first time he had heard it.

'That's it, is it?' he asked.

'That's it,' Grossman said. 'Does it sound remotely like any known language to you?'

Frazer shook his head firmly. 'No,' he said bluntly. 'I wouldn't hold out any hopes of me making much sense of that.'

Grossman tried to hide his disappointment. 'Oh well, I have a clear tape recording of the whole thing. Perhaps if you hear it over a few times you might be able to start tying it in with the short passage you translated.'

Frazer shrugged. 'I can only try,' he muttered, without enthusiasm. He turned away from the chanting children and followed Grossman into the building.

Grossman headed straight for his office, pulling a cassette tape recorder from his desk drawer. He switched it on. Frazer listened intently to the tape for several minutes. Finally, he stabbed the machine off and looked up, shaking his head sadly. 'No, there's no way I can make any sense of that, Heinz. It sounds like gibberish to me. Perhaps if even a couple of the sounds matched up with the words I might be able to make some sort of a start. As it is, nothing!' He switched the tape recorder on again, to play the chant over one last time.

Grossman glanced down at Samantha; her lips were moving in time with the recording. A sudden hope struck him. He bent over, gripping the child firmly by the shoulders. 'Listen, Sammy, you know this song, don't you?'

Samantha looked at him blankly for a few seconds, then nodded faintly.

'Do you think you could write it down for your daddy, so he can understand it?' Grossman went on. 'Like you wrote down the little part, in my car?'

Samantha pouted. 'When am I going to see the dolphins? You promised me I could see the dolphins.'

On impulse, Grossman played a hunch. 'You won't see the dolphins unless you write down the song for your daddy,' he threatened. 'As soon as you do that, we can go to see them.'

Tears began to prickle out of Samantha's eyes. 'You promised,' she repeated, in a sullen accusation.

Grossman handed her a pen and a piece of paper. 'It's entirely up to you,' he said, sternly. He ran the tape back to its beginning and started it again.

Samantha glared at him for a few moments, defiantly testing her powers, calling his bluff. Then, giving in, she began to scribble symbols upon the paper.

When she had finished, Grossman scooped up the sheet exultantly, handing it to Frazer. 'Does it look right to you?'

Frazer scanned the paper, nodding excitedly. 'Yes, I can recognise the passage we have already translated,' he said. 'With that to work from, I shouldn't have too much trouble working out the rest.'

Grossman whirled on Samantha, hugging her. 'There's a good girl,' he said, smiling. 'Now let's go and see the fish in the aquarium before we see the dolphins. Would you like that?'

The child nodded, pacified. Grossman took her by the hand, leading her towards the door. 'I'll be back in about fifteen minutes,' he called over his shoulder to Frazer.

'I've got it,' Frazer shouted as Grossman returned. 'The whole passage begins to make a little more sense, although that final section is still too damned cryptic for my liking.' He handed the translation to Grossman, who studied it carefully.

'The time of the first time is come again. There is death in dark waters. The liquid world awakes in anger. When the Great Fire burns in the frozen waters, only the mountains shall be free.'

Grossman looked piqued. 'Did you say it made more sense?'

Frazer shrugged. 'Well, reading between the words, there is a kind of rational statement of fact,' he said, somewhat defensively. 'That at least is encouraging, don't you think?'

Grossman still seemed dubious. Frazer took the paper from his fingers, scanning the words again. 'Look, ignore the actual words and look for a looser meaning,' he suggested. 'For this "time of the first time", let's say "a beginning, a new beginning". Putting the whole thing into a more vernacular framework, I'd read it something like this: "It is time for a new beginning, for the seas are dying. They are fighting back."' He broke off for a moment. 'Don't you see, Heinz . . . that is a clear, rational statement of the existing facts.'

Grossman nodded uncertainly. 'Sure, but it still doesn't help us much, does it?' he pointed out. 'And this final bit about fire in frozen water still makes no sense at all.'

Frazer looked chastened. 'No, I admit that I can't figure that part out,' he admitted. 'I can only assume that it is a warning of some kind, or a threat.'

'Of what?' Grossman thought carefully, then remembered Samantha. He handed her the pen and paper again. 'Sammy, what is the Great Fire? Could you draw it for us?'

Mutely, the child took the pen and laid the sheet of paper on Grossman's desk. Quickly, she drew a simple shape and handed it back to him with a flourish.

Grossman stared at the drawing without comprehension. A roughly dome-shaped object, supported on a short, thick leg, or stalk. Silently, he handed the drawing to Frazer.

'Looks like a toadstool,' Frazer muttered. 'Or a very bad umbrella.'

'My God!' Grossman blurted out, suddenly. He snatched the paper back, staring at the picture again. His face paled. 'No, Clive, not a toadstool. It's a mushroom, for God's sake . . . a mushroom cloud! That could be a picture of an atomic pillar.'

There was a stunned silence, broken at last by Frazer's nervous, uncertain laughter. The idea was so preposterous, so totally incredible, that only ridicule stood a chance of exorcising it. Even so, some doubt remained.

'The Great Fire,' Grossman breathed in awe. 'Can you think of a better way to describe it?'

'No.' Frazer shook his head violently. He could not, would not allow his mind to harbour the craziness. 'Samantha couldn't possibly even conceive of an atomic holocaust. She's only five, for Christ's sake, Heinz.'

Grossman wasn't listening. He had turned to Samantha, his ashen face pressed close to hers, his eyes stern and commanding. 'Listen, Sammy, we're going out to talk to the dolphins now, do you understand? You have to let them know that your daddy and I are friends, we want to help. We do not want to harm them, or any of the fish in the sea. Can you tell them that for me?'

The child nodded, slowly.

Gripping her hand, Grossman led her out of the administration building, towards the pool which housed the pair of dolphins.

Chapter
Twenty-Six

The two dolphins swam listlessly, moving only enough to keep their bodies lubricated and cool. They could just have been reacting adversely to their recent upheaval, but Grossman sensed that the creatures' sullen behaviour went far deeper than that.

He stood on the very edge of the pool, holding Samantha by the hand. 'See them?' he asked her, forcing a carefree smile.

The child nodded, beginning to look happy again.

'Do you know their names?' Grossman asked, gently.

Samantha nodded. 'Sally and Swift,' she murmured. She pointed a finger at each dolphin in turn. 'That's Swift, and that's Sally.'

Grossman looked up for a second, his eyes meeting Frazer's and exchanging a knowing glance. He had deliberately not mentioned the pet names of the two dolphins in Samantha's presence. There was no way she could have heard them.

He bent down to Samantha again. 'They don't seem very happy, do they?' he murmured.

Samantha shook her blonde curls. 'They're not, they're very sad,' she said quietly, her voice edged with concern. 'All the dolphins are very sad.'

'Why, Samantha?' Grossman prompted. 'What is it that makes the dolphins so sad?'

The child's face creased into a puzzled frown. 'I'm not sure,' she murmured uncertainly.

Grossman shook the child quite savagely. 'Concentrate,' he hissed at her. 'Think about it.'

Samantha squeezed her eyes tightly shut, facing out over the pool. After a few seconds, she spoke again. 'I think it's because they have a brother, and he may be going to die.'

Frazer stepped forward, grasping Grossman by the arm. 'Heinz, this morbid preoccupation with death, drowning, destruction – it can't be doing Sammy any good. Maybe you ought to stop now.'

Grossman threw his friend off violently. 'Leave us alone,' he shouted angrily. 'We may be getting somewhere.'

Even as he spoke, Grossman was surprised at his own

vehemence. He was getting jumpy, neurotic. Maybe the tension was getting to him, he reflected. That, and the dull headache which had started to throb in his temple.

Frazer stepped back, staring at Grossman in amazement. He had never seen the man like this before. He was normally such a placid individual, invariably retaining a reassuring inner calm, a quality of utter sanity. Now, he was rapidly becoming quite antagonistic. His eyes seemed to flash with a dull fire, betraying a growing mental disturbance.

There was something wrong. Frazer knew it instinctively. 'I'm going to fetch Dr Bell,' he muttered, but Grossman didn't seem to hear him. Frazer turned away from the pool, and began to run towards the main administration building.

Grossman relaxed his grip on Samantha's arm, finally dropping it. He raised his hand to his forehead, gently massaging either side of his eyes. He squinted, tensing his facial muscles against the growing pain in his head.

Samantha glanced up at him, an understanding and sympathetic smile playing on her lips. She spoke quietly, but with a calm assurance, in a measured, authoritative voice which was most certainly not that of a five-year-old child. 'You have to relax. You must not fight it.'

Dimly, as if from a great distance, Grossman heard her. His conscious mind struggled to obey, fighting against a rising panic, a terrible fear of being engulfed by a huge and powerful wave. He wanted desperately to give in, but his inner self fought like a demon to stay in control. Conscious and subconscious thought battled furiously, neither willing to give ground. The pain grew in intensity, becoming like white-hot needles being pushed through Grossman's eyeballs, probing about inside his brain. Grossman began to groan with agony as the two needles came together somewhere between his eyes.

Abruptly, Grossman broke free. The pain disappeared as though a switch had been thrown. Grossman returned to himself, feeling weary with sadness and bitter with frustration. He had been so close.

He turned slowly, as Frazer and Bell approached him, walking briskly towards the pool. Behind them, the Swedish and German scientists strolled at a more sedate pace.

'Are you all right, Dr Grossman?' Bell asked, noting the strained look on his colleague's face.

Grossman nodded miserably. 'I'm normal, even though I

don't want to be,' he muttered.

Bell looked at him askance. 'Perhaps you'd better go home and rest,' he suggested gently. 'You seem to be suffering from a little strain. Rest, or even a mild sedative, might help.'

Grossman's eyes flashed. 'Yes, a sedative,' he repeated, somewhat excitedly. 'Something like that, something to lower the mental resistance.'

Frazer looked at him with concern. 'Are you sure you're O.K., Heinz? You're not making a lot of sense.'

Grossman ignored him, he concentrated on Bell. 'That's it, don't you see? They get through to the children easily enough, but they can't quite pierce our mental barriers. If we artificially lowered those barriers with some drug it would be a different matter.'

Bell shook his head sadly. 'I really think you ought to go home and rest, Dr Grossman. In fact, I think we all ought to go home, close this place down for the weekend. We've got a virtual riot on our hands outside the main gate. It's about time I called the police, I think. Then, perhaps, everything can get back to normal.'

'Riot?' Grossman queried.

'There are over a thousand children out there now,' Bell said. 'They seem to be getting more and more agitated.'

The information only made Grossman become more excited. 'We have to let them in,' he blurted out. 'They'll help as well.'

Bell frowned. He was rapidly becoming convinced that Grossman had cracked under the pressure of work.

Grossman saw the hostility in the man's face and withdrew from him, turning to the other two scientists. 'Herr Graunglich, would you be willing to join me in an experiment? Dr Jossen?'

Graunglich spread his hands. 'What sort of experiment, Dr Grossman?'

Grossman controlled himself with an effort, stating his plans as calmly as he could. 'I suggest that we all inject ourselves with a mild dose of sodium pentathal, just enough to make our minds more susceptible to external stimuli. Then, using the children as mental amplifiers, I feel convinced that we should be able to tune in to whatever this mental influence is which has been affecting them.'

Dr Jossen shrugged. 'A small dose would not do any great harm,' he conceded. 'I would be willing.'

Grossman looked at Graunglich, phrasing a mute question with raised eyebrows. The German stared back thoughtfully for a moment, finally nodding curtly.

Grossman returned his attention to Bell. 'I need your approval,' he said simply.

There was a long silence while Bell considered the suggestion. He stared at Grossman morosely, unable to quite make up his mind.

'Look, what have we got to lose?' Grossman insisted, after a while. 'All our research so far has yielded absolutely nothing worthwhile. We're at a dead end, our backs are up against the wall. Even if my idea doesn't work, we're no worse off, and it doesn't involve any great waste of time or effort. It may be a shot in the dark, Dr Bell, but there's a hell of a lot of darkness crowding right in on us just now.'

Bell grunted thoughtfully. Grossman made a kind of sense, even if the idea itself seemed a little crazy. 'All right, Dr Grossman,' he said finally. 'You have my permission to go ahead. I will supervise the injections myself. Perhaps you would try to get the children into some sort of order while I prepare four dosages.'

'Make that five,' Frazer murmured. 'It can't be any worse than going to the dentist.'

In the very heart of the liquid world, Nah-Ep knew that the time had come and he summoned his great powers in readiness. Energy radiated out from his central source, infusing all the oceans of the earth with the ultimate message, the blueprint for survival. Psychically linked, twelve million dolphins prepared themselves to relay his thoughts to their two captive fellow creatures, hopefully to be passed on to the pathetic handful of the great dry-creatures who were at last prepared to listen.

The children were remarkably quiet and controlled. They stood, a dozen thick, around the perimeter of the small pool, their eyes fixed firmly upon the two dolphins which floated, immobile, in the water.

The five adults waited patiently as the drug seeped into their systems, making their bodies lethargic and bringing a strange tranquillity to their minds. Behind them the children began to murmur and chant, their thousand voices blending into a choir, gradually increasing in volume.

Grossman listened to the unfamiliar words anew, as if hearing them for the first time. Strangely the chant no longer sounded ugly and guttural. It had taken on a soft, musical quality, a flowing, gently moving grace of rhythm which reminded him of glittering fish swimming in crystal waters, or delicate seaweeds waving gently in an underwater current. His whole body seemed to respond to the new rhythm, relaxing, drifting, letting it wash over him in warm, gentle ripples.

There was no pain now, only a delicate prickling somewhere deep inside his head, spreading gradually outwards. It was not unpleasant. Grossman put up no resistance as it crept around his brain, putting conscious thought to sleep.

He gazed at the two dolphins, marvelling at their sleek beauty, the warmth and compassion which seemed to glow in their soft, dark eyes. Irresistibly, he felt himself drawn towards them, both mentally and physically, until he could feel the comforting coolness of water against his skin, share the freedom of the vast liquid world.

Grossman sank down into clear blue waters, seeing the pastel colours of the corals, the brilliant hues of the dancing angel fish. Deeper and deeper he sank, his body weightless. Suddenly, it seemed that he no longer needed a body at all. Smiling with a sudden inner knowledge, he abandoned it, allowing his mind to drift free, no longer restricted by physical attachment.

He lived and died a thousand times over, changing form constantly to inhabit new bodies. He was a microbe, a single cell, a shapeless mass, a fish, a whale. Grossman became the very living chain of the sea, knowing life and death and rebirth in a constant flow, moving at the slow and solemn pace of time itself. There was a beauty of simplicity, an absolute rightness about the feeling. Instinctively, Grossman knew that his mind was in tune with infinity, vibrating to the perfect cosmic rhythm of life at its most idyllic.

Grossman hardly had time to appreciate this glimpse of perfection before it was rudely snatched away from him. His thoughts were torn away with a sudden, savage jolt – out of the smooth, pulsing rhythm of life into the ugly, staccato beat of death.

He was plunged into a terrible maelstrom of pain, anguish, sorrow and suffering as he shared the death throes of the poisoned oceans, knew the desperate, terrible loneliness of the last survivor of a species facing the endless darkness of extinction.

In angry, violent surges of imagery, Grossman faced the fury of the liquid world and Nah-Ep's ultimate power. His brain reeled as the horrors assaulted him, confronting him with the collective guilt of all mankind.

The chant swelled inside him, and now Grossman knew the meaning of the strange words, understood their horrifying message. 'The time of the first time is come again. There is death in dark waters.' Grossman knew the final anger of Nah-Ep, felt the rising anger of the sea and all its creatures. 'The liquid world awakes in anger.' He realised, at last, the total power of nature and faced the awesome knowledge that he and his species were expendable. 'When the Great Fire burns in the frozen waters, only the mountains shall be free.' Finally, Grossman understood even that last cryptic message, and saw, in all its terror, the ultimate threat and the manner of man's extinction.

It was unbelievably ironic. Man had himself placed the technology for his destruction in the places of dark waters.

Suddenly, as the images faded and Nah-Ep's power began to withdraw from his mind, Grossman began to laugh, bitterly. He continued until he was exhausted and gasping for breath, struck by the incredibly poetic justice of it all.

Chapter
Twenty-Seven

It was a week later. Grossman and Frazer walked slowly along the sea front, each deeply immersed in his own thoughts. They stopped together, leaning on the promenade wall and staring moodily out across the calm surface of the sea.

Frazer spoke first, in a distant, querulous voice. 'Can we do it, Heinz?'

Grossman smiled faintly. 'We have to do it,' he answered quietly. 'We either do it . . . or we die. We have two years of grace as a last gift from the liquid world. Two years in which to clean up our mess, undo the damage we have caused to the oceans of this planet, and formulate some workable global plan to conserve the total ecology. Otherwise . . .'

He broke off, not bothering to spell out the alternative. Both of them knew that, only too well. Soon, the whole world would have to know. Already, the newspapers had published a dozen stark pictures of the arctic waters, thick with the huge black bodies of the whales going about their task.

In a matter of a few more weeks, every scrap of nuclear waste that man had ever dumped into the sea would have been transported by the whales to this one point, packed around the polar ice-cap in readiness. If man failed to honour his obligation to the liquid world, the canisters and concrete containers would be smashed open, so that the fissionable materials could begin their terrible havoc. A great fire would burn in the liquid waters. The incredible heat of atomic fission would melt the vast deposits of ice, virtually flooding the entire planet. Only the tops of the mountains would remain above the surface.

'What will you do now, Heinz?' Frazer asked, quietly.

Grossman shrugged. 'There's so much, I can't even start to work out an actual plan yet,' he admitted. 'I'll get back to work on the gill-unit, of course. Development of that is going to make our work a lot easier – if we can surmount the first problem of getting the world leaders to see sense. Right now, though, there's one thing I want to do above all else.'

Frazer regarded him curiously. 'What's that?'

Grossman laughed. 'Go for a swim,' he said.

Desmond Bagley

'Mr Bagley is nowadays incomparable.' *Sunday Times*

THE ENEMY 85p
THE FREEDOM TRAP 85p
THE GOLDEN KEEL 85p
HIGH CITADEL 85p
LANDSLIDE 85p
RUNNING BLIND 85p
THE SNOW TIGER 85p
THE SPOILERS 85p
THE TIGHTROPE MEN 85p
THE VIVERO LETTER 85p
WYATT'S HURRICANE 85p

Fontana Paperbacks

Duncan Kyle

'The outstanding thriller-writer discovery of the seventies.'
Evening News

WHITEOUT! 75p
A CAGE OF ICE 80p
FLIGHT INTO FEAR 80p
TERROR'S CRADLE 80p

Fontana Paperbacks

Fontana Paperbacks

Fontana is a leading paperback publisher of fiction and non-fiction, with authors ranging from Alistair MacLean, Agatha Christie and Desmond Bagley to Solzhenitsyn and Pasternak, from Gerald Durrell and Joy Adamson to the famous Modern Masters series.

In addition to a wide-ranging collection of internationally popular writers of fiction, Fontana also has an outstanding reputation for history, natural history, military history, psychology, psychiatry, politics, economics, religion and the social sciences.

All Fontana books are available at your bookshop or newsagent; or can be ordered direct. Just fill in the form and list the titles you want.

FONTANA BOOKS, Cash Sales Department, G.P.O. Box 29, Douglas, Isle of Man, British Isles. Please send purchase price, plus 8p per book. Customers outside the U.K. send purchase price, plus 10p per book. Cheque, postal or money order. No currency.

NAME (Block letters)

ADDRESS
